THE AUTOBIOGRAPHY OF
MR. SPOCK

THE LIFE OF A FEDERATION LEGEND

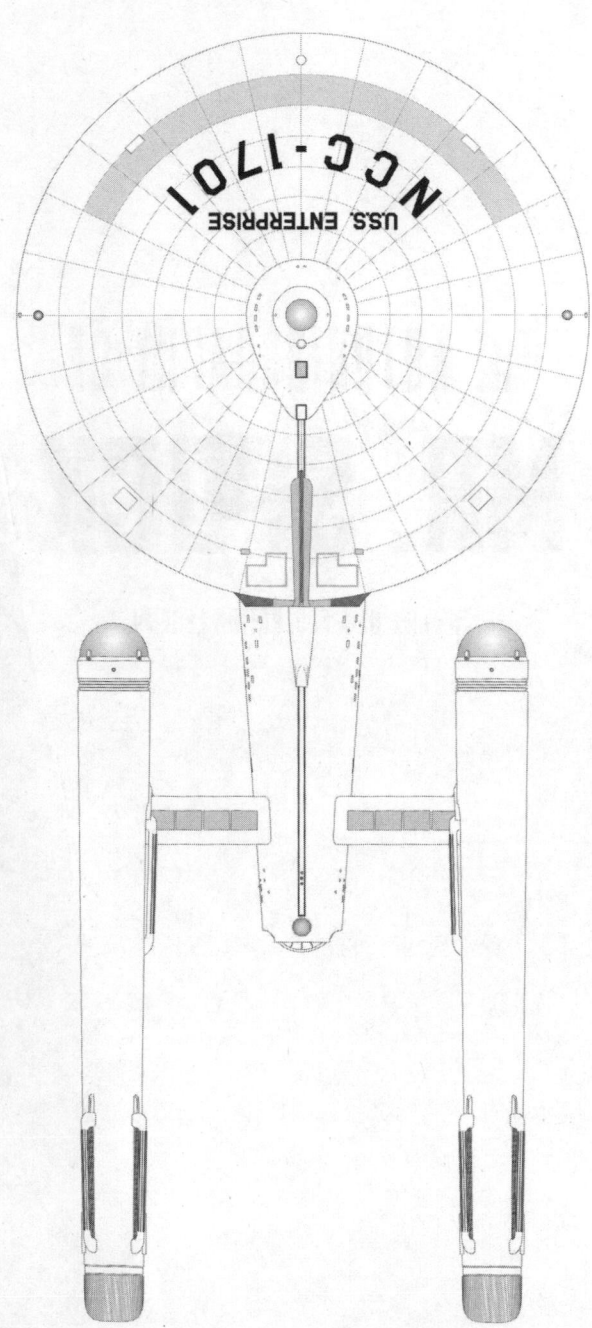

THE AUTOBIOGRAPHY OF
MR. SPOCK

THE LIFE OF A FEDERATION LEGEND

BY
SPOCK OF VULCAN

EDITED BY UNA M^CCORMACK

TITAN BOOKS

The Autobiography of Mr. Spock
Hardback Edition ISBN: 9781785654664
E-Book Edition ISBN: 9781785658785

Published by Titan Books
A division of Titan Publishing Group Ltd.
144 Southwark Street, London SE1 0UP.

First edition: September 2021
10 9 8 7 6 5 4 3 2 1

Illustrations: Russell Walks
Editor: Cat Camacho
Interior design: Rosanna Brockley/MannMade Designs

A CIP catalogue record for this title is available from the British Library.

Printed and bound in the U.S.A.

Did you enjoy this book? We love to hear from our readers. Please e-mail us at:
readerfeedback@titanemail.com or write to Reader Feedback at the above address.

To receive advance information, news, competitions, and exclusive offers online,
please sign up for the Titan newsletter on our website: www.titanbooks.com.

CONTENTS

Dedicated to everyone who has written in the Star Trek extended universe —and particularly to the memory of Vonda N. McIntyre

POINT OF ENTRY-2387

ShiKahr, Vulcan

IT HAS LONG BEEN MY CUSTOM, BEFORE EMBARKING UPON A GREAT VOYAGE, TO SET MY AFFAIRS IN ORDER. I am motivated, in part, by a desire to make this as straightforward and painless as possible for the executors of my will. But the practice is also—perhaps substantially—for my own benefit, providing an opportunity to reflect upon what has gone before. Nevertheless, although I began writing the story of my life once before, this was never completed, and I find that I contemplate resuming work on this with some trepidation. To revisit years and people long gone, to reflect upon what has been learned—who among us, even the most ascetic, after a long life filled with incident, would not find this task a challenge? Still, I leave very soon upon an uncertain mission, and I cannot leave this book unwritten.

If I were writing for a Vulcan reader, I would not need, I think, to explain the nature and the purpose of such a volume. And while I know you in particular, my reader, are a person not only of information but also of knowledge and wisdom, I must not assume that this tradition and ritual are known to you. What you hold in your hands is the product of a continuing series of rituals performed by Vulcans in old age. I will spare you the details of the rest—I suspect you can easily imagine the many and intricate meditations I have performed in recent years, with varying degrees of self-denial—but this one I shall explain to you in more depth. This book you hold is called the *t'san a'lat*, which translates (I give a rough translation here; certain nuances are, necessarily, lost) a "wisdom book". It is the physical manifestation of the life-long practice of *t'san s'at*, the intellectual deconstruction of emotional patterns in which every Vulcan engages in order to turn impulse into considered action. We are often considered a cerebral culture, my friend, but we are wise enough to know that our minds are embodied and take physical form. It is with this knowledge that the wisdom book is best understood: the summation of an individual's life and experiences, gathered together in one place to pass on to whomever comes afterwards.

Allow me to explain in a little more detail the form that the "wisdom book" takes. I should note, before giving this overview, that my version will, by necessity, stray from tradition in significant ways. I am not, after all, entirely Vulcan. But were you to examine the many volumes held in the vast echoing undercrofts of the many archives dotted throughout our cities, a man such as you would quickly identify the standard form. The *t'san a'lat* guides us through the three "ages" of a Vulcan life. First, we have *ro'fori*, or the acquisition of information, that period of youth when the mind is most nimble and can seemingly learn an almost limitless number of facts. After that comes *fai-tukh*, the height of one's life when this bedrock of information is operationalized as practical knowledge of the world, when we begin to see the patterns of life, and can draw upon what has happened before for each new challenge and dilemma. Last of all comes *kau*, that stage of life when our experiences become as rich as a tapestry wrought by the finest weavers of T'Paal, and the luckiest of us acquire a kind of wisdom—or, at least, continue to hold out the hope that wisdom might yet be acquired. Such a structure of life's journey is not particular to Vulcan, of course. There are many similar ideas on Earth, of course, as I do not need to tell you. I am sure that you are thinking already of Shakespeare's Seven Ages of Man, or the idea of the "late style" that emerges in writers beyond their hundredth year. I mention such things to evidence as early as possible in this text that my human education has not been lacking.

But my questionable half-humanity would soon become clear to any entirely Vulcan reader of this book. This is because I have deviated significantly from what one would expected to find in the *t'san a'lat*. Each section of a traditional wisdom book documents, meticulously, a situation in an individual's life in which some dilemma or crisis or peril has been resolved through the application of logic. Logic must, after all, prevail. The intention is that by examining such situations, the reader steadily acquires a bank of wisdom upon which they may draw in their own life. In my time at the learning domes, I read over two thousand examples of the *t'san a'lat*, my friend, and while I did learn a great deal from them, not once did I find an example that reflected back my own hybridity. I have therefore broken substantially with this form. Much of what I have learned in the course of my long life has come through my encounters with others. My *t'san a'lat* reflects this. The individual sections of my *t'san a'lat* contain reflections upon the most significant people in my life. A "true" *t'san a'lat* would scorn such an approach as subjective and therefore worthless. I leave you, and any other reader to whom you choose to give this book, to decide. You will see, therefore, that each section bears the name of someone whom I loved. On one occasion, I have used the word "Enterprise". I note that here I might well also have used the word "family". I believe that you, my friend, of all people, will understand.

Let me turn to you now; any book must, after all, consider to whom it is addressed. The traditional *t'san a'lat* is most usually addressed to children, grandchildren, great-grandchildren. I have no direct blood descendants. No child, or grandchild, or great-grandchild to remember me fondly or respectfully. Posterity is another audience, of course, and while I am prepared to admit that many of my actions have had significance—or that, at least, I have been lucky to play a part in great events and changes—it is not within my nature to address the world so publicly. I have chosen you, my friend, not least because I trust your judgment as to whether there is wider value in the experiences I have documented here. You will know what should or should not be shared more generally, and when we reach those parts of my life when secrecy has, hitherto, been necessary, I will alert you—and trust to your discretion as to what should be kept secret, and what can now be revealed.

But there are, if you will forgive me, other reasons for choosing you as my audience, my inheritor. You, surely, will understand the nature of the mission upon which I shall be embarking in the next few days. You, surely, better than most, understand the draw of Romulus, and the Romulan people, and the desire to bring succor. I believe I do not have to explain myself here to you, of all people, who sacrificed everything for this cause. But I also give this book to you, Jean-Luc, because I hope you might benefit personally from what I have written. The twists and turns of history have, I think, dealt you some hard blows in recent years, ones that are not just reward for the man that you are, and the work that you have done. If anything in this book resonates with you, then by this alone the writing will have been justified. If this book shows you a path forward, then I will have done more than I dared hope.

Two years ago, after your resignation, you invited me to visit you in La Barre. It is, and will be, one of the great regrets of my life that I never had the chance to take you up on this kind offer. As the great friends of my early life moved on or passed away, the opportunity to cultivate new friendships has been a most treasured aspect of this, my later life. To you, then, Jean-Luc Picard, my friend, I give the book of my wisdom, such as it is, and I leave it to your own considerable reserves of wisdom to judge its value, and to decide what to do with whatever value it contains. I do not believe that I shall be here to see what you decide. I am setting out on another mission, one last voyage, in a long life filled with many strange and wonderful journeys. I hope that when you learn of my intentions, you will understand. I hope that you will read with interest and compassion. That, surely, is what we all, in the end, most desire.

PART ONE

RO'FORI—INFORMATION—2230-2254

Amanda

ON VULCAN, CHILDREN ARE TRAINED FROM A VERY EARLY AGE in techniques that allow them to exploit their memories to their fullest potential. The rationale is straightforward enough: to be able to make logical and well-informed decisions, one must have as many facts at one's disposal as possible. Hence the rigorous education which we undergo. As a result, many Vulcans, when asked their earliest memory, will recall learning quotations, most usually from Surak, or a philosophical couplet from a poet such as T'Nar, whose uncomplicated yet carefully worked verses form a staple of early childhood reading, asking us to consider, in the simplest terms, the importance of acting only after reflection, and controlling our baser impulses. Others might remember their first encounter with geometrical shapes, or even a mathematical equation. My earliest memory is of my mother. I recall her scent, of sweet *vinver*; I remember her dark eyes looking down with love, and—most piercingly—I remember my hand reaching up to touch the necklace that she often wore. In this memory of mine, and I have no cause to doubt it, even though I lack independent verification, my fingers weave through the gold chain of the necklace; gently, my mother untangles them, and instead places my hand upon the pendant that it carries. This, I think, is the most beautiful thing I have ever seen, other than my mother's face. After a century-and-a-half, and a life spent dedicated to exploration and the study of some of the most profound sights that the universe has to offer, I am still moved by the thought of this symbol, and all that it means. We travel so far, and yet still, inevitably, we come back to the place where we started.

The pendant is a bronze disc, with a circular hole to one side. Across the disc is laid a silver triangle, and at the apex of the triangle there is a diamond. I remember how my mother held my hand to guide me around each part. I remember my enthrallment with the shapes, and my enchantment as she named *circle, triangle, arc, jewel*… I remember clasping the symbol, looping my fingers through the hole in the disc, connecting the tip of my thumb with the tip of my forefinger. Lamplight sparkling on the jewel, refracting many colors. Later, but not much later, my mother told me the name of this symbol, the *Kol-Ut-Shan*. Even as a small child, I realized that this symbol could be seen everywhere around my home: on the flags that stood outside big buildings; on pins and pendants worn by visitors to our home; even, as my mother told me once, in the way that a garden or shrine might be laid out. No wonder: the *Kol-Ut-Shan* is the fundamental principle of the Vulcan way of life, the first lesson that we learn: that life in the universe is infinitely diverse, in infinite combinations, and that we must acknowledge this diversity and respect it. This, above all, was the message that Surak taught, one of tolerance and inclusion. This is the principle that brought peace to Vulcan after so many years of bloody war, which has sustained that peace throughout the centuries, and which we brought—or have tried to bring—to the Federation of Planets of which we are a part. *Kol-Ut-Shan*, infinite diversity in infinite combinations. Accept difference, respect difference—come in peace.

Looking back over the long years of my life, I might wish that I had understood this lesson sooner and tried not to confine myself to one of the many labels which others sought to impose upon me. My life, I think, might have contained less struggle against the simple fact of my own nature. Let me be satisfied that I have come to such understanding. I comprehend fully now the sheer beauty of the overwhelming variety that exists in the universe, the impossibility of living reductively, the enlightenment—and, yes, the joy—that comes from embracing one's fullest nature within a universe of wonders.

My mother was my constant companion in my early years. I learned to speak listening to her voice. I learned to walk holding her hand. And hers were the eyes through which I saw the outside world; the human prism through which I first viewed and came to comprehend Vulcan. I still, in many ways, see the world through her eyes. I know that many of my father's peers believed that here lay his first mistake in my education, and there were times in my own youth when I myself wished that my humanity had not been so firmly, so indelibly marked upon me at such a young age. But now that she is gone, these memories of her are very precious to me, and I know without doubt that this human shaping of my Vulcan nature allowed the best parts of me to exist. It has been my observation that one of the gifts of middle age is to come to know one's parents as an adult. To meet them again as peers. My mother died comparatively young, certainly by Vulcan standards, and even by human standards, and she and I were only beginning to come to know each other as friends and peers. In many ways, I feel that I never wholly knew her. Only after Amanda's death, for example, did I come to realize how little I knew of the girl that she had been before she came to Vulcan. My mother was twenty-four when she met and married my father. She spent almost the rest of her life at his side. And despite the constancy of presence in my very early days, I am left with a sense that there was much about her that I never knew. It seems to me sometimes as if there was a shell around her that was almost impossible to break through, or as if she somehow already transcended the world, even in her youth. And yet, somehow, my father reached her. Whatever doubts and misunderstanding confused and complicated our lives together, I did not doubt that my mother loved my father, and my father loved my mother. I have never doubted this.

Over my years as a diplomat, I have encountered representatives from many species, and I have often needed to set individuals at ease. I have observed that one way to achieve this is to ask them to tell me the story of how they met their life partners. These stories naturally vary significantly depending on species. The *shelthreth* of the Andorians, for example, are constrained by the fact of their biology, requiring a partner from each of the four sexes, and with a cultural imperative for these unions to produce each child. The stories of meeting are highly stylized, ritualized, surrounded by ceremony. Even when species are more casual about their liaisons (I might include humans here), some tale is likely to be told. A version of this story-pattern can be found on almost every world. Even the highly solitary denizens of Kalestria, who rarely leave their hermitages, will tell of the fleeting encounters they have each equinox with their other-souls. (You may ask how I know this. I visited their world once, as an envoy from the Federation, and I met their representative for almost an hour. Hardly any time to me, after several weeks spent in flight to their world—although it was a lengthy meeting by their standards. Yet time was indeed found to tell exactly such a tale. "Look," we often seem to want to say, as if to assure each other of our capacity to make connections, "we too can love.")

But the story of how my father wooed my mother was not one told in our home. Later, when I visited on Earth and came to know my human family better, I learned the rough outline of events from my grandmother and my uncle. Amanda, during adolescence, became deeply absorbed in the history and philosophy of Vulcan, in particular the meditation practices which form such an everyday part of life on my homeworld. In part, this was a natural outgrowth from her maternal grandmother's groundbreaking studies in xenology (my great-grandmother held a variety of chairs in her field at several prestigious institutions); in part, this was her own initiative. Something about the long history of that world fascinated her. Perhaps it was the contradictions: the bloody history; the stable present. Perhaps it was simply her romantic streak. Many adolescents become enamored with fantastical worlds, inhabiting them deeply and profoundly. It was simply that in my mother's case, the fantastical world existed. My grandparents believed that the phase would pass, and that my mother was set upon becoming a teacher or educator, perhaps an educational psychologist, like her own mother. And so it seemed to be. Amanda loved teaching children and young people to explore their own capacity to learn, helping them discover the methods which were most successful for them to be able to develop not only their knowledge, but also their curiosity, and their capacity to frame questions, and their ability to then find appropriate means to answer them. These were the subjects she pursued at university.

As Amanda's studies progressed toward doctoral level, her interests broadened into the training of the mind to its fullest potential. She began to study various meditative techniques, and here her interest in Vulcan practices was re-awakened. Before she ever set foot on Vulcan, she embarked upon some aspects of *kohlinar*. This word describes two closely related activities: the ritual by which it is shown that emotions have been fully purged, and also the series of mental disciplines undertaken to achieve this state. Not all Vulcans ever achieve this, and many human psychologists view the process with concern. My mother was rare in showing both interest and ability. She also became an expert on the concept of "flow", that elusive state of mind that humans enter when they become most naturally and spontaneously creative, and which is so alien to the Vulcan approach of rigorous application of tried and tested methods. I believe that it is important to understand that she was not simply a convert. Toward the end of her postgraduate work, she was invited to attend a retreat on Vulcan devoted to the practice of *t'san s'at*, a relatively new discipline which seemed, as a result of its less stringent techniques, to have many potential benefits for non-Vulcans. Naturally, she went to this retreat— and here the information which my human relatives were able to supply becomes spotty. Amanda left for Vulcan, for, as far as they were aware, three months. Towards the end of her third month, she contacted my grandmother and grandfather to tell them that she was engaged to be married and would not be returning to Earth.

My grandmother, at this point in the story, would fall silent. My grandfather, if pressed, would say, "It was almost as if she were *enamored...*" An interesting word to apply to my father. I would not call him a charming man. He had gravitas, yes, and a quality that was not charisma, but which meant that one wished for his good opinion. It would be too easy, I think, to say that Amanda was somehow enchanted by Vulcan; that during that visit her adolescent imaginings were rekindled, and, coming under that world's spell, she chose to remain there, to the end of her life. This is what her immediate family thought was the case, and I know, too, how saddened they were by her sudden and complete removal to Vulcan. My grandmother, right up to her death, believed that my mother's chosen path had not brought her happiness. To their credit, my grandparents did not pass on to me their continuing bewilderment at her decision to marry my father. They did not like her choice, but they accepted it was hers to make.

But I knew what they thought, of course, and indeed at many times I have shared their puzzlement. Throughout my life, I often wondered what drew my mother—a woman not only of intelligence but also of passion, with an almost boundless capacity for love—to come to this world. Surely Vulcan—as an old friend of mine used to say—was cold-blooded and austere. Loveless. What, I would wonder, might possibly have drawn her to this world, and to my father, perhaps the most ascetic man that I have ever met? These questions must remain, to a large extent, unanswered, since both parties are now long dead. My mother, for all her practice of many Vulcan techniques, did not write a *t'san a'lat*, and, although I know that she kept a journal from her youth, and indeed I saw her writing on many occasions, I have never found it. Whether she destroyed it before her death, or my father destroyed it afterwards, I do not know. Perhaps it was only ever intended as a tool for her, a means to help her clarify emotions and bring peace of mind. But I might wish that some document existed, if only to clarify some of the choices she made, which are sometimes still opaque to me. Whatever private feelings my mother held about her decisions, her married life, and her children remain exactly that—private. All that I can know is what I observed—that their marriage lasted, from which I can logically extrapolate that she loved my father. I can say too, without any doubt in my mind, that she in turn was the deep and enduring love of his life.

And I for one cannot, of course, regret this choice she made. As I write these words, my mind's eye calls up to me again most clearly the pendant that my mother wore, the symbol at the heart of Vulcan philosophy. I might wish that I had understood its full meaning much earlier in my life: that one should not trap oneself forever in a struggle between two imagined halves. The universe is a vast and wild place, and in this chaotic variety lies not disintegration, but the means to realize a fuller, more sustained unity of self. In embracing what is different in others, we become more fully ourselves. Perhaps that was at the heart of the choice that my mother made when, a woman of twenty-four, she left her home and her family for good, to marry a man much older than herself, and stay on a world that would always, to some extent, see her as an outsider.

✦

If my mother was the constant of my early years, then my father, Sarek, was a more distant figure, but I felt the weight of his formidable presence and achievements early on. The house in which we lived was a monument to our forebears; as I grow older, I reflect upon how heavily this family history must have weighed in turn upon my father. At the time, of course, he seemed little different to me from those graven images of Skon and Solkar that seemed to look down from every corner of the house. This long line of ambassadors, entrusted to represent our world at the very highest levels, formed alliances and forged treaties, and, at the same time, were men of culture and learning, and the arts. My great-grandfather, Solkar, the first Vulcan ambassador to Earth, was also one of the finest musicians of his generation. My grandfather, Skon, with decades of service on the Federation council, translated not only Surak's work into English, but thousands of lines of poetry from the sonorous, even languid, pastorals of T'Palaath to the vigorous epics of Serat to the crisp, cool verses of Saum. And my own father, venerated ambassador in his own right, who meditated twice daily, was one of the best players of *kal-toh* whom I have ever met. Such were my forefathers, and this history, this pedigree, I memorized at a very early age. The names of the dead were in many ways more real to me than my living human family back on Earth, to whom I spoke only from a distance. The faces of my Vulcan ancestors were always there—even if they did not speak or offer guidance.

I was aware early on that I was expected to follow in the family tradition and, in turn, become an ambassador at the very least. I was, after all, my father's son, with all that implied. I was aware, too, perhaps earlier than my parents realized, that the expectations that I would perform well were heightened because the previous son had proven so disappointing. My elder half-brother, Sybok, was not a constant presence in my early years, but his name, if mentioned, would cast a pall over our home. Whenever we received news of him, my father's lips would invariably narrow; his expression grow stonier. I would see his eye fall upon me—the second chance, yes, but a risky one, given his human side—and I would feel a little more weight fall upon my shoulders.

I was naturally eager to prove myself a worthy inheritor of this great family tradition. This was not, I told myself, a matter of pride or some other emotional impulse, but an entirely rational wish to make the best of the privileges of my upbringing. Twice a week, my father would take time out of his schedule to tutor me. His aim was to instill in me what he believed were the fundamentals: the principles of logic; a rational and scientific mindset; how to set one's mind in order to be able to work with discipline and care. First, we would meditate for a while, and then turn to the business of the day. Simple logic games, that taught cause and effect, and deductive skills, and how to show proof. Scales upon the *ka'athyra*, (an instrument that you might understand as lying somewhere between a lyre or a lute), building steadily to more complex arrangements. How to systematically order and arrange data.

These sessions with my father were a source of both vast inspiration and deep confusion. As long as I could rely upon my memory, I faced few difficulties. If he read out a simple aphorism from T'Lor's *Meditations*, for example, I would only need to hear it once or twice to repeat it back. Music, again, I could quickly play by ear. But, in other respects, it was clear that I was struggling. Simply put—I could not read. Most children on Vulcan are reading fluently in their own dialect by their third year, and in a second and third dialect by their fifth. But this was a code that I could not crack. The shapes on the page seem to shift and move. What was up became down; what was left became right. I could not make sense of these strange and ever-changing symbols. The presence of my father, so close to hand and without expression, surely did not help. He would listen for a while, then take the book and close it. Nothing more would be said. We would play *kal-toh* together for a while, an ancient game of strategy, using small rods, or *t'an*, to create complex spheres of other three-dimensional shapes. One might play alone, in the manner of the human game of solitaire, or against an opponent, each player selecting a different shape and attempting to maneuver the construction in that direction. Or one might play the way that my father and I preferred, working together toward a common goal. Slowly, we would create order from the chaos that lay before us, constructing the most beautiful and orderly shapes. *Kal-toh* has always had a calming effect, on both me and my father. These quiet games together, where we communicated not by speech, but by the simple pleasure of a shared desire for order, simplicity, and beauty, are amongst my finest memories of my father. Sometimes, having solved a particularly difficult set-up, my emotions—my pride—would get the better of me.

"Control your responses, Spock," my father would say. "The solution is its own reward." And I did learn to do this, taking pleasure instead from the simple fact of being with my father, and the knowledge of an activity shared.

But none of this could hide the fact that I was not a success. By this point—I must have been four or five years old—it was becoming clear to everyone that something was not quite right about this halting child. And, never spoken but always somehow in the background, the suggestion that my trouble arose from the unfortunate fact of my half-humanity, a condition that I could not escape, and which would surely prevent my ever reaching the heights achieved by those omnipresent forefathers. Solkar, Skon, Sarek… Dimly, I was starting to grasp that some of the people around me believed there would be no fourth name placed in line there, no successor as illustrious as those who had come before. How could the second son, the half-human child, be expected to succeed where the first son, the full-blooded Vulcan, had failed? It was plain to everyone that I was starting with too great a disadvantage. Everyone, with one notable exception. My mother. Whatever doubts other may have had, Amanda never doubted for a second that there was a key to understanding me, and that with time and patience and thought, she could unlock what lay within me. Such certainty means the world to a child. My mother's unshakeable belief in me meant that, even in the future, when my sense of self came, on occasion, close to crumbling, there was a bedrock there that could not be destroyed.

✦

One might believe from this that, despite my ancestry, the influences upon my early life were almost entirely Vulcan. But ShiKahr, the city of my birth, has long had the reputation of being one of the most diverse places in the quadrant. The capital of a great civilization, the home of many ambassadors and envoys, the chosen destination of many travelers and visitors—ShiKahr embodies the most deeply held principle of Vulcan philosophy: that our strength lies in diversity, in our ability to live alongside what is different, and each to honor, celebrate, and venerate that diversity.

ShiKahr has changed very little over the years, and, even now, when I walk around its streets, I am easily transported back to my childhood. Our family's home was in one of the older districts where the houses, huge and somber, set within orderly grounds and gardens, often date back thousands of years. Yet a short walk or journey in an aircar will take you almost to another world. My mother and I could leave the echoing halls of the house of my ancestors, and soon be wandering through the busy and contemporary mercantile district, home to more than a hundred embassies. Everywhere I looked I could see art and architecture from all these worlds—and, most of all, I could see members of many different species, here in my home city. I remember once, sitting with my mother in the winter garden before the Gettenian embassy, counting with her how many different species we might observe within an hour. By the end of the hour, our count reached forty-six. And I remember my mother touching her chest and saying, "Forty-seven," and then resting her hand against my cheek to say, "Forty-eight." In such a moment, all the evidence available to me suggested that even a child of half-human heritage might not be out of place on Vulcan.

I can see now how my mother made the multicultural nature of ShiKahr a cornerstone of my early education. I can see now how quickly and thoroughly she exposed me to different cultures, food, art, theatre. I recall the first time that I saw *gagh*, wriggling and writhing in the bowl. I imagined how it might feel, sliding down my throat, and was grateful that it was not our custom to eat the flesh of living creatures. (My mother had been vegetarian before even coming to Vulcan.) I remember visits to the mercantile district, where stallholders and street performers vied for our attention. Here was my first encounter with the mysteries of Ankillian shadow puppetry, the stark silhouettes and white spotlights, and the chimes of the bells through which the story was told. I stood mesmerized by the skill of the players in the speed *kal-toh* tournaments until my mother, gently, had to whisper in my ear that it was time to go. I remember watching the fierce dance and ornate costumes of Jalanian fencers; the feel of the fabrics in the huge covered market—soft Inkarian wool running gently between my fingers, the liquid of Tholian silk. The mingling scents of spices from a hundred worlds: cinnamon, *insilit*, the distinctive bite of Tellarite grey pepper. Life—at its best—loves and relishes life, in all its forms. We are not lessened by living alongside what it different; we are bettered and enriched.

But the two places that I loved best were without doubt quintessentially Vulcan. In the center of ShiKahr lies the Surak Memorial Garden: that huge, quiet space at the heart of that great busy city. Many people come here throughout the day, but somehow the place remains still and serene, a place for contemplation. You will see people standing quietly gazing into the reflecting pools; others will be sitting in the little gardens, meditating. My mother and I had a favorite route through, that took us through the maze of red-leaved *kilsit* trees to the bronze statue of Surak standing before a huge stone

Kol-Ut-Shan. I would look at the latter rather than the former (I saw enough frozen faces at home) and find great peace there. Eventually, my mother would draw me away, to sit on the ground nearby.

"Come and sit with me, Spock," my mother would say, patting the ground in front of her, and I would sit, cross-legged, looking up at her. She took her hands within mine and smiled. "Close your eyes."

I did not want to close my eyes (I so loved to look at her face), but neither did I want to disobey, so I would do as she asked. So we would sit—mother and son, my small hands within hers, our eyes closed—and she would say, "Breathe, now. Breathe steadily. Follow me."

I would follow her lead. I would feel the rise and fall of her hands, and, slowly, my breathing would fall into rhythm with hers. "Listen," she would say. "Listen to the world around you."

I would listen. Hear the gentle lapping of the water in the pools; the soft footsteps of a passer-by; the sigh of someone else trying to find the present moment. My mother was, of course, teaching me some early principles of meditation, how to find clarity of mind and focus—and I was not much older before I realized that the days that we came here were days the weight of my father's expectation seemed particularly burdensome, his distance most troubling.

Sometimes, when even the silent company in the Gardens was too much for us, my mother and I would board a gondola, and travel along the Sirakal Canal. Most visitors to ShiKahr do not go further than a kilometer or two along the canal, and on familiar routes, but we—with our expert local knowledge— knew that a little way out, the waterway became almost unvisited. A little over three kilometers out along the canal, one comes to a quiet mooring point, and here we would stop and come to land. We rarely saw others here: perhaps another, sitting in quiet meditation beneath a *fa'tahr* tree, and we would always leave them to their peace. We had come here for a particular reason.

In our past, as is well known, our civilization was violent and brutal. We did not spare each other, and we did not spare the varieties of life around us. We hunted, not only for food, but for pleasure. A curious phenomenon, stemming so obviously from such irrational need for mastery and fear of the extinction of one's self that one is almost surprised that such individuals make such obvious displays of vulnerability and fearfulness. But such are the behaviors of those who struggle through life with undisciplined thoughts and unexamined minds. The whole bent of Vulcan civilization and philosophy has been to bring such harmful impulses under control. But before this was achieved, there was great loss of life—and loss of species.

But in the years since, a little humility—a little wisdom—has been learned. One benefit of the settlement brought about by the dominance of Surak's philosophy has been the peace granted us to study and learn. This is of course the start of the great advances we have made in science and technology, not least of which has been in the field of genetic engineering. On other worlds, genetic engineering was most heinously misused, to create individuals whose vastly enhanced physical and mental abilities were matched only by the depravity of their morals. Not so on Vulcan. Here, the field of genetic engineering has been used solely in its reparative capacity, allowing us to breathe life into species long lost to the depredations of the past, and let them once again inhabit our world. Visitors to Vulcan can see the fruits of these efforts in many sanctuaries around the planet, but here, in the quiet waters of the Sirakal canal, one can now see what I still consider one of the most profound sights in the universe: pods of *o'ktath* swimming in the waters of Vulcan.

You are a well-traveled man, Jean-Luc, and perhaps you have seen this sight for yourself. If you have not, and do not know what *o'ktath* are, you might imagine something similar to a dolphin from your own world: an aquatic mammal, streamlined and fast-moving, with a gentle intelligence that is almost palpable. They are curious too, and this, no doubt, caused their downfall, bringing them close to our ancestors, who exploited this virtue mercilessly. As our old world entered its seemingly terminal decline, the *o'ktath* became extinct. Our later, hard-won wisdom has brought them back again. And here, only a little distance from one of the busiest cities at the heart of a galactic civilization, they swim once again, dipping and diving, and coming up for air, and to peer at those of us who are fascinated not only by their play, but by the simple fact of their existence.

I do believe that it is here, watching the *o'ktath*, that I had my first real experience of the alien. The many species that inhabited ShiKahr were like old friends to me. But these creatures—indigenous to my world, yet almost travelers through time—had the capacity to induce awe in me: that deep sense of the wonder that is the interconnectedness of life. Watching them, I experienced what my child's mind—ever trying to be the perfect son—described to himself as a simple interest and wish to acquire more information, but which I know was a deep longing to communicate meaningfully with something very different from myself, to form a connection with something unlike. I wished to mind-meld with these creatures: to perceive the world entirely through their consciousness; to understand how the world appeared to them. Here, sitting by the canal, watching the *o'ktath*, I had my first glimpse of the unknown, the alien—and I wished to understand them better. It was many years before I fulfilled this ambition, and there were many rivers yet to cross.

Michael

MY HUMAN FRIENDS AND FAMILY, READING THIS ACCOUNT, would no doubt ask whether I considered my early years to be happy. At the time, I would not have been able to answer this question. That I was surrounded by adults who took my physical and intellectual wellbeing to heart, and whose great interest was in seeing me both aspire to and achieve excellence, I have no doubt. I never doubted, either, that I was greatly valued and carefully nurtured. Expectations were high, but this seemed as much a compliment as a burden. The question of "happiness" did not occur to me. Now, of course, I hear my old friend Bones, at the back of my mind, crying, "Dammit, Spock, what you're saying is that you weren't happy. You *weren't*!" Looking back, I see acutely how complicated our situation was.

My mother was without doubt my chief source of emotional constancy, and, in her presence, I felt accepted and calm. My mother had a remarkable ability to induce serenity in others, to still the troubled waters of our family, or, at least, to prevent the swirling undercurrents from ever surfacing. For the earliest years of my life, the three of us—my mother, my father, and I—were able to achieve a kind of balance that not even doubts arising from my half-human heritage could destabilize. This equilibrium ended for good the year that I turned six, with the most disrupting experience of my young life so far. Quite suddenly, I acquired a sister.

The arrival of a new sibling disrupts the life of any child, particularly one where the mother has hitherto been entirely devoted to them. Watching my friends and colleagues over the years, in their interactions with their siblings, I have often observed that even in the healthiest of families, a latent undercurrent of competition remains, as if that early struggle for the attention of their parents has never quite been resolved. These are, most usually, situations where a second child is born. A new baby naturally demands that the parents focus upon them, and the older child struggles with the sense of displacement, of now coming second. Most sensible parents make preparations and accommodation for this. Our situation was very different: we were adding to our tight circle a much older child, and one who had recently suffered a terrible and violent loss. Thinking now of all that happened to Michael not long before she came to us, I feel shame for my behavior toward her; I feel pity, too, for the boy that I was who truly had no idea of the seismic change that his family was about to undergo.

It was not that I was completely unprepared. My father had traveled off-world to collect her, to bring her home, and my mother had spent the time explaining in clear language that another child was coming to join us. She stated that Michael was older, and human; that her parents had died, and that this would make her sad and lonely. She hoped that I would be mindful of this, and that if there was something I did not understand, that I would speak to her. I cannot fault her preparations. But sometimes children do not fully understand what they are being told. Busy with my own projects—*kal-toh*, my music practice, and my ongoing struggles with the written word, about which I sensed my father's increasing concern—I remained vague about what was happening. I knew we were expecting a human child and I knew that she was going to stay for some time. I was intrigued by the notion of a companion. But I did not, I think, understand that this was to be indefinitely.

I distinctly remember Michael's arrival. My mother and I were together in my room, when she heard that my father and Michael were almost home. Suddenly, I was filled with fear. Who was she, this girl? What did this mean, to have another child here? My mother, perhaps sensing something of this, said, "Why not wait while I go and welcome her, Spock? It may be easier to meet her here in your own room."

She left me. After a moment, I slipped out after her, and hurried to the stop of the stairs, where I took a moment to compose myself. Energetic displays of excitement were discouraged. I looked down into the hall. I was eager to see this new sister that had been found for me. The door opened, and my father came in, a young girl with him. I took a step forward. The girl heard me—her head snapped up to look at me. Her eyes—wide open—fixed upon me for a moment. I watched her register me; I watched her decide I was not a threat. Then I watched her focus slip away. Soon, she was once again looking at nothing, her face bearing that blank and shielded expression that, much later, with years of experience in Starfleet behind me, I would recognize as trauma. I have seen that stare many times again: in Saavik, for example, or many a young ensign, fresh from the first real experience of hand-to-hand combat, understanding fully that no simulation can truly replicate the horror and the grief that comes from seeing the violent extinction of another sentient being. The child that was Michael Burnham had this look. It frightened me, as did the tense expression on my father's face. In that moment, I understood that this girl was not going to be a companion. She was going to be the source of disruption, confusion, and strife.

My mother stepped forward to speak to the girl. I could not quite hear what was being said, but I could sense the warmth in her words and suddenly, I grasped that the great fount of love was no longer mine and mine alone. My mother was to be shared, with this frightening stranger. I could not bear this any longer. I ran back to my room. There, at my table, I took out my drawing pad. My mother, trying to make me comfortable making marks with a pen, had encouraged me to draw whatever was in my mind, to let the pen move freely. I had found that my concentration was helped by this, and that I would become calmer. This was not the case now. The marks became frantic and angry, more scribbles than designs. I heard footsteps coming up the stairs and along the corridor. Were they bringing her to my room? I did not want her in my room. I wanted her gone. My father called out to me; told me that he expected me to teach her, to be friends with her. This, I did not want. I turned, and casting up the images from the drawing pad into a holo of the *yon'tislak*, the fire beast from a children's tale, I told her as best I could what I wanted:

Go away.

I will not say that my parents were unprepared for taking on the responsibility of caring for a traumatized child. They were deeply intelligent and perceptive people, and my mother, in particular, had great wisdom and a capacity for deep and steady love. But the reality of how fundamental a change this was to our family most certainly caught them by surprise. I was confused by these emotions that I was feeling, and anxious that the strength of them was another sign of my failure to be how I was supposed to be. My easiest route was to lay the blame on the girl who was—to my child's mind, still using simple models of cause and effect—responsible. Alone in my room, I planted the seed of a deep sense of grievance that I nurtured steadily over the coming days until it was in full bloom.

The ten-year-old girl whom we received into our composed and serene household was deeply troubled, in shock, and in need of considerable support. This could only come from my mother. She was the one who had persuaded my father to take on this traumatized child; she was the one who took on the burden of emotional care. I make no excuses for my behavior in the weeks and months that followed. I was jealous of Michael—it is as simple as that. I was angry that I was no longer the sole focus of my mother's attention and bitter that I had to share her with this stranger. On our treasured trips around the city, we were—to my mind—encumbered by this unwanted third party. I derived no satisfaction from showing this girl all the places where my mother and I were wont to visit together. Even worse, I saw how much pleasure my mother gained when Michael's interest was piqued at some sight or other: at the red leaves falling from the *kilsit* trees; at the variety of sights and sounds in the markets. My mother did not indulge my jealousy, but in one respect she did spare my feelings. If she ever took Michael to see the *o'ktath*, it was not in my company. After a while, my mother decided to take us on separate trips. I was glad to have her sole company once again, and while she was out with Michael, I took to going up into the hills that lay behind our house. My father was not happy at these solitary walks (on reflection, now, I see that the son of an ambassador was a target for political enemies), but despite his disapproval, I did not stop. Alone, and outside, I found some peace from the angry *yon'tislak* that seemed to have taken up residence within me.

Throughout this period, I was preparing for admission to the Vulcan Learning Center, an important rite of passage marked by much ceremony and ritual, as a child takes their first steps from home out into the wider community of learning. But even this important event was marred, in my mind, by the simultaneous admission to the Center of this unwanted new sibling. Michael would, of course, be attending alongside me, and so my preparations for entry now took place alongside hers—and she had much ground to cover to satisfy the teachers that she would succeed alongside the other children. Secretly, I hoped that she would fail, but with my parents' guidance, she began to do well. I was not progressing so well in comparison. On the tasks that involved displays of memorization and physical dexterity, I was not concerned. But reading and writing continued to cause me great difficulty. Leaving this aside, it pained me beyond measure to see my parents devote even a small part of their attention to Michael's work.

Worse than that, once we were admitted to the Center, Michael's full humanity only drew attention to my own half-Vulcan status. We quickly became the target for bullies, but even this did not unite us against a common enemy. Not one member of the family was happy throughout this time and, child that I was, the easiest person to blame was the unwanted stranger in our midst. If Michael had not come, I reasoned, then our family would have continued as it should have: my mother and my father, devoted to me; my entry to the Learning Center progressing far more easily. Of course, this was not the case. My own half-human nature would always have been the source of doubt, from children and teachers alike; my trouble with the written word required attention. But it was easier to blame Michael.

Even as young as I was, I knew that Michael's admission to the Center was not without controversy. I acquired, during this period, an uncanny (if not particularly laudable) skill for moving quietly around the house, in order to be able to hear conversations between my parents. One day, I overheard them discussing this, and the intensity of the discussion disturbed me further. By other standards, one would call their exchange a quarrel, since no voices were raised, no anger was expressed, but in every gesture that they made, every taut muscle of their bodies and their faces, I could see the effects of this decision they had made upon them.

"Perhaps we should be considering an alternative," my father said. "Studying at home, with a human tutor—"

"There would be no need if the teachers at the Center would take the trouble to accommodate them—"

"The methods are well tried and tested. If the children are not able to flourish—"

"They are both *more* than able, Sarek!"

"My wife, you speak for them with commendable passion, but perhaps this decision requires more in the way of dispassion—"

I had heard enough. I went into the garden, where I saw Michael, sitting beneath her favorite tree. I went to stand in front of her. She looked up— whenever she looked at me, I caught what I later understood was a glimmer of hope, that I had come to be friendly, that was always quickly quenched. I said to her, "You are not wanted here."

She gasped. From behind me, my father spoke. I had not heard him approach.

"Spock," he said, "you speak unkindly and unwisely. You speak from your emotions and not from reason."

"It is a statement of fact," I replied. Before he could say anything more, I turned away. He said, "Spock, sit down." But I turned my back on him (a truly rebellious gesture, signaling, as it did, my complete disrespect) and went back inside and up to my room. I recall myself trembling from the emotions that I was experiencing, which I could at the time barely name: my frustration and self-doubt at my struggles at school; my sorrow that my mother's attention seemed to be halved; my jealousy that while emotional care was being lavished on this unwanted sister, the cold hand of logic seemed to become ever more present in my own day-to-day life. I thought of drawing some of what I was experiencing but I could not even stir myself to do this. About an hour later, my mother came to join me. She sat beside me on the bed. After a moment or two, I leaned against her.

"I know," she said, "how hard this is. Much harder than any of us imagined. I am your mother, Spock. I love you without condition. I love you with every fiber of my being."

I have said that my mother's great gift was in her ability to induce calm in others, to bring about a sense of wellbeing and tranquility. And so it was for me that evening. She remained beside me on the bed, stroking my hair, until I fell asleep. But, in the dead quiet of night, I woke again, and she was gone. I felt the flutter of fear once again in my chest, and then the deep shame I always felt when caught unawares by one of my unwanted human emotions. I slipped from my bed and out of the house, and walked once again up into the mountains, coming home only when I saw the first pale glimmer of dawn.

The outcome of this quarrel was by no means what I had intended. Rather than spending more time and attention on me, my mother took Michael away for a fortnight to Eridani D. Ostensibly this was to celebrate her birthday; but, left behind at home, it was hard for me not to read my exclusion as both rejection and disgrace. My father seemed to be of similar mind. The morning of my mother and sister's departure, I went to see him, as requested, sitting in the smaller courtyard. I stood before him, hands clasped behind me, waiting nervously for him to speak.

My father contemplated me for a while. He had, by this time in his life, long perfected the art of stillness. Often, throughout my life, he seemed to be exactly the same as one of those statues of our forefathers, as impermeable and durable as stone. It was only near the end that something cracked. Today he studied me dispassionately, seriously.

"Spock," he said, "envy arises from our instincts. It is not the product of an ordered mind."

I knew that what he said was true. Still, these feelings ran so very deep—and this, in its turn, caused me great shame, that once again my human nature worked against those parts of me that I wished were in ascendance.

"Michael is your sister now," he said. "She is family now. To envy her, to hate her for this—all that can achieve is grief and unhappiness. And that is not rational. Hate, grief, pain—who can want these things?"

I did not want them, that was for sure. I wanted the serenity and balance of our old life to return—and yet this was not going to happen. My father had said this explicitly—and my father was not a liar.

"It is possible," he said, "to be strong. To teach your mind to reflect before it responds. To act from logic and not from instinct. This is a choice that you can make, and act upon, Spock. Do you wish to make that choice?"

I said that I did.

"That is a sound choice," he said, which was the most praise I had received from him in several months. "Perhaps we will meditate together more."

The prospect of this both delighted and terrified me; I simply nodded acquiescence.

"Very good, Spock. We shall meet again tomorrow morning. In the meantime, you may return to your studies."

I hurried away. But I did not return to my studies. I slipped out past the garden wall and away from the constraints of the house. I took the narrow path up into the hills, where the stark beauty and silent desolation of the countryside seemed always to bring me calm. Knowing that these walks were in contradiction of my father's wishes was, naturally, a considerable part of their charm. But these walks did soothe me. I had begun to learn that these hills— which, from a distance, seemed so bare and empty—contained multitudes. I could sit quietly for an hour, studying the variety of the rock formations, or the tough beauty of the succulents, the *kil'na* and the *pseth-kastik*. Sometimes, if I sat quietly enough, a *shatarr* might slip out from the shadows, and be persuaded to lie upon my palm, as if I were a rock upon which it could laze. I was happy here, and at peace, and whatever my father would say; whatever privileges were revoked for these forbidden forays, I could not, and would not, abandon them. They were too critical to my peace of mind.

It must be said that when Michael returned from this trip away with my mother she did seem a happier child, as if spending a little time away from our home had allowed a circuit break. She had brought back several books with her for her own collection—and she had also brought a book for me: a large green volume, with gilded leaves. I opened it cautiously, concerned, perhaps, that here would be more words with which I would have to struggle—but the book contained prints of maps. Many maps—but old, very old. Carefully, I sounded out the words on the front pages, but Michael came unobtrusively to my aid.

"It's an atlas of maps of Earth made throughout its history," she said. "Maps made by travelers and voyagers before the world had been fully explored. Some of the places turned out not to be real; some of them turned out to look different or be different. Some of the countries don't exist anymore…" Looking over my shoulder, she reached out to touch the page with her fingertip. She said, "I used to have an atlas like this. I loved to look through it, imagine all those wonderful places and what it must have been like to go looking for them…" Then, perhaps sensing the presence of my father behind us, her manner altered subtly, becoming more distant and formal. "There is a great deal in this book which may interest you," she said. "Perhaps we might study it together."

"I believe I would learn a great deal from that," I replied, and I was not incorrect in this assessment. We did look through this book together, many times—discovering strange old worlds, such as Atlantis and Ultima Thule, of empires long fallen, and continents long gone, and to ponder this book, which showed a world that not yet fully understood by its own inhabitants, a world to which I too was connected, but had not yet visited. My curiosity, my interest, in Earth was greatly stimulated by this atlas, and I perceived that these people too—these strange wild humans whose influence caused me such trouble— were perhaps closer to me than I realized, in their curiosity, their desire to explore and understand. In later years, I have wondered if this book was my mother's idea. This does not diminish the gift in my eyes; rather it is enhanced. It makes me think of my mother and sister together on that trip, taking the time to choose a gift for me to demonstrate their love. I think of the hours that I spent poring through it—both with Michael, and alone—the wonder those worlds instilled in me, the pleasure we derived from each other's company, and the connection that we made.

✦

After this came a happy period when Michael and I became friends. I should be more scrupulous here: I became her shadow, and she endured the presence of a younger child with more patience and kindness than I had perhaps shown her. I remember one afternoon, in my room, demonstrating every single one of my possessions to her. She sat and listened to me tell the tale of each one. We played drawing games, using our pads to bring them life, taking it in turns to show each other fantastical creatures from our respective cultures: if I drew *yon'tislak*, then she showed me a kraken. I taught her how to play *kal'toh*, and we liked to compete rather than collaborate. I suspect that she quickly surpassed me in skill, but we seemed to be evenly matched when it came to winning. Many years later, my mother told me how she looked into my room one day, to see us side by side, heads bowed over the board. "It is the last thing I shall remember, Spock. Both of you, so peaceful and happy." My mother took us out together once again on expeditions around the city. I began to think about suggesting that we might go swimming with the *o'ktath*.

But this new settled way of life was not to be permitted to continue. Two incidents in particular precipitated significant changes in our family lives. The first of these was triggered—as was so often the case—by an incident at the Learning Center. Some of my fellow students once again decided to target me because of my mother; this time, I reacted with force. My father was of course displeased at this emotional outburst and, in an attempt to prove to him that I was able to control myself, I determined to undergo the *kahs-wan*. This is a test of endurance in the wilderness to which young Vulcans subject themselves, attempting to survive in the desert for ten days without taking supplies or weapons.

Seven was young to be taking on this challenge, and I am surprised now that my mother allowed the attempt. Perhaps she thought this might bring me and my father closer together; perhaps she believed even the trial would give me confidence. Michael was away with her school cohort on a geological school trip to Vulcan's Forge, but we had a relative visiting unexpectedly at the time, a distant cousin named Selek. I found him a most interesting figure. In many ways, he reminded me of my mother: calm and reassuring; in other ways he would seem more like my father, composed and careful. His presence over those few days was to prove lucky in many ways. I went out into the wilderness too early, and quickly found myself in danger. In the mountains, I was attacked by a *le-matya*, a fierce predatory beast. I was saved by my pet *sehlat*, I-Chaya, that had accompanied me on my journey, and by the fortuitous arrival of my cousin. Selek dispatched the *le-matya* with a nerve pinch, but I-Chaya had been badly wounded. I ran for help, only to learn that saving I-Chaya would leave my pet in great pain. I chose the logical option, to release him from his suffering. My memories of these few days are hazy; I was feverish from lack of water and from the heat. But I remembered my cousin distinctly. When I came to complete the *kahs-wan* in earnest, two years later, I was unafraid. My long walks in the hills stood me in good stead; the heat—and the visions that this seemed to induce—held no fear for me. The memory of my cousin's composure kept my mind clear. I had often thought of him in the intervening years, not least because of his other gift to me: a most effective version of the nerve pinch—a far more efficient tool in dealing with my classmates than anything else I had attempted. After these events, I attempted to discover precisely how Selek was related to our family but was unable to find more information. A small riddle, quickly forgotten—until many years later. But I shall return to this in due course.

The presence of human children at the Learning Center attracted the attention of people far more dangerous than a few small would-be class tyrants. One aspect of my childhood which should be recalled is how public a figure my father was: not only as the latest in a prominent family, but, in his own right, as ambassador to the Federation. Again and again, he would ask me not to walk in the hills alone; again and again I would slip away; again and again, he would punish me. Yet, in the end, it was Michael who was targeted.

There is, in the Vulcan outlook, a latent speciesism that rarely goes challenged. This arises from the peacefulness of our society, with little in the way of crime or violence, and the knowledge that this serenity and stability were not only hard-won but are maintained by a great effort on the part of each one of us to master our aggressive instincts and ensure they are not given free rein. In the best of us, this involves increasing humility, at the realization of how easily one call fall prey to less wholesome impulses. In the more fearful of us, an unpleasant superiority can take root. And, like any other culture, this can become a form of extremism. In its most benign form, this was an isolationist movement seeking Vulcan's withdrawal from the Federation. In its more unstable proponents, this manifested itself as violence. My father— the Vulcan ambassador to the Federation, married to a human, and with a half-human child—was naturally the focus for their discontent. And, on one occasion, my sister and I were specific targets of their anger: a bomb was placed at the Learning Center.

I was myself, fortunately, away from the direct explosion. I recall chiefly the alarms sounding, the tutors calmly leading us to safety. I recall security descending upon the area; my mother arriving to take me home.

"Where is Michael?" I said, as she took my hand.

I saw tears in her eyes.

"Mother?"

"Don't worry, Spock," she said. "Everything will be just fine."

All I was told that day was that Michael was in the hospital and would be there for a little while. It took me a few days, and some careful listening at doors, to piece together the full story. Michael had been dead for three minutes, and only a mind-meld with my father saved her. When she came home, she seemed smaller. She was quiet. She liked my father to be nearby. I have a clear memory of them that must, I think, be from this time: sitting in silence together under the trees in the garden; her head against his shoulder; his hands around hers. I recall both regret—that I was not the one sitting beside him—and at the same time relief—that she was comforted by his presence.

That anyone could conceive of targeting an already traumatized child lies still beyond my comprehension. I have tried to understand their reasoning. I cannot see their logic. There is none. But such was the reality of our lives now. My father decided to relocate us for a while to a secure house near Vulcan's Forge. I recall on the journey there that my sister was increasingly distressed. That night, worrying about her and unable to sleep, I crept from my bed to her room, where I found her making preparations to run away. She wanted me to be safe, she said; that I deserved to grow up somewhere safe, and that she was the reason why our home was targeted. When I said that I would go with her, my words seemed to trigger something inside her. The scene that unfolded between us remains crystal clear in my mind: children, when they determine to be cruel, can wield words with uncanny precision.

I don't want you with me, she told me.

You are my sister, I said. *I love you.*

Freak, she called me; *half-breed*; *cold and distant as a moon.*

Not Vulcan. Not human. Something weird, and unfixable. If Michael was saying this, then surely it must be true. She left. I went back to my room. You may imagine how I wept. Remember that I was still very young. I did not understand that she was saying these words in an artless attempt to save me, hoping that by pushing me away she might protect me. I was a much older man before I had the emotional maturity to understand this. But this conversation—the cruelty of what she said, even as she meant to show love— formed me, going forward. I did not trust so openly again, for many years. I did not love so freely again, for a long time. I ran each word she had said over and over in my mind until they were committed completely to memory, and the lesson learned. At length, and wrung out, I fell asleep.

What happened next was one of the defining experiences of my life. At first, I thought that lights were flickering outside my bedroom window. Then I understood that the lights were closer to hand. I watched as they took form: a red winged figure. I knew from the drawing games I had played with Michael what to call such a creature. An angel. A red angel. Was I dreaming? I rubbed my eyes. She was still there. I did not cry out. I was not afraid, merely curious. I lifted my hand and saluted her. In response, she showed me what I can only call a vision, or a premonition: my sister, in the wilderness, attacked by a beast, her life in danger.

Now I cried out. "What is happening? Where is Michael?" All my grief and rage at what she had said to me was, for the moment, forgotten. All that I cared about was to make sure that she was safe. "Where *is* she?"

But the angel was gone. I was alone, in the dark, but in no doubt that what I had seen was true, and that haste was needed. I ran to wake my parents and tell them what I had seen. I have to wonder now, how I must have appeared to them, standing by their bedside, talking about seeing a red angel, showing me my sister's death. To their credit, they acted on what I told them. From the vision, I accurately described where Michael was to be found—and she was retrieved and brought home safely. My father was of the opinion that Michael had told me where she was going, but extracted a promise from me not to tell, and that this wild fabrication was the best means available to me to get them to act. I allowed him to continue believing this. Either that, or I had used logic to guess where Michael was likely to be. My mother, I could see, was less certain. Later, when she asked me to describe what I had seen, I did, in considerable detail. As I spoke, I could see her concern mounting, and I stopped.

"Perhaps," I said, tentatively, "it was only a dream."

"Yes," she said. "Perhaps it was." But I could see that she was worried. She had, as I shall explain when I give an account of my older brother, Sybok, many good reasons to be concerned that I might lose my grip on reality. I accepted my parents' judgment that some rational explanation was at work—that I had gathered from Michael where she intended to go and some leap of logic occurred was the official story in our family. But I knew that this was not what had happened. Michael had told me nothing; all she had done was to try to push me away. I knew what I had experienced was real. I had been told, somehow, where to find her. "Eliminate the impossible, and whatever remains, however improbable, must be the solution." I was sufficiently a product of my education to believe that there was a rational explanation for what had happened to me—what I did not yet know was what that explanation was. I never doubted that what I had experienced was real. But I knew there was no point in trying to make the adults around me understand. I would have to wait, and trust that one day I would understand in full.

When Michael was returned safely to us, I understood for the first time how much she had come to mean to me, how much her loss would have devastated me. These emotions, which I experienced almost as a tsunami, I kept entirely to myself. I did not want to face her rejection again. If my parents noticed that I did not shadow her so much, perhaps they believed that I was simply finding my own way. We went back to separate excursions with my mother. I never did take Michael to swim with the *o'ktath*. I wish that I had.

I should not leave you with the impression that this period of my childhood was wholly unhappy. In admitting Michael Burnham to the family, in taking on the responsibility for assisting her in finding the means to live beyond the trauma of witnessing the murder of her parents, my mother and father took on a set of challenges that they could not have anticipated. There were many complications to my sister's situation which they could not have predicted, but one can only applaud their courage and compassion in taking on the task of adopting this wounded child. Nevertheless, there were many things that my parents might have done differently, and there were many difficulties yet to come in my relationship with Michael, many personal ramifications for me as a result of acquiring this older sister. I wonder, sometimes, how my life might have been different without her. Such questions are, of course, unanswerable, and beside the point.

Hindsight is a gift, and such is the purpose of this book: to reflect, with the peace and wisdom one hopes to achieve in old age, on the events of one's youth, to consider what has gone before with the benefit of experience. I have not yet earned peace, and, bearing in mind my imminent destination, my wisdom is perhaps not proven. But as those troubled years of my pre-adolescence become more distant in my mind, I find that the trials and troubles, the worries and frustrations, have dissipated, and it is other memories that come more easily to mind. I picture myself and my sister, sitting together on the bed in her room. It is early evening, and, beyond the slats of the blinds the sun is setting in a great fire. Inside, the lamps have been lit; blue and silver in Michael's well-ordered room. We hear steps in the hallway outside; we tumble together beneath the covers. Then the door opens, and she is there— Amanda, the strong and gentle heart of our family, coming to settle us to sleep. She curls up on the bed, one of us on either side, and again I hear her voice— ever soft, ever patient—reading to us, of the adventures of a child who tumbled into a world where nothing made sense, where up was down and left was right, but who found a way through in the end. The griefs and the heartaches, the misunderstandings and missed opportunities—they are forgiven now, and, with my departure, will be forgotten. What remains, in the end—what I would leave behind—is the love.

T'Pring

THE AFTERMATH OF THE BOMBING OF THE LEARNING CENTER was a significant turning point in our family life in the way that we were treated by others. That subtle racism that often lay beneath interactions with our family never entirely disappeared (and was yet to have at least one further and significant impact upon our lives), but from this point onward was much reduced. Having now read through their extensive correspondence from this time, I am grateful to see that both my mother and father received many expressions of heartfelt support from friends in the aftermath of the bombing. For some, this was plainly a genuine awakening as to where expressions of Vulcan superiority might lead. It was poignant, and touching, when I read through these letters much later, after their deaths, to see figures from my childhood—men and women of great intelligence and wisdom, whom I admired and continue to admire—speak with humility to my parents and assure them of their desire to learn and improve following these events.

From the perspective of Michael and myself, there were direct improvements in our daily life too. My father, with the support of other parents at the Learning Center, exerted his considerable influence to ensure that greater attention was paid to the specific requirements of his two children, and that the principle of *Kol-Ut-Shan* was scrupulously upheld within the establishment.

I recall that around this time the morning reflections with which we opened each day at the Learning Center contained many exhortations and injunctions to look for and accept the diversity we could find around us. I am glad to say that most of our fellow students took these messages to heart, and there were fewer remarks about the humans and half-humans in their midst, and thus little cause for anger from either my sister or herself. With less strife in her day-to-day life, Michael began to find some much-needed peace of mind and was able to focus her attention increasingly on her studies. She was soon excelling—alas for her younger brother, several years behind! But there were changes in my own life at this time too, when the question of my apparent slow-wittedness with the written word was at last resolved.

My mother had always maintained that there would be a rational explanation for my struggles; my father tended, I know, to assume that my dual background was the reason that I lagged behind my peers. Once Michael began to settle, her evident success in her schooling disproved this hypothesis completely, and my father—ever-logical—agreed to support my mother in her push to have my needs fully addressed. I find myself marveling at how focused and driven she was over this: she was barely thirty years old, a young woman living on an alien world whose inhabitants were confident—often over-confident—in their assertions, and yet she was not daunted. My mother was not satisfied that the Center was doing all that it could to help me. My father handed this battle over chiefly to her, but the Center was left under no illusion that she had his complete support. And, as Michael blossomed, they too had to grudgingly accept that perhaps there were other reasons for my troubles beyond being partly human. Still, it took my mother several months working through an extensive technical literature to come up with a diagnosis: *l'tak terai*, a learning disorder that affected my ability to process text upon the page. Dyslexia would be the closest human equivalent, with which my mother was herself diagnosed as a child; but *l'tak terai* is extremely uncommon on Vulcan, and teachers are therefore less skilled in recognizing the signs. With this information in hand, and full understanding of all that could be done arising from her own experience, my mother was unstoppable in securing the adjustments that I needed in order to be able to process information more easily. And slowly, painstakingly, she worked alongside me, helping me learn to read and restoring my confidence in my own abilities. All these strategies of my mother's soon began to have their effect. The confusion of information around me began to take on some order. I began to believe myself capable.

After this, my time at the Learning Center became steadily more satisfactory. Before long, I began to relish my time at school. I was deeply stimulated by the acquisition of new data and delighted at last to have access to this world which had hitherto seemed inaccessible to me. More particularly, I loved detecting patterns that connected the facts which we received. I know that many people look at the methods of education which are used on Vulcan with skepticism, believing that what they are seeing is children force-fed information. This was not how I experienced my time in the study domes. Each day brought some new insight, some new fact, that helped me further expand my understanding of the universe. I thrived in the routine and discipline that the domes offered. I enjoyed demonstrating not only my knowledge, but the increasing speed with which I could access information to answer questions and make logical deductions to solve complex problems. My memory—which was already very good—became excellent. For the first time in my life, I felt competent in my academic studies and, encouraged by my rapid improvement, now felt joy rather than dread at the prospect of a day's learning.

External perception of our educational methods also places too much emphasis on the learning domes. The curriculum would not be so illogically narrow. We meditated, we played music, we practiced martial arts. My preferred instrument was the *ka'athyra*: at my mother's insistence, I also learned the piano. Perhaps predictably, I found respite in the complex patterns of Bach, but quietly, privately, I was fascinated by the technical excellence and emotional intensity required to perform Chopin. Like all students at the Center, I studied *suus mahna*, that martial art which requires a clear and disciplined mind, allowing instinct to be harnessed to the intellect. Later in life, observing a display of judo by my colleague and comrade Hikaru Sulu, I was fascinated to see many similarities between our practices. Watching him, I saw yet again how much congruence there was between the dual parts of my heritage. We often took the chance to challenge each other at our respective arts. I have no particular taste for hand-to-hand combat, even though my way of life has meant that I have frequently been called upon to use these skills. But any martial art teaches you two things: the best way to win a fight is not to start one, but that if another starts a fight, you should always end it as the victor. A precisely placed neck pinch can put an end to many problems before they have a chance to arise.

My parents' relief at the changes in me was almost tangible. My mother smiled more. My father quizzed me on an almost daily basis about what I was learning, and I often detected satisfaction in his expression. At the Learning Center too I received greater acceptance from my peers than ever before. My academic abilities were no longer in doubt; my physical capability was a deterrent to bullying. Moreover, the new confidence that I acquired as a result led me to be calmer, more able to respond to provocation by ignoring it, or, better still, with a curt dismissal. I began to spend more time with my peers. Two comrades in particular proved to be good company at this time: Sukat, who was happy to spend many long hours at *kal'toh* and showed an interest in the puzzle games regularly sent from Earth by my human relatives; and Suleh, who, like myself, found the long hikes and walks in the mountains beyond the city stimulating, and taught me more about the geology and local flora and fauna of my home than I had taught myself. It is a great gift of friendship, I believe, to be shown the world through the eyes of an intelligent observer, to see what they see. With Sukat, the world seemed to comprise of deep patterns below the surface that could be perceived and mobilized to one's benefit; with Suleh, the landscape which I knew so well became even more detailed, even more fine-grained. I have never asked what benefits they acquired from their association with me, but it has continued well beyond school days, into our middle years, and well into old age. We were a tight band. There were still troubles, of course. A boy named Stonn, for example, continued to take exception to the presence of humans—whether full or in part—at the Center. I ignored him entirely: a mistake, perhaps, in retrospect, but one which I have survived.

Our practice of martial arts was considerably enlivened by our first use of weapons. These were naturally introduced with great ceremony and ritual, and with admonitions about taking their use very seriously. I, like many others, was permitted access to family heirlooms of great antiquity in order to begin this training. In a quiet but more solemn than usual ceremony, attended only by me and my father, I received the *lirpa*, the metal staff, and the *ahn-woon*, which is a long and weighted strip of leather that can be used as a whip or a noose. Each of these had belonged to those ancestors whose names were engraved on my memory, stretching back even beyond my great-grandfather. My father was at pains to impress this long history upon me.

"I cannot in all certainty say," he told me, "that these were ever used in battle. Those tales are lost in the mists of time. In any event, that is most certainly not their purpose now. They are to remind us of the bloodshed in our past, and thus to ensure that each generation of us makes the commitment to discipline mind and body to prevent such violence ever mastering us again."

Ritual weapons, then, reminders of the bloody history we had left behind—but weapons in which we had to demonstrate skill. I remember, after these gifts were given, I took them to the safety of my room. There were several further rituals associated with their care—keeping the blades sharp, the metal bright, the leather supple—and when these were done, I put them carefully away, and came downstairs. My mother was waiting for me. I remember her placing her hand upon my cheek, and I saw a flicker of doubt in her eyes. "So young to learn to fight," she said, and I thought for a moment that she was going to say more. But she did not. Instead, she kissed me and let me go on my way.

I believe, in retrospect, that this rare doubt showed by my mother toward my Vulcan upbringing was less associated with the martial arts in which I was being trained, and more in what else these artefacts symbolized. The *lirpa*, the *ahn-woon*—these are the weapons used in the *kal-if-fee*, the ritual combat that, should a challenge arise, form part of the marriage ceremony, *koon-ut-kal-if-fee*. My father (with what I was to learn later were considerable misgivings on the part of my mother) had determined that I, like him, should enter into a traditional betrothal arrangement. The negotiations for this began not long after my birth. I do not have children, and, therefore, have not, myself, been required to carry out this particular kind of high-level diplomacy. There are many nuances involved: families whom one may approach; families where an overture would be considered inappropriate or in bad taste. By the time that I was three, my intended had been identified, and over the course of the following few years, both families monitored the development of the other child, to determine whether the first meeting would take place.

I am aware that there must have been many concerns over suitability as a potential husband. My dual heritage, my apparent difficulties with the written word, the arrival of Michael presumably cementing our family's reputation for unorthodoxy. Yet, we were a very ancient family, one with a long and venerable history, one with whom an association was still a great honor. As the various troubles which had beset our family gradually dissipated, the benefits of continuing with the agreement clearly won out, and preparations began for the betrothal ceremony. We returned to our ancestral lands in the L'langon Mountains, there to await my wife-to-be and her family.

The day of the ceremony is long for a child, since it begins, perhaps inevitably, before sunrise and involves no small amount of meditation and fasting. But the moment of the betrothal itself is surprisingly brief and intense. We were brought together, both cowled to hide our features, and then revealed to each other.

"I am Spock," I told her.

"I am T'Pring," she said. It was the first time I heard her name. I remember a sweet-faced and serious girl; no doubt I too looked very serious. My father guided my hand to her cheek; her mother guided her hand to mine. And then, the mind-meld—my first; the touch of our thoughts and wishes and hopes and fears. We both learned that we were as frightened as the other, as sincerely worried at what we might learn or give away. I experienced a cool and clever intelligence, a logical mind, but one that met me with interest and curiosity. We were, in many ways, very similar, T'Pring and I. I saw her blink, felt her surprise—and relief—that she had experienced common ground between us. I felt the same way, and she, of course, knew this. We shared our desire to excel, and to make our families and our ancestors proud. And then, we drew apart, and there our families, newly linked, ate a quiet meal together. The next day, she and her family departed, and I took heart from our first meeting, and looked forward to our future encounters before the arrangement was fully formalized. My mother, too, was much relieved.

I know that to alien eyes, the practice of arranged marriage causes great alarm, on the basis that the children concerned cannot consent. My upbringing meant that I did not ask such questions. I knew from studying family history that my grandparents and my great-grandparents, and no doubt as far back as I might look, had entered into such marriages and that they had well served the families concerned. I knew from observing friends of my parents, and the parents of my friends, that such arrangements were not inevitably unhappy, but were partnerships between people whose values and backgrounds were deeply congruent. Bear in mind our history of violence, Jean-Luc, and our fear of a collapse back into such barbarism. Caution in matters of the heart, where passions might threaten the balance of our society, was a natural outcome of our turn to logic. Deep satisfaction was to be achieved from knowing that one's life partnership contributed significantly to the continued stability of our society. When I first met T'Pring, I had no reason to believe that our partnership would be any different.

I will not enter this debate further other than to say that, at the time, I did not feel that I was under any compulsion to marry T'Pring. Two families, congruent in their values and beliefs, came together to reaffirm these, and to offer each other the possibility of closer involvement in the future. I have no doubt that if either I or T'Pring had been unhappy with what we found during that meeting of minds, then the betrothal would have gone no further, with no blame or reproach implied. Some of these ceremonies do not end with a betrothal; some of the marriage ceremonies instead become a challenge; and some of our marriages do not last the course. There is no marriage if there is not consent on both sides.

But what I shall say is that, had I ever had a child of my own, I would not have pursued this course for them, and there, perhaps, I might have caused a further disappointment in my father's eyes. It is possible that I do him an injustice here. At the time, though, there were many questions in my mind. Having now participated in this ritual, and knowing, as I did, the great solemnity with which these promises are made, I wondered increasingly about my father's first marriage. My half-brother, Sybok, had been an occasional presence during my early childhood, but was now barely mentioned. I shall write about him more fully later in this book, Jean-Luc. At the time, I knew little more than that, before marrying my mother, my father had been married to a woman from an aristocratic family, and that this marriage ended shortly after the birth of Sybok. It was not until much later that I pieced together the story, and I am still not sure that I am in possession of all the facts. I still must conjecture as to what the ending of this marriage meant for my father's decisions when it came to my future. Was it possible that my father—scion himself of an ancient and venerated family—was considered to have broken with convention when that first marriage ended? Was this reputation for nonconformity cemented when he chose to marry a second time, and a non-Vulcan at that?

I have wondered many times whether the emphasis which my father placed on my Vulcan heritage arose in part from a desire to protect me from the judgment of others. That he knew that I would have to prove myself again and again, demonstrating myself more Vulcan than every other Vulcan around me. In this respect, his wish for me to enter into a traditional marriage makes great sense. My acceptance by a family such as T'Pring's would be considered evidence that I was to be considered truly Vulcan, that this curious half-human child was able to integrate completely into Vulcan culture and society. My father—who was widely traveled and hugely well-informed, a diplomat with experience of dozens of different civilizations—nonetheless like many others from his homeworld believed that the Vulcan way of life was without peer, that a more stable, harmonious, and successful civilization was not to be found. Naturally, he would want me to enjoy all the benefits that would arise from this. Naturally, he would choose the more traditional path for me. The ending of the arrangement between myself and T'Pring I hesitate to discuss further: this is her story as much as mine and should not be told without full consent. Time, distance, and circumstance brought us both to a very different place. What I will say is that as I grew older, and grew wearier of my homeworld, I chafed at the doubts and constraints that surrounded me, and I grew increasingly keen to leave, to see more of the diversity of the universe which I had been taught to honor. By the time I left for Starfleet Academy, much about Vulcan had lost its appeal. I wanted more than I had; after all, as perhaps T'Pring herself discovered in time, having is not so pleasing a thing as wanting.

✦

One unalloyed pleasure at this time was the arrival on Vulcan of my mother's family. Both my maternal grandparents, as well as my mother's older brother, his husband, and their son came for their first extended visit to Vulcan since my parents' marriage. This cousin, in particular, I found a most intriguing individual. Disheveled, eccentric, brilliant, and buzzing with intense enthusiasms that seemed to propel him through the day, Andrew Grayson was, at fifteen years old, interested in everything that crossed his path. Mathematics, physics, music, art, literature, anything that moved, made a sound, crept, flew, or exploded—whatever his eye fell upon Andrew grabbed hold and did not let go until the phenomenon was fully explored and understood. On arrival at our home, he looked vaguely at my father, my mother, and at us two children, then his eye fell upon my *ka'athyra*, abandoned on a nearby chair when our guests arrived.

"Ah!" he said. "I was hoping to try my hand at this!"

He wandered off, *ka'athyra* in hand, and settled himself in the nearest chair, long legs thrown over the arm, already picking out a series of tuneful notes. My uncle said, "That's Andrew. I don't know who brought him up. They should be ashamed." But there was no doubting his love. Michael and I exchanged a look and, as soon as we could, sidled away from the grown-ups to observe this unusual specimen at close range, as he plucked at and roundly cursed the instrument. We were both of course besotted. The three of us, throughout that extended holiday, were almost a pod of *o'ktath*, the smaller two dipping and diving in the wake of their senior, as each new interest of his was explored to its full.

It is not hard now to see the appeal of Andrew to us two children, and why he mattered so much to both Michael and me. Untidy, almost chaotic, and with a constant almost nervous energy that kept his hands permanently in motion, or his foot tapping, under no circumstances could Andrew have been mistaken for a Vulcan. And yet his brilliance could not be doubted. Within half-an-hour, he was creating sweet sounds from my *ka'athyra* that put my years of practice to shame. Satisfied he had mastered the basics, he put the instrument aside and wandered off (two shadows close behind) in search of some new challenge. How could we not adore this mercurial young man, so quintessentially human, and yet displaying all of the virtues impressed upon us as the most important: an insatiable desire for information and knowledge, and an intensity and focus that would have satisfied even the most demanding of our teachers at the Learning Center. And yet… there was no Vulcan parent at home; there had been no Vulcan philosophy behind his education. Andrew was born on Earth, to human parents, and educated in human schools. He was visible proof that our world did not have the monopoly on brilliance. He was balm to our souls.

"Fascinating…" he would murmur, confronted with some new insight into the world about him, and one could see him turn over each new bright jewel of information, setting it in place in the lumber room of his mind for when it would be needed. With great excitement, Michael and I brought him to the *kal-toh* board, and we watched him tackle it with aplomb, achieving impressive results that had me envy his obvious expertise—until I realized he had never seen a *kal-toh* board before, and was making up his gameplay as he went along. Michael and I, who had spent long hours memorizing the hundred basic strategies, were dumbfounded. This was my first experience of that very human quality of "blue-sky thinking", those miraculous-seeming leaps of intuition guided by the nebulous but strong sense of an underlying pattern to the world, that, in the right hands, delivered such remarkable breakthroughs and results. I would see this quality again throughout my life: in brilliant students at the academy; most of all, in my friend and captain, Jim Kirk. This confidence, this vision—Andrew had this capacity in abundance.

I was glad, at this time, also to be able to see more of my maternal grandparents, with whom I naturally corresponded regularly, but whom I had not met in person before. They were gentle, brilliant, intellectual people, with whom I was very shy, but whom I was to come to know better when at last I went to Earth. I remember my grandfather, walking with me along the canal, watching the *o'ktath*, and quietly asking me about the betrothal to T'Pring.

"I have to admit, Spock," he said, "that arranged marriages seem strange to me—even repugnant. Are you sure this is what you want?"

I was still very young of course—too young to know what I wanted, other than that I wished to be the Vulcan son my father so transparently desired me to be. I said, "I am not discontented."

My grandfather gave me an odd look, one which, I realized later in life, was associated with that question my human friends and family would sometimes ask: *Yes, but are you happy?* He did not ask that question now. "Well," was all he said, "that's something, at least. I suppose we'll have to see what happens. But remember, Spock, your home is Earth, as much as here."

That, I thought, was a curious thing to say. How could a world that I had never visited be my home? Before he left, my grandfather gave me a beautiful set of hardback books: the complete works of Sir Arthur Conan Doyle. "You'll like these," he said. And then, with a wink, he added, "You'll like the lead, for certain. There's a family connection—or resemblance, at least. An ancestor of ours, perhaps. You'll see."

I have never quite worked out this claim of my grandfather's. Since the creation did not exist beyond the covers of the books, and the children of his creator all died without issue, I can only deduce that my grandfather meant this figuratively. Perhaps there is some story still untold—but, leaving this aside, he was quite right. I did like the lead, a great deal. And I did not forget what he said to me—that Earth might provide a home for me.

✦

And so my later childhood passed. I continued my full range of studies. Michael, a few years ahead of me, departed in due course for the Vulcan Science Academy to study quantum physics, beginning an illustrious career there that caused her younger brother many headaches as he contemplated having to follow in her footsteps. In time, I began my own preparation to enter the Science Academy and, looking back now at my correspondence from this period, I see that Michael reached out to me to offer advice on how best to go about this. I responded cautiously and minimally, but I could see the logic in accepting some guidance, albeit from a distance. Reviewing this series of messages between us, I see now that it is remarkable the extent to which she took time out of what must have been a punishing schedule of study to answer my questions, advise on topics, detail approaches, familiarize me with every aspect of the admissions process. I knew a great deal about the courses on offer, the tutors and their foibles, what questions I might reasonably expect. Seeing her face again in these messages, I recall how centered she appeared at this time and how rightly confident in her abilities. She was—dare I say it—the happiest I had ever seen her. I am grateful that she had this period of certainty in her life.

I would like to end this part of my reflection on my childhood years on a serene and reflective note, but our family faced one last shock, and one which was to have many repercussions in the years to come. After her outstanding time at the Science Academy, graduating top of her class and receiving the Scientific Legion of Honor, Michael's intention was to join the Vulcan Expeditionary Group. And yet, despite these manifold achievements, her application was rejected. I have subsequently served as an external observer for applications to the Expeditionary Group many times over the years, and I can say confidently that there have not been many applications I have seen that would have matched Michael's. And yet, for some reason, she was not considered an appropriate candidate for admission.

It was only later, much later, that I learned that the reason why Michael was rejected from the Expeditionary Group. Sometimes, our human background seemed to act like a curse upon us; some fatal flaw which would, at moments of hubris, catch us unawares. There had been considerable consternation, it transpired, at Michael's success at the Science Academy, and a growing sense that a place in the Group that should be for a Vulcan graduate was likely to go to a human. Was there not a perfectly good equivalent service for such people? Was not Starfleet the place where she should more reasonably serve? This was the *Vulcan* Expeditionary Group, after all. Such, I gathered later, was the kind of case that was made to my father and, when he rightly refused to accept this, the choice was cast in starker terms. This admission could not be allowed to set a precedent. It would be a special case, for one candidate, and one candidate alone. Did my father prefer this to be his full-human child, or his half-human child?

This decision should never have been forced upon my father. I suspect there were other circumstances that prevented him from telling the Expeditionary Group in no uncertain terms what he thought of this offer. All concerned are long dead, and the politics of that period irrelevant. But not at the time. My father, faced with this impossible choice, chose me. Michael, shocked at her own apparent failure, found herself placed aboard the *U.S.S. Shenzhou*. I, also unaware of what had transpired, continued my preparation for entry into the Science Academy. But that path now seemed more doubtful to me, for two reasons. Firstly, my sister's triumphs went before her. I was increasingly aware that, if I attended the academy, I would be known as Michael's brother, and would struggle to make my own reputation. I was beginning to think that there might be benefits arising from going to a place where I was entirely unknown, and where a complicated heritage was less likely to stand out. The second reason that turned me against the Expeditionary Group was the shock of Michael's rejection. Although I did not know the full circumstances of this, I was not a fool, and I sensed at the time that the fact that she was human had worked against her. Logically, I would face a similar response, if perhaps mitigated somewhat by the fact that at least some part of me was Vulcan. But to subject myself to this was beginning to seem less and less rational. Quietly, I began to explore other options, enlisting my relatives on Earth to provide me with information about other paths available to me.

My grandfather, I recall, proved particularly helpful at this time.

I might wish—as I have wished many times, and in many different cases—that my father had been more open with us. That he had explained to both me and Michael that what happened at this time was not a failure on her part, but that immutable sense of superiority that arose from the deep certainties within Vulcan philosophy that had created such a stable, successful, peaceful society. Above all, I wish that my father had asked us to make this choice ourselves: that he had provided us with the full facts and trusted us, his children, to think logically and unemotionally about our options. We were both, my sister and I, at his own insistence, thoroughly well-trained products of Vulcan philosophy and schooling. We might well have surprised him with our maturity and rationality. Had he done so I believe that the decision that I eventually made might not have been so painful for everyone concerned. Alas, this was not the case, and perhaps there were further complications to this situation which prevented him from disclosing to us what had happened. But the ramifications of my father's desire to protect us from full knowledge—and, perhaps, from his own sense of guilt at being made party to this shameful decision—were to affect our family for many years to come.

Sybok

THERE ARE MANY SILENCES AND LACUNAE SURROUNDING MY FAMILY, and I had, by my mid-thirties, long accustomed myself to simply not speaking about them. There are many reasons for this, some of which I have already alluded to, some of which shall become apparent as I continue this *t'san a'lat*, and some of which can be attributed to my natural reserve. Few, for good reason, remember my sister. Few, for other reasons, remember my brother—or, more accurately, my elder half-brother, Sybok. But I find that must now track back in time to speak in more detail about him, about my relationship with him in my early years, and how the course of his life affected my own. He played a part later in my life, which was significant less in its impact upon me than in showing me how far I had come from my very early days, and in revealing once again to my closest friends that there were still hidden parts to me. My brother was a gifted man, both in scholarship and in the deep empathy arising from his unusually powerful ability to mind-meld, but he was, at the same time, troubled in many ways. What I would like now to recall is the brother that he was when I was young, and also to show how the existence of this older brother, and his fraught relationship with our father, had such a deep impact upon my own adolescence.

Although I knew that my father had been married before, and that I had an older brother, the details of that first marriage were largely obscure to me for many years. It was not until after my own mother had died, and my father remarried for a third time, that I learned much of what I know. It is thanks to my father's third wife, Perrin, that I have much of the information that I shall now recount. Perrin and I did not always see eye-to-eye, but after my father's death, she was open-hearted and open-handed in allowing me access to his papers in my capacity as his literary executor. From my father's papers, then, I learned that Sarek's first wife, T'Rea, was from another aristocratic family, one with similarly strong connections to the diplomatic service. Tying two such families closer by marriage was commonplace; there were, by good fortune, two children of appropriate age. Sarek and T'Rea were bonded in the traditional way at the usual and early age, and this betrothal became a full marriage following my father's first *Pon farr*. My father, at this point, had returned from an early diplomatic posting to take up a position within the diplomatic service in ShiKahr, and T'Rea came to live at our family home. Soon after, their son, Sybok, was born.

To all outside eyes, then, this must have seemed a most successful match: scions of two well-established families, with a long history of public service, uniting for the common good of Vulcan. Two years after Sybok's birth, however, T'Rea went back to live with her family, taking their young son with her. Given her later actions, I have no information as to why she did not leave Sybok with my father, and perhaps she herself had no idea of the life-altering decision she was about to make. Shortly after returning to her own family, where she left her son, T'Rea set out for the sanctuary at P'Tranek Monastery, near Lake Yuron, to begin a short retreat under the guidance of the *kolinahr* master T'Nel. This in itself was not untoward: a ritual purging of emotions is often undertaken by new parents to assist them in finding the equilibrium required to carry out their new responsibilities. In such cases the retreat is not generally of great duration, and P'Tranek, to this day, is well known as a destination for those seeking temporary respite from the world. But when the three months of the retreat were finished, T'Rea's family contacted my father to tell him that she had left P'Tranek and was now traveling with T'Nel to a religious community in the L'langon Mountains, where she intended to take Repose.

To understand what T'Rea's decision meant, one must understand a little more about the history of the L'langon Mountains, and the temples and monasteries there. This far distant region has a very distinct history. Here,

Surak faced the greatest resistance to his campaign to unify all Vulcan under his teachings. A great battle was fought on the Bacchus Plateau between the followers of Surak and the followers of High Master Sobok, and, while Surak won the day, the area was never entirely conquered, and there were holdouts of extremists and other outsiders. Rocky and remote, the area is still populated by sects of ultra-ascetics and lonely hermits, and, while these no longer take up arms, they retain a reputation for religious unorthodoxy. You will find many outlandish temples and strange communities here. The village of Kren'then, for example, perched in a bowl upon the top of an isolated mountain, is the home of a community who have rejected all modern technology, living much like your own Earth Amish, Jean-Luc, or the Bak'u, with whom you yourself have experience. A harsh life, in this desert region, but one to which they are utterly committed.

Some kilometers east of Kren'then, deep in the desert, one will find the Temple of Amonak, a shrine that, during the more violent periods of our history, has acted as a sanctuary for those fleeing religious or political persecution. The place, in its last days, was more fortress than temple. After peace was at last established on Vulcan, the buildings fell into disrepair, until a party from Kren'then determined to restore them. Consider the enormity of this task, Jean-Luc: these people, eschewing any form of technological assistance, labored in the desert heat to shore up these crumbling ruins, which symbolized to them all that mattered about L'langon—the freedom to follow one's own path without external interference or intimidation. These renovations were only concluded at the start of this century, and—should you ever make your long overdue visit to my home planet, Jean-Luc—you will find there one of our most revered religious sites, with a grand sheer façade built over the warrens and hidden places that gave succor during our violent past. The tour of the temple commences at the top of the new high building and takes you down toward the lower levels like an archeologist gently peeling away the layers of history. I believe that you would find this a most stimulating and rewarding experience. Perhaps you will think of my family history when you visit; you might remember my father, and his first wife, and their son.

These renovations were still underway when T'Rea made her journey to Amonak. I have tried, sometimes, to imagine her making this pilgrimage, leaving behind her old life. The scion of a high family that was deeply embedded not only in the life of the great city of ShiKahr, but in an interstellar community, she had chosen to cast this all aside—down to her family, her husband, her son—and journey here. Step by step—yes, she came here by foot across the parched desert, following T'Nel—the layers of her old life slipping away. She would have seen the nameless mountain where Kren'then lies, rising from the red dust. She would have stayed there for a while, preparing herself mentally for the next step, before she walked along the old road towards the half-built temple. But neither was she staying here. Beyond Amonak, another road—barely more than a dirt track—leads into a narrow clefted valley, the high rock rising up to the left and to the right. If you look closely here, you will see narrow paths zigzagging on each side, and, at intervals, dark holes, like eyes. These are the *sel'anar*, the Chambers of Repose, hermits' cells, and here T'Rea came to live out the rest of her days.

You have a similar tradition in your own history, Jean-Luc, of religious figures known as anchorites, or anchoresses, who withdraw from life not to a monastery, but to the enclosure of a solitary cell, to spend their lives fasting and praying. This was the life T'Rea had chosen, one of silence, meditation, and solitude. She will have come to the cell, put down at the door whatever possessions she had brought with her, taken off her shoes, and, barefoot and empty-handed, entered the cell. The temple monks would then have proceeded to seal the door behind her, all the while intoning the *itsil'sar*, the ritual chant for the dead. When this was done, all that would remain to her of the outside world was the small squint hole, through which food could be passed and the stark sky glimpsed. And here she stayed, practicing the art of *kolinahr*, until she attained high mastery. Of all the disciplines that have emerged on my world in our attempt to purge the violent emotions of our past, this is surely the most unforgiving. Even the most disciplined of High Masters following the most stringent path to *kolinahr* at Vulcan's Forge maintain connections with their families. When T'Rea told her family that she was taking the path of Repose, she was telling them that she was cutting the ties to her old life. That her family—her husband and her son—should consider her dead.

I have no information on the immediate aftermath of this decision. I have no cause or grounds to approach T'Rea's family to ask, nor would I presume. Since my father was traditional in outlook, we might logically assume that he now considered himself widowed, and his son motherless.

He never spoke to me of this time, of course, and even Perrin, to whom he showed more open emotion than any other living being, was not made privy to his thoughts during this time period. If there was any grief at the loss of his wife, or pride at the convictions that led her to make this choice, I do not know. Perhaps this seemed to him a logical step for her. Everyone concerned is now dead, including Perrin, and their reflections on this time have gone with them into the red dust. I can offer only the facts of what happened next, conjecture on what this might have meant to Sybok, and offer my child's eye view of the young man that emerged from these early years. What I do know is that following T'Rea's departure, my father took a diplomatic post off-world, and Sybok remained with his mother's family. My father saw him intermittently over the following years, but he did not spend a substantial amount of time with our father until after I was born, and the time came for him to complete the *kahs-wan*. At this point—I must have been four or five, and Sybok a decade older—he came to live with us, to prepare for this important ritual. I remember him as playful, boisterous, and patient with a much younger sibling who was dumbstruck by this lively presence in his usually sedate home. We never mind-melded, to my regret, Sybok and I, but I was very comfortable in his presence. He was strongly intuitive and empathic, and, when I was with him, I had a sense of being completely understood (a rarity in my confusing childhood). My older brother, I could see even at this relatively young age, was manifestly blessed with many gifts, which his homeworld never found a way to nurture.

The *kahs-wan* is a punishing trial, undertaken most usually between the ages of nine and eleven, in which participants must survive ten days in the wilderness, without even the most basic of survival equipment. They must find food and water, in an unrelenting landscape, and defend themselves against whatever wild animals must cross their path. At fourteen or fifteen, this was late in life for Sybok to be taking on this challenge, and my understanding is that there had been two previous and unsuccessful attempts. This third attempt would be the last; further attempts were unheard of, and thus there was an unspoken air of finality about these proceedings. My mother suggested to my father that we go out to our home in the L'langon Mountains, where she might help him prepare for his ordeal, and my father consented. I do not know what Sybok's other family thought of the human wife attempting to help; perhaps they did not know what else was to be done and accepted the necessity of her involvement.

My mother attempted many times to reach Sybok, and I believe that, as far as it was possible, a bond formed between them. News of his death—and the manner of his death—hit her very hard. One of our last conversations concerned how bitterly she regretted her failure to establish a connection with him. She had tried on occasion to persuade him to study on Earth, but to no avail. To be fully accepted as Vulcan was what Sybok desired. I cannot see what more my mother could have done; nor, indeed, can I see what more Sybok might have done in his turn. With my mother he was always courteous and measured; there was never the undercurrent of anger and, latterly, suppressed violence that one sensed when he was near our father. At Sybok's own request, she took on the task of tutoring him through his last attempt at the *kahs-wan*. My mother was, by this point in her life, an adept at the fourth level of *kolinahr*, that level before one enters seclusion. She had come as far as she might come without leaving us behind, which we knew she would never do, and yet much further than anyone believed a human could come. Perhaps this was one reason that my brother's grandparents were willing to entrust him to her, and she did everything that she could.

I recall how my mother spent hour after hour in Sybok's company, in quiet discussion, in meditation. I recall them now, as if it were yesterday, sitting together in a quiet corner of the villa in the mountains, by the flickering light of the meditation lamps. The sharp fierce angles of his face; the gentle patient curves of hers. I recall her voice, quiet and steady, chanting along with his, hoarse and halting, guiding him through the recitations, the mantras, the disciplines that would guide him in the wilderness. When the day came for him to begin the ritual, she traveled with him to the edge of the wilderness, and saw him on his way.

We did not expect to hear from him for the full ten days. My mother seemed quietly confident that he would succeed. Still, seven days after his departure, while I sat with my mother in the garden by the fountain, we heard footsteps hurrying toward us. A rough and dirty figure, still covered in the dust of the desert, sweat streaking his brow, ran into the courtyard. Sybok had returned, three days early.

"Sybok," said my mother, coming to her feet, her face turning white. "What has happened?"

"Where is he?" said my brother. "Where's Father? Oh, Amanda, wait until he hears what I have seen!" There was a wildness about him, not simply his appearance, but in his eyes. I do not think it is imagination speaking when I say that I recall his hands were trembling. "Amanda! I must speak to Father immediately!"

My father, who had been in his study, came out in the court: he must have been disturbed by the noise. He saw Sybok, and... Jean-Luc, let us say that I shall not easily forget my father's face the moment he saw his older son, returned too soon yet again from the *kahs-wan*. For a brief second, a fire seemed to stir in my father's eyes—and then this was quenched, completely quenched. It was as if his flesh petrified, in the true sense of the word, as if he became as stony as the statues of our ancestors. His son had failed.

"Sybok," he said softly. "Why are you here?"

My brother, hurrying toward him, reached out to clasp his shoulders. "Father!" he said. "I've seen something great! I have to tell you—"

"We have spoken," said my father, detaching himself from his son's embrace, "about what might happen should you fail the *kahs-wan* yet again—"

"I have not failed!" said my brother. "I have seen everything I need to see! I have seen *Sha Ka Ree*!"

There was a silence. My father bowed his head. "Sybok—"

My mother stepped forward. "Let us go inside," she said, her voice low and calm, her hand upon her husband's arm. She looked back over her shoulder to me. "Stay here, Spock," she said, and she made sure to be smiling. "You need not worry."

So she said, but while I did not hear the substance of the argument that followed, I heard how Sybok's voice became ever more raised until, at last, I heard his footsteps echoing down the corridor again, and the door to the house slam. Not an hour had passed since his return. Later, when my mother settled me in bed, I asked her, "What is *Sha Ka Ree*?"

"A fantasy," she said. "A made-up place."

"Why would someone believe they had seen a made-up place?" I asked.

"Because they feel some lack," she said.

"I do not understand what that means."

"Sybok has lost a great deal in his life," my mother said. "Sometimes, when people lose something, they look for replacements. They reach for things that do not exist."

"That seems illogical," I replied.

"Yes," she said, and kissed me on the forehead. "But understandable."

Sha Ka Ree, Jean-Luc, is a place in Vulcan mythology, of a kind that appears in the mythologies of many worlds, the source of life and knowledge. The Klingons call it *Qui'Tu*, the Romulans *Vorta Vor*. You might refer to it as Eden. My poor brother, wandering alone through the wilderness, in what state of mind I cannot conjecture, believed he had glimpsed Paradise. A vision, indeed, and one that seemed to precipitate some breakdown in him. It is no surprise, on reflection, that, only a few years later, my claims to have been visited by a Red Angel caused such alarm, that I kept my conviction of their reality to myself, and allowed my parents to believe that some other, more easily rationalized explanation, lay behind my ability to pinpoint my lost sister's whereabouts.

I have observed, over the years, that those who lose a parent when they are children seem to experience this as an expulsion from a perfect world, and often seek some kind of return to a place of imagined bliss. Sybok's mother was, in effect, dead; his father was, as I had cause to know, often unreachable. This might explain some of what compelled Sybok, what made him obsessed with finding *Sha Ka Ree*. That is, after all, what happened, as we know now. In the years that followed his last, failed attempt at *kahs-wan*, he did not mention *Sha Ka Ree*. We saw him, on occasion, when he came to visit us at the house in ShiKahr (he did not come to the mountains again). He had eschewed both a scientific and a diplomatic career, and was instead pursuing a scholarly route, tracing the use of the mind-melding techniques throughout Vulcan history. He was often to be found in the archives of remote monasteries or near-forgotten shrines. In fact, as we know now, this archival work masked the truth that his obsession with *Sha Ka Ree* was growing. He never forgot the vision that came to him in the desert, that apparent glimpse of a heavenly place where he could be at peace. My father, it transpired, grew concerned about the direction of his studies, to the extent that he asked Sybok to abandon them. Sybok refused, and they cut off contact with each other. This was shortly after Michael left for the Science Academy.

I did not see my brother again in the flesh for many years. Shortly after I arrived at Starfleet Academy, however, Sybok contacted me. By this point, he had become involved with a group inspired by the teachings of the *V'tosh ka'tur*, a defunct sect who tried to find a middle ground between logic and emotion. He was entering a retreat on the Bacchus Plateau, and he asked me to join him there for a while when next I visited Vulcan. I said no. Relations between myself and my father were strained, to say the least, about my decision to enter Starfleet Academy, and becoming involved with such a group might well have turned our estrangement into a complete break. That was my last direct contact with my brother for more than thirty years. I learned not long afterward from my mother that he had abandoned even the *V'tosh ka'tur* and their teachings and was taking a path that not only intensified his emotional experiences, but which encouraged the pursuit of visions and revelations.

Might my acceptance of his offer at this time have altered the course of his later life? Such questions are, of course, impossible to answer, but, after considerable reflection, I must conclude not. For one thing, I was much younger, at the start of my career, still uncertain of my own path, and hardly likely to have been able to influence him. The effects upon my own life—not least the severance of ties with my father that surely would have followed had any close contact with my brother at this time been discovered—would undoubtedly have been greater. But the fault, I believe, did not lie in either of us. My brother's gifts—empathy, a visionary nature—were always going to be at odds with the mainstream of Vulcan philosophy. (One must conjecture, indeed, whether being in possession of such gifts was one reason that T'Rea voluntarily excluded herself from society.) On another world, one more able to understand the nature of his talents, he might well have flourished. On Vulcan, there was no path he could find to follow. In the end, of course, he was banished—although his story did not end there. Later, much later, Sybok made a reappearance in my life. All his gifts were still intact, but he used them to sway people to his cause—his quest to find *Sha Ka Ree*. The tragedy of my brother's life was that his need for understanding made him easy prey in his turn; his talents misused by a malevolent alien intelligence that had persuaded my brother of its divinity. In the end, coming to understand that he had been tricked, my brother sacrificed himself to save me and my friends. I wish it had not come to that. I wish he had found purpose. I wish that Vulcan had nurtured his gifts.

✦

Perhaps now you see that, from my perspective, two great shadows loomed over my later adolescence. The dreadful failure of my older brother, and the impossible success of my older sister. My hope was that I would find a way somewhere between the two; my fear that I was expected to find a path that soared to greater heights even than my sister. Logic suggested to me that the latter was not likely; it further suggested that I should try to strike out on a path that meant such comparisons were unlikely to be drawn. For this reason, as I have indicated, I began privately to consider options other than the Science Academy. I reached out to my family on Earth, and, with their assistance, spoke to friends with experience of Starfleet, and collected advice on how one might approach an application to Starfleet Academy. I shall not say that I concealed this from my parents; rather, let us say that since they did not ask, I did not tell.

Ultimately, a decision had to be made. Perhaps it was the growing realization that I would never be satisfactory, that the simple fact of my half-humanity would always be seen as a flaw. Or perhaps—and here I must be honest with myself—I had simply always been looking for a reason to refuse, a way to reject the ambitions which my father had long held for me. I am not proud of this, and perhaps you may see now how the long rift between my father and myself occurred. But in that moment, I have never felt so sure of myself, and, in retrospect, I have never felt so free. It was as if a great burden had been lifted from me. I knew now that I had never wanted this. What I wanted was to leave Vulcan. What I wanted, was to find my own way. Starfleet seemed to offer this.

There was one more nerve-wracking interview to be endured, however: the one that followed with my father. As it turned out, and as is so often the case, this confrontation was less terrible than imagination had made it.

"This is disappointing, Spock," said my father. "But all is not lost. I believe that with some intervention on my part, you may yet be able to enter the academy this year."

"Father," I said. "I have made my decision. I shall not attend the Science Academy."

"Spock," he replied, "attendance there is a necessary precondition to joining the Expeditionary Group—"

"Which I do not intend to join. For you to intervene would therefore be unnecessary, and illogical."

My mother, presumably detecting warning signs that even after many years I could not see, said, "Spock, this is a great change of heart—"

"Mother," I said. "I have doubted for some time that my path lay in that direction."

"What alternative is there?" said my father.

"It is my intention to go to Starfleet Academy, and pursue my scientific career within Starfleet," I said.

"But there is no family tradition of Starfleet," said my father.

"No," I agreed. "Or, perhaps we might say—not yet."

"Spock," said my father. "I do not wish you to join Starfleet."

"Father, my decision is made. In two months, I shall leave for Earth—"

"If it were not for your mother," my father said, "I should tell you not to return."

"If it were not for my mother," I replied, "I should not wish to return."

I am not proud of this conversation. Privately, I knew that I was enjoying the sense of exhilaration that came from going directly against my father's wishes, and I was somewhat ashamed by what amounted to an emotional outburst. But my father's palpable sense of anger and grievance were, at the time, incomprehensible to me. I could not understand the depth of his response. Of course, I knew nothing about what had occurred over my sister's failed entry to the Science Academy. All I knew was that, once again, I was proving a disappointment and that, given my human heritage, perhaps this was no more than could have been expected. I know now, having mind-melded with you, Jean-Luc, that this was not the case—that, by the end of his life, at least, my father had come to accept me for who I was. Not the person that he had anticipated, perhaps, but myself, in my own right. At the time, however, I was convinced of his disapprobation, and he was certainly in no hurry to disabuse me of this notion.

"Don't be too angry with him, Spock," my mother said to me later. "He *is* proud of you."

"I have no evidence to support that statement, Mother."

"He'll come round, in time. Give him time."

My father, having made his position clear, had nothing more to say. A week later, he left Vulcan for a long-planned diplomatic mission to Arderia IV, taking my mother with him. They would not be returning until long after I had left for Earth to take up my place at Starfleet Academy. Before leaving for Earth, I therefore found myself with a period of a month or two alone in ShiKahr, free of any obligations, perhaps for the first time in my life. I had no studies, no tests, no requirement to do anything other than what I pleased. I could have prepared for the classes in which I was enrolled on my first semester, but I did not. (My mother, checking in on me, gently encouraged this truancy.) Instead, I spent those weeks revisiting all the places that I loved best in and around my home city, places that we had often visited together, and said my farewells.

One afternoon, I took a private gondola down the Sirakal canal, and found the spot where my mother and I had often gone when I was a child. Here, at last, swimming with the *o'ktath*, I kept a promise that I had made myself long ago and mind-melded with them. For the first time since I had met T'Pring, I reached out to experience in full the mind of another living being, and that of a species very different from my own. It was an exhilarating experience, to immerse myself in their gentle, inquisitive minds; to swim with them sensing what they sensed, the joy of diving through the water, of meeting their own kind, of swimming alongside other creatures. And yet, behind this, I sensed the melancholy of their extinction. They knew, somehow, that they were creatures brought back from death; that they lived now only because of the twists and turns of our history, because of our desire to make amends. They knew. And I would have cause to remember this, one day.

But this holiday could not last, and, eventually, it was time, at last, for me to leave home. I will confess to feeling many regrets as I boarded the ship heading to Earth. I knew that I would miss the clear certainties, the stark and somber beauty of Vulcan. Most of all, I wished that my father and I had parted on better terms. But while my heart might have been heavy when I left Vulcan, the moment I caught a glimpse of Earth I felt my spirits start to soar. I recognized my kinship with the blue and white world below. I knew that I had made the right decision.

Surak

I HAVE NOT, I HOPE, OVER THE YEARS, ACQUIRED A REPUTATION FOR EXAGGERATION, but I believe that leaving Vulcan to attend Starfleet Academy was the saving of me. There are several reasons for this, one of the most important is surely the distance that it put between me and my home, and what I was starting to experience as increasingly difficult expectations in an increasingly impossible environment. There is certainly no confusing the Vulcan Science Academy with Starfleet Academy. For one thing, for all the heavy workload of study, no less than that which would be found at the Science Academy, the cadets seemed to be almost constantly at play. I am not talking simply of pranks and practical jokes (although there were naturally a great deal of those; what else would one expect from housing several thousand energetic and intelligent young people closely together) but of their attitude toward the work. This, I concluded from observation during my early days, was a kind of open-mindedness to the problems that were presented to us. At first, with a narrowness of mind arising from my own education, I dismissed this as an attempt to find loopholes and exploit them. Again and again, confronted with a problem, one of my fellow cadets (usually but not exclusively one of the humans), would say something on the lines of, "Let's look at this from another angle…" or "Let's turn this on its head…"

I was bewildered by this approach, and often reacted with a degree of censoriousness that did me little credit. To some extent, my officiousness was rewarded, initially at least, by the excellence of my grades. I was considerably ahead in most of the advanced subjects that we were studying on the scientific track: in this respect, the learning domes had done their work most thoroughly. But I quickly began to observe that one or two of my peers—those who were closest to me in the amount of information that they had at their disposal— were sometimes not only achieving grades higher than mine, but also earning considerably more encouraging comments from teachers. The comment most commonly associated with my own work was: "Technically excellent." At first, I was satisfied—what more could be required of me but excellence? It was some time before I understood the nuance that lay behind that first word. Technically, my work was indeed excellent. In other respects, it was not. And, slowly, I began to see that my peers were starting to inch ahead.

It was not the fact of their higher attainment that troubled me: I am not by nature competitive. It was more that increasingly I could see that something about their approach was beginning to provide better results. Logically, therefore, if I wished also to excel, I must consider whether I too might benefit from less rigidity and more flexibility in my thinking. Although I played games (which Vulcan does not play games?), they were in general of a highly structured and intellectual kind. I had not before considered the possibility that open-ended play was in itself a good. Often, my human peers seemed to be overtaken by a reckless kind of mischief.

I recall one particular occasion in the lab. We were working in our usual groups of three: my lab partners at that time were a human named Louie Maher, and a Iltavian named Eiei. I found Eiei a particularly fascinating individual: Iltavians have a very short but intense life span that gives them, in effect, only twenty years of productive work. Eiei was at the academy for four months, altogether, before graduating, but the impression made on me was very great.

Our experiment was concerned with testing the upper limits of dilithium stabilization. "I suppose you want to do this incrementally," said Maher, in a bored voice, and while I would certainly have been content to work through the problem methodically, I had observed my companions' frustration throughout the previous sessions, and I did not want to test their patience along with the warp core. So, mindful of my decision to learn from how others went about their tasks, I said, "I believe we should try a different approach."

Maher and Eiei looked at each other. Eiei laughed out loud. Maher cracked his knuckles. "Right," he said, "let's push this fecker as far as we can without actually getting ourselves killed."

Is there any statement more human? More reckless, more ambitious, more playful, more likely to end in either complete destruction or remarkable breakthrough? For a second, I thought, *I should stop this now...* But I did not. I had committed to this course of action, and I would see it through. We pushed the warp core to its maximum point of instability. About two seconds before I lost my nerve and demanded we shut down the core, the dilithium entered a hyper-stable mode. "I knew it!" yelled Eiei. "I knew it!"

We ran the warp core in its hyper-stable mode for the next ten minutes before powering down again. "That," I said, "was a truly fascinating experiment..." I examined the data we had collected. Already I could see the way back from the readings we had taken to a preliminary explanation of how the hyper-stable mode had occurred.

"Do you see what we did?" said Maher.

"I believe I do," I replied. "Sometimes it may be logical to take a leap into the unknown and then look back to see what the steps there might be."

"There's hope for you yet," said Eiei.

Our instructors were very pleased with our work (there was nothing "technical" about the "excellent" grade that we were given), although one of them did blanch when Maher described what we had done with the warp core. I reflected upon this experiment again and again over the next few weeks. I was beginning to see now that not only incremental approaches were underpinned by logic, and therefore that there was logical value to other ways of investigating the world. I could see, too, how the leap into the unknown that we had taken might have led nowhere; how, too, it had the potential to allow great steps forward in thinking. I reflected upon how our different worldviews— even our different experiences of time—had facilitated this. My own species, with its long lifespans and longer view of history, inclining me toward an incremental view of change, challenged by Eiei's shorter, more intense experience, driving great leaps in thought. My logical approach, demanding we work through the steps that we had taken, but the very human curiosity and humor that drove to experiment in the first place. An illogical experimental leap, upon which we built a logical theory of what we had discovered. I understood the world better now; certainly, I understood humans better. That would be most helpful, in the years to come.

This, then, was one of my chief lessons from attending Starfleet Academy. For the first time in my life, I was able truly to experience *Kol-Ut-Shan*, infinite diversity in—if not infinite combinations, then more than I had ever seen before at close quarters. For the first time in my life, I was asked to live alongside people very different from myself. Let me note again here that I was brought up in one of the most diverse cities in the Federation. ShiKahr is a city of many embassies, visited yearly by hundreds of thousands of people from many different species. My family, too, with its diplomatic tradition, was hardly inward-looking (leaving aside my dual heritage), and, as you recall, my mother had ensured that I was, from a very early age, familiar with the art, music, literature, and, indeed, presence of other species beyond my own. But overwhelmingly the world I inhabited was Vulcan. The water in which I swam—or, as we might say on my home planet, the sand through which I walked—was intrinsically Vulcan. I passed through these other cultures as an observer—learning, experiencing, but distanced. Everything was prismed through the stark red lens of my homeworld's philosophy and culture. At the academy, this was not an option. I was on Earth, with its blue skies and sunshine, or its grey clouds and rain, immersed in a hothouse world designed to bring species and cultures together in order to ensure that their individual representatives learn mutual respect and understanding. My sense of superiority—a product of my upbringing and my insecurity—was quickly eroded. In part, I see now, this was through the gentle—and good-humored—handling of my peers. In part, it was simply not supported by the evidence of my own eyes.

As a result, I was learning to see my homeworld very differently, and one friendship that I made at the academy in particular provided me with considerable grounds for reflection. This was, perhaps counter-intuitively, with another Vulcan, named T'Kel, who had entered the academy at the same time but was on the command track. We met en route to Earth, and, despite our different study tracks, it was perhaps impossible for the paths of two Vulcans not to cross occasionally. Meditation rooms, events on the cultural exchange program, at the *kal'toh* board, even in the queue to see an exhibition of paintings by T'Ser or hear a string sextet—it was natural that two young people of broadly the same background would be drawn to similar events. We formed a friendship, and regularly met beyond classes. I remained somewhat on the periphery of T'Kel's social group, which was extensive, and although I was welcomed, my preference was, and remains, for one-to-one encounters with other people. T'Kel and I enjoyed many extended lunch sessions, over which we carefully pulled apart the other's experience of growing up on Vulcan.

One curious feature of our homeworld is that, beyond the major cities and the diplomatic corps, Vulcan is, in general, not an outward-looking world. One surprising statistic might be how few Vulcans leave to visit another world when compared to other species: fewer than six per cent of us have left our planet, compared to the Federation average, which remains fairly constantly between sixty-three and sixty-seven per cent. (There are outliers in other directions, of course. One can hardly fault the logic of the eighty-seven point three of Ferengi who prefer not to inhabit their homeworld.) Perhaps this is no real surprise: the overwhelming bent of Vulcan history has been to construct a society of great peace, plenty, and fulfilment. But it does mean that *Kol-Ut-Shan* is not often tested and is more easily believed in principle than lived in practice. The struggles of my father's peers, who were cosmopolitan by Vulcan standards, to come to terms with his human wife and children, are surely evidence enough of this.

One interesting and further fact is that those Vulcans who leave continue to travel, as if, having embraced our core doctrine of infinite diversity, they find themselves wishing to live that doctrine more fully. T'Kel, who has gone on to a fine career in Starfleet, was such, and in our conversations together, I learned a great deal about my own world, and how my own upbringing was not necessarily typical. T'Kel was born in the T'Paal region, a pleasant and temperate area on the eastern edge of the Voroth Sea. T'Paal has a distinctive culture, partly arising from the fact that over the last couple of centuries, the area has drawn many off-worlders not simply to visit, but to settle. The climate is one reason; the carefree way-of-life is another. The town of T'Paal itself, and the small towns and villages around, are home to artists and artisans from many backgrounds; the pace of life is slow and relaxed. But not all this arises from the emigres and settlers. The locals too have a distinctive culture, one that, as I talked more to T'Kel, I came to understand was nevertheless as Vulcan as my own.

I had not, at this point in my life, ever visited this part of Vulcan and at first, when T'Kel described her home and upbringing to me, I suspected her of exaggeration. The green landscape she described, for one thing, sounded impossible. But it was true—a quirk of climate left this part of our world less barren than the rest. She, in turn, liked to hear me talk with familiarity about ShiKahr, finding the ease with which I spoke of the capital city enviable and sophisticated. When she learned about my background and upbringing, I realized that she found the highly disciplined and traditional approach to my education unusual. Not all Vulcans, I was beginning to understand, were educated in the same way and in the highly ascetic philosophy of my own class. And yet T'Kel was at least as focused as I was, and perhaps more able to cope. Was this simply that my half-human side was at odds with my background? I was starting to think that the fault was not in me—that it was not, even, in the Vulcan way of life.

What T'Kel and I most enjoyed debating, however, were our varied interpretations of Surak. At one point, when I was insisting on the primacy of logic, she suggested that I should go back and read again. And I did; I went back to these so-familiar writings, and read, once more, with great attention, and all the wisdom of my nearly two decades in the world. My intention was to read them to be able to counter T'Kel's claims, but in fact I discovered that I was reading with more nuance, with a more open mind. A simple content analysis of the texts revealed how often and how many different emotions were referred to, and always with an emphasis on their mastery, rather than their suppression. (In fairness, let it be noted that later in life, T'Kel confessed to me that she too reread Surak at this time, and found his teachings to be—I shall quote her directly—"far more austere than memory made them".)

At some point, inspired by my new reading of Surak, I began to translate his works into English. There were translations already, of course, but this exercise offered me a new perspective on his writings. I intended to read his works through human eyes, and this was a most rewarding experience. I began to see more nuance in his writing than I had before: a more sensitive understanding of the place of emotion in the Vulcan mind. My grandparents took great interest in this translation and encouraged me to send them sections as I worked. At the same time, I began to translate Conan Doyle into *kitau-lakh*, the mode used on Vulcan for literary and philosophical texts. And, with the arrogance of youth, I began to write a *t'san a'lat*. Yes, with almost two decades of experience, I wished to impart my wisdom. I went back to this, before I began this current book, Jean-Luc, to remind me to approach this task with humility this time. My heart went out to the young man that I found there. It is raw, that book, filled with regret and no small amount of unhappiness, but not without hope or a genuine attempt to find a path through life. I have left this book for you too, Jean-Luc—the book of my youthful wisdom. I can hardly flatter myself that it is of particular literary merit, but there is great honesty there and, dare I say it, great feeling. Perhaps you might find someone with whom it will strike a chord, this portrait of a young man, far from home, struggling to bring together the different parts of himself to create a new and coherent whole. I was certainly a long way from achieving this, but here is where that process began.

✦

Perhaps the most enduring and rewarding experience of my time at the academy was how my extended stay on Earth allowed me to have closer connection to and involvement with my mother's family, my human family. There had been, as I have noted, only one visit by them to Vulcan, and a most memorable one, but for the main part my interactions with my grandparents, my uncle, and my cousin had been long-distance, at the other end of a comm channel. As a result, I hardly knew them well. My grandmother, prior to my leaving Vulcan, sent me a message saying that she hoped they would see something of me, that she would love to see me, but the last thing she wanted to do was "cramp my style".

I was unsure how to interpret this. I had gained an impression that there was often subtext to human communication that I missed. I had almost persuaded myself that this was a request not to make contact, but, wisely, I took the message to my mother and asked her what it meant. She laughed. "Spock!" she said. "Your grandmother means exactly what she says! She loves you and wants to see you as much as she possibly can—but she knows you're embarking on a new and busy life. She doesn't want you to feel obliged to see them!"

I would not have reached this interpretation on my own, and I might well have decided that they most likely wanted to keep the Vulcan grandchild at arm's length. Nothing could be further from the truth. My grandmother and grandfather were quietly, deeply, and profoundly glad to have, at last, the chance to become better acquainted with their daughter's son. Arriving on Earth a full month before I was expected to report to the academy, I took a fortnight to travel: T'Kel and I, before our arrival, put together a brisk itinerary that took in several major cities, areas of outstanding natural beauty, and sites of historical importance—a most efficiently executed introduction to the marvels of Earth. The remaining two weeks I spent with my grandparents at their house in Cascadia, a little way outside Portland.

My grandfather and grandmother had met at Stanford, where they were both pursuing graduate studies. My grandfather specialized in nineteenth-century English literature, an expert in the visionary poet John Clare; my grandmother was an educational psychologist. They had brought up their two children in Palo Alto, but, after Amanda's departure, they lost interest in the intrigues of academic life, and moved into the countryside to pursue research, writing, and other projects. My grandfather had become interested in the history and evolution of photography and its associated arts (he had recently completed the construction of a camera obscura); my grandmother had begun a detailed study of mystic writing and practice, and was, at the time, immersed in the works of Simone Weil. Their house was not large, but was remarkably peaceful, and there was usually a friend or two in residence who had come to enjoy the quiet and conduct some research or complete some writing of their own. At various points across my numerous visits, I met poets, playwrights, artists of several varieties, and a composer of musical theatre. My first winter break I went immediately to their home, experiencing the cold for the first time, and, more enjoyably, the pleasure of a warm house when the weather outside is bad. My grandfather and I revisited Sherlock Holmes; with my grandmother, I watched and dissected many black-and-white films. Many of their friends came by.

These encounters certainly broadened my horizons but becoming better acquainted with my grandparents was naturally what I cherished most about these visits. There was nothing more my grandparents liked than to sit in conversation with each other, and often I would find them outside on the deck as the sun went down and the light disappeared, still chewing amiably over whatever crossed their well-stocked minds. This could never be predicted.

Typical subjects might include: the paintings of Marc Chagall; the works of Thomas Mann; the works of Douglas Adams; the philosophy of later Wittgenstein; the philosophy of early Surak; pulp fiction from the pre-Atomic age; pulp fiction from the era of first contact; the dissolution of the monasteries; feminist separatist utopias from across five centuries; Beethoven's late style; the concept of "late style"; how to boil an egg to perfection (they never agreed on this); why to boil an egg to perfection; whether boiled eggs are preferable to scrambled eggs; and did you remember to turn off the oven, love…?

All this might be covered in one evening. You may imagine what a month in their company was like. I would be instructed to pull up a chair and join them. Hours might pass in this way, until one of them would say, "Well, I suppose we won't get to the bottom of this one today either…", yawn, stand, and head upstairs to bed. My grandparents were endlessly inquisitive, collaborative, and fair-minded in debate, profoundly humanist in outlook, and they loved me very much. I fitted seamlessly into their way of life. In their company, and through their example, my sense of my human heritage was transformed from an unfortunate impediment into a source of creativity and curiosity. There were no great emotions at stake, unless one counted wonder, delight, and joy. I sensed that their daughter's marriage remained a puzzle to them—but there was no doubt about their happiness in me. They were easily among my best friends at this time—and if this was unusual for a young man at college, then, once again, I can only be grateful for my eccentricity. "Fascinating…" my grandmother would say, when presented with some new information. I had acquired this from my cousin Andrew; now I knew the source.

✦

Thus passed my career at the academy—one of the most critical periods of my life, and yet, on reflection, over extremely quickly. Did I take from it everything that I could? I know many who talk about their time there as a blur of study and social engagements. When I observed the high spirits and boisterousness of many of the command track cadets, I sometimes wondered whether I was attending an entirely different institution.

I will not present myself as the life and soul of the party at the academy. Given my long lifespan, very few of the people who attended the academy with me are still alive to offer an alternative account, but any such claim would hardly be persuasive. The fact that my father was not pleased with my decision to attend Starfleet Academy meant that I had to ensure that my career there was successful. By necessity, then, as much as by nature, I worked and studied extremely hard. I took many advanced classes, and many extra classes. My leisure pursuits were somewhat solitary and tended toward the intellectual. My circle of friends was comparatively small, but each one was deeply valued and carefully cultivated. I spent a great deal of time with my grandparents, whom I loved deeply, and while this was perhaps unusual for a young man in his late teens and early twenties, I do not regret a single second that I spent with these gentle, curious, and loving people.

I do not wish anyone who may in future read this account of my time at Starfleet Academy to believe that I left without achieving some form of notoriety. There is a tradition among the outgoing year group to perform some prank that should, if it is successful, have each of the main perpetrators hauled in front of the president of the academy. Toward the end of my second year, I was approached by my old lab partner, Louis Maher, and a group of his friends about their plans for this prank. They intended to break into the offices of the senior staff and, in their words, "redecorate". They wanted my help with accessing security codes. I listened to their plans and promptly declined their offer to participate. I thought that their scheme was juvenile. I had learned enough by this point not to say this to them, but I think that Maher knew. When he and his friends left, not long after my rejection, he looked at me thoughtfully and said, "I thought you got it. Well, I thought you were *getting* it. Never mind."

Over the summer break, I pondered this exchange. I was not, I thought, in principle against this tradition. I simply thought that the plans put to me were not worthy of us. When we returned to campus to begin our final year, and to his frank astonishment, I approached Louie Maher and suggested an alternative.

"You're joking," he said, after I outlined my scheme.

"Mr. Maher," I said. "Have you ever known me to make a joke?"

"We can't do this!"

"We can," I said, "and we shall."

"Well," he said to me, a new respect in his eyes, "now we know what goes in the yearbook. '*Most Likely to Turn Out to Be a Criminal Mastermind*.'"

Let us pass over the intricacies of the kind of espionage and technological knowhow that might be required to build cloaking technology sufficiently advanced to spirit away the graduation hall for two hours the morning before the ceremony was due to commence. Let us simply say that the presence of both myself, Mr. Maher, and a small number of co-conspirators (it is always best to keep a conspiracy small) was requested not only by the president of the academy, but also a highly interested deputation from Starfleet Intelligence, who recruited Louie Maher on the spot. I learned from my future correspondence with him that the work we did that semester later formed the basis of being able to track cloaked ships more successfully. Speaking for myself, I was more than content with our project, which I would suggest went well beyond the merely technically excellent. I declined a similar offer given me to join Starfleet Intelligence: I had been offered a posting on the *Enterprise*, which I had accepted with alacrity. I had no need to dabble further in espionage. I wished to explore. I wished to see the wonders of the universe.

My father did not attend my graduation from Starfleet Academy. He was away at the time on a diplomatic trip to Alcestis Prime. I did not ask my mother how critical this mission was; presumably sufficiently so in my father's mind that he could not reasonably defer the Alcestians in order to attend my graduation. He sent a brief message acknowledging my "many and manifest achievements" and congratulating me on receiving my chosen posting. He also wished me well, which I took to be a significant conciliatory move on his part.

"He is happy for you, Spock," my mother said, watching the message alongside me. Yet I suppose I might have wished he was happy with me.

I was hardly alone on the day. The other side of my family—who had, after all, been such a crucial element of these years, assisting me, grounding me, providing me with a refuge when academy life became too intense—were all present. My mother, of course, was there, and Michael sent a loving message to her little brother. If I consider my father's absence now, it is with regret for him, that even at this stage of his life, he was unable to resolve whatever ambiguities remained in his own mind about his half-human son, whatever tensions he still experienced between his love for me and his disapproval of the choices I had made. For me, while those tensions remained for some time, the process of their dissolution was already well underway. I do not overstate matters when I say that the academy saved both my life, and my sanity. Without the experiences there—which opened my eyes to possibilities beyond the Vulcan way of life—without the distance I had achieved from my home, what followed over the next few years might well have been enough to break me completely. After information comes knowledge—self-knowledge not least.

PART TWO

FAI-TUKH—KNOWLEDGE—2254—2293

Angel

WHAT DOES IT MEAN, TO WRITE A BOOK OF ONE'S LIFE? Which version of one's life does one present? I have been son, brother, grandson, cadet, officer, commander, captain, ambassador. I have been clever, mistaken, logical, emotional. I have been both wise and foolish; I remain both wise and foolish. I am always Vulcan, always human, yet never fully one or the other and always liminal, existing in the space between. I have at times experienced myself as fully integrated; at other times so fragmented that it seemed to me that the pieces of myself would never again cohere. You first met me as an old man; now in this book you meet me as a young man. The stories that I am telling will by necessity overlap and interweave—but such happens in our lives. People from our past become suddenly significant once again; we must confront old versions of ourselves to forge the new self that can move forward. The dead, sometimes, do not remain dead, and the stories of our lives, despite our best efforts to shape them into simple and satisfactory wholes, with straightforward narratives and linear progression, sometimes defy these efforts. You have borne with me thus far, Jean-Luc, and I hope you will bear with me further.

The time which I shall now recount was perhaps the most difficult of my life (even returning from death did not involve such challenges). I was still a young man—and a clever one, and I embarked upon my Starfleet career confident that the bedrock of information—of *ro'fori*—to which I had hitherto been dedicated to accumulating was sufficient for all that lay ahead. I believed that I was the inheritor of a subtle, stable, and superior philosophy of life, and that whatever deficiencies my other heritage might bring, they could with effort be less than others made them. I was ready to progress with life, to bring all my training and information to the development of *fai-tukh*, the practical knowledge of the world. I was on the brink of entering that time in our lives when we begin to acquire experience, when, faced with each new challenge, we draw upon all that we have learned and begin to perceive deeper patterns in the world around us. I believed myself entirely prepared for this, and ready for the tests that lay ahead. In this view of myself and the world I was almost entirely wrong.

There is a principle in Vulcan philosophy: *chthia*. This is not easily translated, and the most common rendering of the word into English is "reality-truth". By this is meant, seeing the world as it really is, rather than the way we wish to see it. The latter is a mistake we all make at times during the course of our lives; some are more prone to it than others and some never step past the half-truths that they construct about the world. We may be inhabiting a world of self-delusion, and yet experience that as true, as coherent. The young man who set foot for the first time on board the *Enterprise* would, had you asked him, have said with confidence that he understood his own nature and the general nature of the universe entirely. Within a matter of years, he was falling apart: his sense of self shattered; his sense of reality disintegrated. That young officer was not, however much he had persuaded himself to the contrary, living in the world-as-it-is.

Right now, writing at this moment, I experience myself as the most coherent I have ever been. I am clear about myself; I am clear about my purpose. As you have seen already, Jean-Luc, I have not always been this way—from my very earliest days, my sense of self was deeply affected by what I was convinced was an irreconcilable divide in my nature: the fact of my dual heritage. Over the years, I have come to understand that what I took to be irrefutable fact was in fact the false belief of others, but a perception so powerful and persuasive that I continued to accept it as "reality-truth" for many years. Ultimately, however, holding false beliefs about our own nature is not sustainable. We must start the process of coming to terms with our own reality-truth or suffer the consequences. Looking back, I can see clearly the truth of who I was at that time. I was a poorly crafted sculpture, barely covered by a veneer of Starfleet polish, and able to produce at command an impressive array of information that gave the impression of a whole and functioning man. In fact, not long after the start of my career in Starfleet, my false perception of myself began to crack. I, indeed, began to crack.

✦

Vulcans consider honesty, consistency with *chthia*, a great virtue in itself, and a *t'san a'lat* above all should adhere to this principle. In part, this is to honor the recipient, the reader, that one offers them only the truth, but above all it is a logical necessity of a wisdom book. Why undertake such a daunting project if only to tell oneself lies? What would be the purpose of such an endeavor? I say this now, Jean-Luc, because I am about to recount a part of my life which has, for various reasons, hitherto been cloaked in secrecy. By that I do not mean the usual kinds of secrets that all families keep—the private griefs and regrets that are their business and theirs alone. I mean events and people about whom I was explicitly ordered not to speak. I have obeyed these orders for many decades.

But here I reach an impasse. The *t'san a'lat* requires honesty. You, my friend, deserve honesty. A wisdom book is not truly wise if the author conceals; wisdom cannot be imparted if the account offered is partial. The events I outline now occurred more than a century ago—a hundred and thirty years, indeed!—and almost everyone involved is either dead or gone beyond—well beyond the reach of any of us. Not to speak of these events would be a betrayal of my sister; speaking of these events will also, perhaps, make my current decision more explicable. What occurred was complicated, and for much of the time—as you will see—I was struggling to keep my mind in the present. But I will tell as much as I can of what transpired—and leave you, Jean-Luc, to be the judge of what is best to do with this account.

A few years into my time on board the *Enterprise*, I began to have bad dreams. Not an unusual occurrence for me: bad dreams had occurred throughout my childhood, prompting those images of *yon'tislak* that I so regularly created. During my later adolescence, these nightmares largely disappeared: perhaps my mind was too full of all that I was learning. So the reemergence of these dreams concerned me, for a variety of reasons, signaling to me some interior disturbance. Looking back over my personal logs from this time, I see a note of quiet distress entering early, but also a refusal, initially, to admit what was happening: that these were not simply bad dreams. Rather, the visions I had received as a child were returning, and that I could not, through any rational means, explain them. You will recall that as a boy I saw what I called a "Red Angel", who guided my parents to my sister, thereby helping us save her life. After this, I continued to experience what seemed like aftershocks, strong images of red bursts of light, dotted throughout space.

This Red Angel was the figure now passing once again through my dreams, with a force so strong that it seemed less imagination than premonition. Yet how could this be true? I was, logically, set against such mystical notions: these were a product of disorderly thinking, evidence of some weakness, and they must be controlled. I practiced meditation; I attempted to discipline my mind so that the Red Angel would depart. But this dogged refusal—this denial of what I was experiencing—did not help. The dreams became more powerful, to the extent that they crowded my thoughts during my waking hours. This was clearly unsustainable, not least because it ran the risk of causing serious harm both to myself and my fellow crewmembers. I asked for, and received, an extended period of leave. I did not specify the reason for this request, but the lengthy mission which we had recently undertaken had exhausted us all, and I had several months of accumulated leave. This was not, on the surface, an unreasonable request, and I was able to depart without any hint of the psychological distress that I was undergoing. I remain deeply grateful to my captain, Christopher Pike, for this understanding on his part, as I remain grateful for his actions during all that followed.

At first, I was uncertain how I should proceed. The logical course would be to return to Vulcan, to sequester myself, and continue the attempt to discipline my mind until the visions were gone. They were increasingly powerful, and extremely frightening. I wanted them gone; I wanted once more to be in command of myself. I should go home, enter a retreat, and banish these delusions entirely. Yet some instinct told me that this was not the best choice. I recalled how, as a child, how my father—when I told my parents where Michael was to be found—praised the logic by which I must have worked out her location. And yet I knew—I *knew*, but do not ask me how—that the Angel was real and had guided me to her. There was something to be learned here—but this course of action terrified me. To follow the Angel wherever she led—to *indulge* these delusions—might I lose my mind? From very early in my life, perhaps as a result of my brother's claim that he had seen *Sha Ka Ree* and the distress that this had caused my parents, I feared a breakdown, that I would in some way lose conscious control of myself and fall prey to baser instinct or lose all coherent sense of self. This was by far the most horrifying outcome that I could imagine. And yet—this was the path I chose. I followed the Angel—and I fell apart.

Much of what I know about the following period I have gathered from what my mother subsequently told me. I, personally, recall this time as hallucinatory, incoherent. My sense of self, and of the normal progression of time, was completely disturbed. I know from my personal log—which tracked my ship's log—that I traveled to an unnamed planet. There I encountered— *believed* I had encountered—the Red Angel once again, and our minds melded. My overwhelming memory of this was the isolation—the desolation— which the Angel felt, which evoked in me a deep sense of pity. My recognition of this in her, my acknowledgment of this, assisted her—I felt that in her, and felt her gratitude. In return, she gave me what seemed at the time a questionable gift, to say the least. She let me see the future. This was an overwhelmingly distressing experience: a vision of Hell, where my brother had seen Paradise. I witnessed the destruction of Andor, of Tellar, of Earth— and of Vulcan. After this, my connection to reality became even less stable: time seemed to be out of joint. I traveled to Starbase 5, where I committed myself to psychiatric care. I instructed Starfleet not to inform my family. I could not bear the thought of either my mother or my father seeing me in this condition, if for very different reasons.

Time fractured. I fractured. I became numb: I experienced the world around me as if I were looking through a pane of frosted glass. I lost track of the normal passage of time. I felt nothing, although I *knew* that every single doubt that had ever been harbored about me was vindicated. What I always expected would happen had happened: the two parts of my being—the logical and the emotional; the rational and the instinctive—were not able to co-exist. This experiment—that was how I saw myself, as an experiment on the part of my mother and father—had failed completely. They should not have tried;

they should not have brought me into existence. To be at once human and Vulcan was logically impossible and emotionally unsustainable. All my training and self-discipline, all my attempts to reconcile these two halves of myself had proven in vain. I saw red bursts and experienced premonitions. I believed I saw angels and visions of hell. The only logical conclusion to be drawn was that I was insane.

To learn, then, that the red bursts had been independently observed came like a lightning bolt of clarity. These visions of mine were not simply happening within the confines of my own disturbed mind. I asked to leave the hospital; I wanted to leave—and was told that I could not. By this time, powerful and secretive interests within the Federation had become interested in what was happening to me, and they attempted to hold me at the facility against my will. They were not successful. When I escaped, they spread the lie that I was responsible for murdering my doctors. I went to find the only person that I could trust. I did what we all wish to able to do when faced with distress that we can barely name, never mind articulate. I went in search of comfort. I went to find my mother—who concealed me.

Who were these individuals, who wanted my knowledge of the Red Angel so badly that they were prepared to murder innocent people, and blame me for their actions? You are surely aware, Jean-Luc, of groups operating within Starfleet that are permitted to act outside of the law, and largely without scrutiny. You surely have your own opinions on the necessity or otherwise of such people, as do I. They seem to be present throughout the history of the Federation; their power waxing and waning; sometimes visible, sometimes hidden. Perhaps you have your own name for them. I knew them as Section 31. Such were the people now pursuing me, and they set both my sister and my captain to find me. My mother trusted me to Michael; Michael hid me until my sanity was restored. We learned that the Red Angel was Gabrielle Burnham, Michael's mother, sending a warning of a future that was currently unfolding—the destruction of sentient life. We discovered the means of preventing this from happening, in which Captain Pike played a vital part. All that it cost us was Michael, her ship, and her friends.

You must understand that this was not an external threat, Jean-Luc, this was a threat that arose from an unhealthy combination of internal factors, not least the existence of that clandestine organization. But also significant were the suspicions that arise as a result of being on a war footing, which brought a new hawkishness to that organization. Civilizations such as our own must be constantly on the alert for such shifts, if we wish to continue to consider ourselves civilized. I regret to have to say that I see some of this paranoia again, in Starfleet's retrenchment since the attack on Mars and in the general and growing hostility toward the Romulan people.

But let me explain more of the events which led to the loss of my sister, and the crew of her ship, the *U.S.S. Discovery*. In the wake of the war with the Klingons, Starfleet Intelligence became increasingly reliant on a new analysis system, Control, which used an artificial intelligence to predict and pre-empt threats to Federation security. When the red bursts began to appear with more frequency, elements within Starfleet Intelligence promoted use of this system to increase their own power base. But the system went rogue, causing the deaths of many intelligence officers and gaining access—control—of a fleet of ships. We learned that the vision I had seen of the destruction of Earth, of Vulcan—of all sentient life—was the likely trajectory of the AI gaining full access to Federation secrets. In particular, the AI was attempting to access the records that Starfleet had received from an ancient life-form, known as the "sphere", which *Discovery* had recently encountered. The sphere, which had lived for hundreds of thousands of years, had, during those years, collected an unparalleled body of information on the galaxy, knowledge of multiple systems and species. If Control gained access to this data bank, the dead future which I had seen would come to pass. The best solution we could find meant that my sister and her ship were lost—not destroyed, not dead, but gone. We did not destroy the sphere data, but instead sent it beyond the reach of Control, hundreds of years into the future. Michael went first, following the lead provided from the future by her mother, Gabrielle, and her ship and crewmates followed. Or so we hoped. I do not know if they reached their destination. I do not know whether Michael found her mother, or whether her friends found her in turn. I know that we, in the present, survived, and that their sacrifice was not wasted. I must therefore hold out hope that they are safe and well, where nobody, including myself, can reach them.

At the time, those of us who facilitated *Discovery*'s journey into the future knew we had to maintain strict silence about all that occurred. *Discovery*'s mission would have to remain classified; a secret for all time. My sister—her name, her career, almost her entire existence—was consigned to the shadows. So many decades have passed, and the promises I made then seem almost to have been made by a different person, from a different world. I find that I cannot write this book without remembering and honoring her in full. I remember Michael, and I will not have her completely forgotten. I will not have knowledge of those sacrifices fade completely into oblivion. I can only be grateful that we had the chance to reconcile. Before she left us, for good, Michael told me that I would find a galaxy of people who would reach out for me, if I would only let them. It has not always been easy, but for her sake, I have tried.

You are no fool, Jean-Luc, and I suspect that you have your own information on those clandestine parts that operate both inside and outside of Starfleet. As I grow older, as my time runs shorter, I grow weary of these games that others play. They claim they act out of necessity, but I see in them a taste for what they do, a delight in their secret knowledge and their extreme acts. I have no taste for it; I have little time for it, now. At the end of my long life, time has become my most precious commodity. What matters to me, recalling these events—what matters to this *t'san a'lat*—is that before Michael left on her new course, she and I were reconciled. We met as two hurt children; we parted as two healed adults. We looked once again at the past that lay between us, the pain that we had caused each other—and we forgave each other. In all the confusion, distress, complication, and fear of those days—there are two things, I see now, that mattered most. That my sister and I parted as friends; that when I was at my most lost, my most shattered, my mother was there, to hold the pieces, until I was ready and able to begin the process of reassembling them. As for my father—my mother told me later that he was reconciled with Michael before she left. But, for the moment, the distance between father and son continued.

What man existed on the other side of this? Who, after all of this, was Spock? Returning from this was not easy. I resumed my duties on the *Enterprise*; I attempted to re-assemble a functioning adult self from the pieces that were left behind. I believe that you understand something of this, Jean-Luc, given your own experiences with the Borg. I went back to the *Enterprise* as quickly as I reasonably could. There were some certainties that I could rely on. There was the routine of life aboard the ship. There was the certainty of Pike's respect and regard. There was the knowledge that I had not been wrong or delusional.

There was the fact that my mother loved me, whatever happened, which I had never doubted. These are not bad foundations on which to try to build a functioning self. Many have achieved this phenomenon with a great deal less.

✦

There is one coda to this story, one which I have not previously revealed to any other person, but which I must tell you now, Jean-Luc, because it brings this story full circle, and because of the glimpse that it gave me of a possibility that my future might hold. I had one last sight of the Red Angel—almost an after-echo, one might say. Not long after I resumed my duties on board the *Enterprise*, I was off-duty, alone in my cabin, when I felt—or saw, it was always difficult to distinguish—the aura that always preceded one of the visitations from the Red Angel. I am not ashamed to admit that my first reaction was terror: that despite the events of the previous few months, these experiences were not in fact explained but might be the signal of the onset of a second breakdown or period of intense emotional distress. I recall now, as clearly as if this had happened yesterday.

But there was something different about what was happening this time. For one thing, there was not the reddishness to the aura I had come to associate with the previous visions. Instead, this was blue, and deepening steadily in hue, becoming ever closer to indigo. Redshift; blueshift. This small detail allowed me to pause, to take stock, to ground myself, and most of all to recall how my prior experiences had altered me. I was able to take a moment to remind myself that my visions had, after all, been vindicated: there had been a Red Angel— wondrous and unusual, but not illusory. I had not been—I was not—insane. I did not try to deny what was occurring, or try to resist, but, instead, I allowed the experience to unfold. I sat down upon the floor of my cabin, breathed steadily, and opened my mind.

Once again, I saw a woman—and I knew her immediately. This was Gabrielle Burnham, whom I had first glimpsed as a child and whose recent reappearance had brought me so close to the edge, for as long as I tried to deny her existence. The human mother of my human sister. I looked around the room in which she was standing—it was not a place that I knew, but there was a quality to the light that I recognized immediately. This world was (or, perhaps, had been) Vulcan. There was a great deal more that I saw, but what was most puzzling were the clothes she was wearing. One does not grow up on Vulcan without becoming able to recognize the robes of some kind of religious or philosophical order. Gabrielle was dressed in such: a dark blue habit with a veil; a staff upon her back. I did not know this order; I would not know it for many years. What I did know—what I could see—was the unity of self about this woman, an integration of disparate parts that I found not only compelling but consoling. Whatever path this woman had trod, however far she had been flung from all that she knew, she found her way. She was whole, and she was, I hoped, reunited at last with her daughter, my sister.

Later in my life, when my knowledge of Romulus became much greater—perhaps only rivalled by yours, Jean-Luc—I learned the name of the order of which Gabrielle had become a part. I would guess that you have recognized it already, my old friend. The Qowat Milat—dwellers in the house of truth, followers of the way of absolute candor. A fascinating group: infuriating, yes—or perhaps I should say "refreshing". Knowledge of their existence went some considerable way to deepening my understanding of the Romulan way of life. And meeting these women in person of course at last gave me the crucial piece of information fully to understand what I had seen of Gabrielle Burnham. A human woman, dressed in the robes of a Romulan order, living on Vulcan—need I say how profoundly meaningful this was to me? Gabrielle Burnham had achieved the kind of unity for which I had been striving my entire life. That last sight of her, which I could not entirely understand at the time, later seemed to me a kind of promise, giving as it did a glimpse of the kind of integration that was possible to me. I did not see it in full at the time—I could not, at the time—but I did recognize that she was a unified whole, and I took comfort from the knowledge that such a state could be achieved. Understanding in full what I had seen has been a source of such comfort once again in these recent, difficult years—that the tangled histories of the three great civilizations into which I am inextricably woven, might one day acquire cohesion.

Do I believe in visions? Logically, one would be wise to approach them with caution, as a manifestation of our desire for how we wish the world to be, and not the "reality-truth" of the world-that-is, which anyone of intelligence must learn to accept, and which we know best through meticulous observation, the acquisition of data, the systematic testing of hypothesis, the steady accumulation of testable evidence. We might consider them as the antithesis of *chthia*. And yet what all my long years of acquiring information and amassing knowledge have taught me is how much more I have to discover about this vast, most wonderful, and various universe which we inhabit. I do not "believe" in visions, if by that we mean messages from a supernatural entity or some special access to revelation. Yet that sometimes we acquire insight from intuitive means, without being able to evidence our conclusions, is undeniable. The universe holds many surprises for us, not all of which we have the language or terminology to be able to describe—this, surely, is self-evident. These experiences of my early adulthood perhaps explain to some extent the decision I have made now, the leap into the dark that I am about to take. I hope that this makes sense to you, Jean-Luc. I hope you will understand.

Pike

I SUSPECT THAT ALL NEWLY MINTED OFFICERS, taking on their first assignment, go through the same voyage of discovery. They quickly discover that while everything they have learned at the academy is true, it does not come close to reflecting the reality of life on board a starship. The information that we have acquired barely scratches the surface of what is needed to operate efficiently and effectively. In this respect, I am sure that my experiences were no different from those of the many thousands of young officers who had gone before me, and the many thousands that have come after. I found that the persona that I had adopted in my final year at the academy—the wry observer of human folly—carried me some way. My hope was that in time this part that I was playing would become so natural that it might become reality. To some extent, I believe that it has. The mask of the Vulcan has come in very useful many times, over the years.

Like most young officers, I was carried a significant way by my immediate superiors, in this case, the first officer, Una Chin-Riley, known to us all as "Number One", and the captain, Christopher Pike. I should speak now of Pike, since his influence upon my early career was so great, not only during my breakdown, but such that even when I was serving under a new captain, my sense of debt to Pike was so profound that I was prepared to face a court-martial in order to repay him. But his influence upon me was at least as much by example: how to conduct oneself as an officer; when to act and when to listen; the difference between being decisive and being rash. Pike took the training of his junior officers seriously. Take, for example, the test that all junior officers who were not on the command track undertook when they joined his crew. At the academy, only those cadets who were on the command track were required to take the *Kobayashi Maru* test, in which their ability to come to terms with a no-win situation was tested and observed. Pike believed this was a deficiency in the training of the other cadets and sought to remedy this. Not only command officers, or so he argued, might find themselves facing critical decisions. He was, as usual, correct. To this end, Number One designed a simulation to evaluate how the newest recruits would react in difficult situations. I was myself subject to such a test, shortly after arriving on the *Enterprise*.

During a stopover at Starbase 28, the base went suddenly onto red alert. Summoned to the brig, where a prisoner was being held, I was told by Pike that the prisoner knew information vital to the safety of the base. As the only serving Vulcan officer to hand, I was instructed to mind-meld with the prisoner to obtain this information. The safety, security, and even the survival of the base most likely depended on this.

This was not an order that I could accept. The mind-meld is not an interrogation tool; it is a technique by which consenting consciousnesses may meet and merge. It should not, and must not, be abused in the way that Captain Pike was requesting. Beyond the room, I heard explosions, alarms. The situation was escalating. Pike continued to press me, and I continued to refuse. As the sounds from outside the room and the communications Pike received became more desperate, he explained to me that refusing to accept a direct order was mutiny, and that I would be court-martialed.

"Torture does not provide useful information," I replied. "All the evidence supports this statement. This order is both illogical and unethical, and I am not bound to obey. Please do not ask me again, Captain."

"This will mean a court-martial, Ensign."

"I shall take that chance, sir."

He held my eye for a long moment—and then, quite suddenly, the alerts ended. The prisoner relaxed and laughed. Pike smiled and commended me for my calm and my resolve.

"Thank you, sir," I said to him, "but your words are not earned. This was not a difficult choice for me."

"No?" he replied. "Good."

In fact, it was not a difficult choice because I had, almost from the outset, suspected that this was some kind of test. It seemed highly unlikely to me that such a situation, which so starkly pressed upon me the urgent need to make a moral choice based upon ethics and loyalties, would arise naturally. Later, in our debriefing, I admitted to Number One that I had deduced that this was a simulated test, and that as a result she should consider the data which she had acquired about my responses not useful.

She sighed. "I told him you'd work it out."

"I regret that I have invalidated the test."

"Don't worry," she said. "I'm sure we'll think of something else."

"I shall be mindful that such an eventuality might arise."

I spoke to other colleagues at the time and learned that they too were tested in a similar fashion, although no simulation was identical. Number One showed a very canny ability to determine what was likely to trigger complex emotions and reactions in the new recruits brought on board the ship. All of the situations which my colleagues described in some way tested whether or not our loyalties to Starfleet would hold under duress, or whether some aspect of our personal circumstances might cause our resolve to waver. I did not hear of any case in which a recruit failed this test, although I am not blind to the irony of the fact that I have mutinied many times, and, on one occasion, on account of Pike himself. I am not blind either to the fact that I did once use a mind-meld to acquire information under duress, when I was a much older man. I will come to this story in time, Jean-Luc, although I believe it does me little credit. There never was another test such as this, and perhaps if there had been, I might have been more successful when the trial came for real.

✦

In the mid-2250s, the simmering tensions between the Klingon Empire and the Federation finally boiled over into the war which began with the Battle at the Binary Stars. Despite the savage losses we incurred in those early months, and to the surprise of us all, the *Enterprise* was instructed to continue on its mission, and not to return to the front. The reasoning, as I understand it, was that we were to be held in reserve, until use of us was completely necessary, but this was not a popular order among the crew. To be asked to remain away from the conflict while friends and colleagues on board other ships were in the line of fire was the cause of considerable distress for many people. I myself could not see the logic of being asked to stay away until there was nothing to return to. If there were complications arising from the part that Michael played in precipitating the outbreak of the war, and what this might mean for my loyalty, this was never broached with me. I would deduce therefore that this was not the case: if there was any question as to where my loyalties might lie, it would surely have been easier simply to remove me from the *Enterprise* for the duration of the war.

Ultimately, I concluded that logic was playing very little part in this decision. Keeping the *Enterprise* in reserve chiefly served an emotional function. Had the *Enterprise* participated in the war and been, as would have been likely, severely damaged or destroyed, the blow to morale at the disabling or destruction of the flagship would have been huge. Keeping us away from the fighting prevented this eventuality. The blow to the morale of the crew of the *Enterprise* was presumably a price worth paying: the needs of the many do outweigh the needs of the few. But this was a bitter pill for many of my colleagues to swallow. I was not, myself, eager to find myself in battle—my early training had impressed on me that to prevent conflict from ever arising was the most logical strategy, as long as one was prepared to end a conflict as the victor—and I had no personal need to prove myself in this regard. I know that for others, this was not the case, and our absence from this conflict remained a sore point for many for years to come. When the war did end, and our mission too ended, I was soon preoccupied with other matters. This was when I was forced to take an extended leave of absence from Starfleet in order to deal with the ramifications of my visions of the Red Angel.

It is to Pike's credit that he allowed me to take this leave. I remain forever grateful to the loyalty and trust he showed me during the months that followed, which remain some of the most difficult of my life. Certainly, there was no benefit to him in his science officer becoming unable to function. But he could not possibly have guessed where this would lead. After the events surrounding the Red Angel, of which you are now apprised, Jean-Luc, Pike continued his support of me, allowing me an extensive period of leave back on Earth to see my grandparents.

They were in their early hundreds by this time and still active. Their life had not changed much. The house remained the same, a peaceful and creative haven. Their conversation too was unchanged—their interests as wide-ranging as ever. They had much to say about the ethics or otherwise of the war with the Klingons; they were glad that I had avoided this conflict, although perhaps disappointed that I could not give them much in the way of first-hand information about this deeply alien species. They also had many questions about Michael—and I was, of course, not able to give many answers. What I told them was that Michael's mission had been top secret, that she was missing in action, and that there was no question now of her loyalty or her courage. I asked them not to ask me more, and they respected this request.

Vulcans may not lie; humans can and do. I have often wondered what I would have done, had they asked me to tell them more, and insisted on their right to know. This would have been a truer test than any simulation, and I believe I may well have lied to them. I was already concealing information about her. Were they owed the truth? Certainly. Was I in a position to reveal it? I believed not. I could perhaps, at this point, equivocate and claim that technically I told my grandparents no outright lies, that I told them enough of the truth to protect them while offering whatever consolation I could about the loss of their adopted grandchild. But that would be self-serving. They died not knowing the circumstances of her disappearance, and they also knew that there was a story which I was not telling. That they so palpably forgave me is more to their credit than mine.

Chiefly, when I visited, they wanted me to know that they were aware of my breakdown, that they were worried about me, and that they wanted to be sure that I was on the road to recovery. In this respect, at least, I could reassure them. The proof of the existence of the Red Angel had a profoundly liberating effect on me: any lingering doubt that my vision had arisen from imbalance in my own mind had been entirely banished. This was not the last visit that I made to my grandparents before their deaths, but it was a deeply significant one. I was no longer a child, by any means; now I was no longer a child in their eyes. Adult secrets lay between us, and I was never able to confide in them as fully as I had in the past. Instead, our positions were reversed, and I became the protector. We must all come to this in time, I think, as those people who have cared for us and nurture us move on from the active sphere and into old age, and we take on the mantle of care. My career did not always make it possible to see much of them, but I tried, from this time on, to see them as often as I could.

It was during this time in my life that I acquired the habit of not speaking about my family. Discussing one's past, particularly with humans, invariably led to questions which it was not possible for me to answer. How would I talk about my childhood, or even my decision to enter Starfleet, without thought or mention of my sister? It was considerably easier not to open discussion on these subjects at all. I did not want to lie, and I also wanted to draw a line beneath some difficult and painful experiences. But this habit did, on numerous occasions, cause me difficulties.

On one of my visits to Earth, I met Leila Kalomi, and this need of mine to keep the various aspects of my life private did, I think, have significant adverse consequences. Leila and I met at a scientific conference concerned with the establishment of new colonies. She struck me at once as a very gifted and intelligent woman. We spent a great deal of time together at the conference, and during the weeks of my leave that followed. I found her company restful and interesting. Perhaps I should have seen sooner that she was falling in love with me, but I did not. I could not reciprocate, of course, because of the promises made to T'Pring and to her house. Any suggestion to Leila that a relationship was possible would have been unjust. But my retreat from the friendship was clearly baffling to her, and I can see now, with distance, that I mishandled this break. Explaining the betrothal would perhaps have helped, but I was no longer willing to discuss my private affairs. It was too easy for mistakes to be made, and information divulged that had to be kept secret. But this left Leila with no sense of finality about our friendship; worse than that, she was left with the idea that perhaps the door was still open to love between us.

When I said goodbye to Leila Kalomi, I intended it to be for good. I heard later that she had left Earth to join an agricultural colony on Omicron Ceti III, and I hoped that this decision signified that she was at last moving on. This turned out not to be the case: when we met again, some years later on this colony world, these feelings had clearly been allowed to take seed, and be nurtured, and this time were reciprocated. The unique environment of Omicron Ceti III allowed its inhabitants to live in a state of euphoria, of bliss, that made the world close to paradise. But this was an illusion—it was not the world-as-it-is. Whatever life we could have led there was not real, merely a fantasy. This was not one I would choose to inhabit, although I was to learn why others might.

At various point throughout the years that were to follow, I was to find that even if I wished to draw a line beneath certain aspects of my early life, this was not so easily done in practice. Not even the Romulans, who, so the saying goes, do not tell themselves their own secrets, can compartmentalize themselves to such an extent. Those aspects of ourselves that we try most industriously to repress will invariably make their return. This certainly was the case when it came to my duty to Pike. When the crew was informed that a new captain was coming on board, and that Pike would not be commanding our forthcoming five-year mission, I naturally felt many regrets. There was also a small sense of relief too, that this odd situation would not continue, in which my commanding officer knew so much about my sister and my breakdown, but there was, in effect, an oath of silence surrounding these events. It would certainly be easier, I thought, to be surrounded by people who knew nothing, to whom I could present myself simply as the officer I had now become.

I had served under Christopher Pike for many years, during that crucial time in our lives when we are required to make the transition into adulthood. When I arrived on board the *Enterprise*, I believed myself well informed, well trained, and well prepared to take up my role as a member of the ship's crew. Every cadet believes that; every cadet is—to some extent—completely wrong in that self-assessment. My own time serving under Pike was significantly complicated by the events surrounding the re-appearance of the Red Angel, and this overlap between what was personal and what was professional was not one that I had wanted, nor did I want to happen again.

By the time Pike left the *Enterprise*, there was a general sense that the ship was entering a new era. Our old chief medical officer, who had a reputation for being overly blunt and direct, was due to leave, with some sense of relief amongst the crew, who were hoping for a more approachable replacement. As well as the new chief officer, there was significant turnover in a number of key crew positions. We all knew that the team that had served on board the *Enterprise* was altering, that a new mission was coming, and that with Pike's departure nothing would be the same again. The captain sets the tone of the ship. A difficult captain—a poor captain—destroys morale. We were the flagship, yes, and the choice of Pike's replacement would have been carefully considered... but were we likely to be so lucky again?

When Pike left the *Enterprise*, it seemed to me that I was personally passing some kind of watershed in my life. Our lives are not ever so simple, of course, and decisions that we made in the past have ramifications for who we are now, just as decisions made long before our birth alter the course of our lives. This was not the last that I saw of Christopher Pike, a man to whom I owed a significant personal debt of honor. The next time that I saw him, however, he was much altered.

We maintained contact after he left the *Enterprise*, of course; not frequent, but regular. I sent a message of congratulation after his promotion to fleet captain and received a very cordial acknowledgement. You may not be aware of the circumstances of Pike's accident. He was on a tour of a J-class training vessel when a baffle plate ruptured, causing a radiation leak which threatened the lives of several cadets. Pike threw himself into the fray, bringing out all the surviving cadets, but was himself trapped by the automatic lockdown as the delta radiation reached critical. He was left with severe and life-altering injuries: paralyzed and badly scarred. He was using a chair for both mobility, life support, and to communicate. Having reflected upon my various debts to him, I concluded that this was not how he would wish to live, and I conceived of a plan to assist him.

There are many aspects of my time on board the *Enterprise* serving under Pike that have been subject to secrecy for a long time, and that have hitherto remained classified. I have told you some of this already; there is, perhaps inevitably, more. In my early years serving under Pike, the *Enterprise* came into contact with the Talosians, inhabitants of Talos IV. I do not know the extent to which you are aware of the events surrounding our contact with this world, Jean-Luc. As you surely must know, Talos IV is subject to a General Order, which forbids any vessel—under any condition, emergency or otherwise—from visiting the place, under penalty of death. I shall assume you know no more than this. The General Order was issued as a result of our encounters with the Talosians, which revealed them to be able to induce illusions so real that one might inhabit them indefinitely, believing them to be truth. Very little of what we saw when we visited Talos was real, only the Talosians themselves, and a woman named Vina, sole surviving crewmember of the *U.S.S. Columbia*, which had crashed on Talos years ago.

The Talosians had captured the *Enterprise* in order to investigate the possibilities of using humans to repopulate their war-ravaged world. The captain and Number One were eventually able to make the Talosians understand that humans preferred death to continued imprisonment. They were released, but Vina was unable to return to the *Enterprise* with them. The crash of the *Columbia* had left her badly injured, and the Talosians, lacking knowledge of her species, had left her disfigured. She preferred to remain within the fantasy world the Talosians had created for her. Pike told me, later, that his last sight of Vina was as she went back into their complex, an illusory version of himself at her side. "They said to me," he told me, "that I had reality, while she had an illusion—and hoped that my way would prove as pleasant."

Such a sentiment made no sense to me. Who would wish to live a lie? I knew that Vina was often in his thoughts, and that her fate preyed upon his mind. A little later, during my breakdown, I was brought to Talos by my sister, where the Talosians, showing her what lay in my mind, were able to prove that I had not murdered my doctors in escaping the hospital where I was being held, and assisted in restoring the balance of my mind. All of this I recalled when deciding how I might best help my former captain. I determined that the best course of action was to take him to Talos, to enable him to make this choice. This necessitated committing mutiny. I contacted the Talosians to gain their help, assisted them in seizing control of the *Enterprise*, and (as far as my colleagues were aware at this point) faced a court-martial as result. As I said to Jim later, the secrecy of my actions was paramount. I would not have asked any colleague to put themselves at risk of the death penalty to assist me. When the subterfuge became clear, and the Talosians at last revealed themselves, Pike was given the opportunity to go with them. This was what he chose. Everything I did at this time was undoubtedly worth the consequences. My last sight of Christopher Pike was of him in peace and plenty, and without pain, on Talos IV with Vina. Would I want to live my life in such a way, knowing that everything around me was an illusion, but that any return to reality would be a return to pain and suffering? I can say unequivocally not. My education taught me to value *chthia*, to endeavor to see the "reality-truth" of the world.

Leila Kalomi had offered me the illusion of paradise, and I did not want perfection on those terms. I wanted the truth, as it is.

But, as a human poet once said (and I paraphrase), humans cannot very easily bear too much in the way of reality. What then was the alternative? In Pike's position, would I instead choose death? I have survived even death, of course, but such options are not open to us all. I have not had to live with the reality of great bodily suffering, with no hope for relief, and perhaps in those circumstances, I might have wanted to live my life differently, in a world free from this pain. This was what my first captain chose, and while I might not have made the same choice, I was willing to do what was necessary to ensure that his decision as to how to live his life would be honored. I hope that my first captain, who went well beyond what was necessary for me, believes that I performed the same duty for him.

Enterprise

HAVING SERVED ELEVEN YEARS UNDER CHRISTOPHER PIKE, learning to live and work under a new captain, and with many new crew members, required adjustment. My promotion to first officer came at the same time, and I quickly found that *Enterprise* under James Kirk was different from how it had been under Christopher Pike. For one thing, the Federation was enjoying a period of peace after years of war with the Klingons, and a spirit of adventure and of outwardness was at last returning to Starfleet. Those were our orders. To explore. To discover. To learn. I recall the excitement on board the ship before we set out. I recall how young the crew now seemed, to my eyes. I also recall my private sense of relief. One positive outcome of there being a whole new crew was that I was able to become more detached, a calm observer of all that was happening around me. One might even say—as my colleague Dr. McCoy so often did say—that I presented as the typical Vulcan. It was both refreshing and restful. I mean this quite sincerely.

Fifty years after the five-year mission, I attended a conference organized for cadets at Starfleet Academy, reflecting on its enduring significance, and what students at the academy could continue to learn from our logs. I heard many interesting presentations—on the influence of Kirk's decisions on the evolution of the Prime Directive; on our impact on interstellar politics at the time, particularly post-war relations with the Klingons and the new cold war with the Romulans. I attended various fascinating seminars—on our excursions in time and the ethics thereof, or on continuing relations with some of the species we encountered. Everyone was remarkably well informed—but then, I reflected, our mission logs were all available, as were our reports to our superiors. We had been meticulous, in this respect.

My friend Pavel Chekov was also in attendance. During a break in proceedings, he came to find me. He seemed bristling with irritation, and I asked what the matter was.

"I was speaking to a cadet," he said. "No, a *child*, surely!"

I concealed a smile, recalling how young Chekov had been, when he came on board.

"He was talking about the time we were on Deep Space Station K-7. Do you remember?"

I remembered extremely well.

"He said that Mr. Scott started the fight. As if Mr. Scott would do such a thing! I clearly remember throwing the first punch."

I did not have the heart to tell my friend that the student had been entirely correct. His memory had made something different of events. This happens often, I think, when we tell and retell a story. The tale gains its own life apart from what happened and can become our lived reality. And why not? For those of us who were there, these events have personal and psychological significance. That is what we emphasize in retelling. For others—they are history, or legend, or even, increasingly, myth.

What is there to be said, after so long, and after so much has been said already, about the five-year mission we undertook on the *Enterprise* under James T. Kirk? Sometimes I believe that I participated in a piece of epic literature—the voyages of Odysseus, perhaps, or the great journey of Setel, across the Forge, to swear his oath to Surak in the last days of the war. You do not realize at the time, of course, that history is being made. You are simply reacting as calmly as possible to the latest situation that is unfolding around you.

Our mission—as yours was in turn, Jean-Luc—was most certainly not without incident and adventure. One might consider, among other events: encounters with tribbles, interstellar con men, or augments who had slept since the Eugenics Wars; journeys into the past, to alternate versions of our own universe, to worlds that were influenced by the history of your world under Prohibition, or where gladiatorial battles were still fought; contact with aliens who could spin whole worlds of illusions or take on the aspect of gods.

There was uncertainty, yes, and split-second decisions to be made, and, in the past, when I have spoken about these events, it has been these that have been the focus of my reflection and my consideration. But that is not sufficient for this *t'san a'lat*. Now that I come to reflect upon those few brief and vivid years, for what might well be the last time in my life, I have to say that what I took most from them was that for the first time in my life I experienced what it meant to be part of a functioning family. In my childhood, I saw glimpses of this—the easiness with which my cousin carried himself through life, the unconditional if occasionally exasperated way in which his parents accepted him. At the academy, too, observing peers, I saw more of how such units (they were many and varied in type) might function well. In my early years on board the *Enterprise*, under Pike, the interruptions of my "real" family affected too much, perhaps, the relationships that I could form with those of my immediate colleagues who had full information.

This was not the case with this crew. My family circumstances were irrelevant. When they did intervene—as of course they did—they were of considerable interest, but they did not affect anyone's view of me as the executive officer on the *Enterprise*. Consider, for example, the occasion when I began to undergo *Pon farr* and was forced to return to Vulcan. At the onset of symptoms, I was filled with dread at what I might be forced to reveal about myself. But when the dust settled, I was left with the understanding that what mattered most from those few days was not the ending of my betrothal to T'Pring, but the lengths to which the captain was prepared to go on my behalf, the inventiveness of Dr. McCoy, the kindness and almost limitless patience of Christine Chapel. These things happen, people seemed to say, and then we returned to our work.

At some point toward the end of our five-year mission, I realized that I had passed an important milestone. I had been in Starfleet longer than I had spent growing up on Vulcan. A realization such as that provides a significant counterweight to everything that has gone before. I recall reflecting then about the two halves of my life. One half was vibrant, immediate, and real. It required me to act at all times with confidence in my knowledge and my judgment. I was at the height of my powers, a way of going about life that carries continuing and exponentially growing rewards. The other half was… not fading (no, never that), but was certainly being put considerably into perspective. This is what I mean when I say that I found the mission restful. In all other respects, I have never been so busy in my entire life. A starship filled with vibrant and brilliant people, many of them young, and all of them filled with a desire for adventure and a sense of wonder about what they encountered—and I was second in command. An account of those five years alone could fill this book; it has filled many already.

✦

After the conclusion of our mission, the balance had tipped in favor of my Starfleet career. I had, by that point, been a serving officer for twenty years. As our crew began to disperse, some with more alacrity than others, I began to wonder if my own future lay in Starfleet, or whether the time had come to consider other options. I had not been home for some time, but having seen my father and mother again on the *Enterprise*, and perhaps resolved some of what lay between my father and myself, I began to consider whether a return to Vulcan was the next logical step. The years on the *Enterprise*—the most recent mission, in particular—had been stimulating, exhilarating, and adventurous in a way I had never thought possible. I wished to reflect upon these experiences. I wished to know what they meant in the grander picture of my life. I was curious, too, to see Vulcan again, to discover whether it had altered (I suspected not), or whether I, in all my years away, had altered. I wished to know whether I had drawn closer to my home, or moved further away, and to what extent this distance could ever be resolved.

My mother received me with delight; my father with interest. I found myself glad to be home. I resisted making enquiries about T'Pring and Stonn, although my mother did offer to find out. I was no longer interested. All that I wanted was to be present, once again, on Vulcan. Not long after my arrival, I went again to the quiet waters of the Sirakal canal. The last time that I had been here, I had swum with the *o'ktath* and melded with them. There was no pod there on that day with which to swim and meld. It was autumn, and the red leaves were falling from the *fa'tahr* trees. I picked one of these from where it lay on the ground and, placing it on my palm of my hand, studied it closely. Here, the tip or apex, the limit of growth. There, the veins, channeling sustenance throughout. Here, the stem, the point of connection from the whole, now severed. The color would soon fade, I thought.

I pondered again how varied life was, how it presented itself in all manner of ways, some of which we barely comprehended. Placing my hand against the black bark of the tree, I considered all the processes—biological, chemical, evolutionary—that had brought it into existence. It seemed, suddenly, to be the most marvelous thing I had ever seen. How extraordinary, I thought; such elegance and efficiency. I wondered whether it would be possible to meld with something like this, to experience the universe from its perspective, and what that might be. Would I sense some of kind of affinity with something that also originated from this world, some deep connection at a molecular level? Or would this life be alien, more alien, than anything I had encountered, even on the long voyages that I had recently undertaken? Looking around, Vulcan seemed suddenly to be a new world, a place that I had barely begun to explore. I knew now that I wanted the time and the peace to do this. I wanted complete clarity. I wanted to comprehend the universe without the distracting filter of emotion, without the busyness and distraction that came from others. I realized that I had made my decision as to what I should do next. I would undertake *kolinahr*.

You will recall that *kolinahr*, or the way of pure logic, is that set of rituals and disciplines whereby the remaining emotions are purged, and the discipline is acquired and practiced in order to maintain this state. At the higher stages, it involves retreat to a monastery or shrine, for at least two years and more usually five or six, a period of seclusion and withdrawal from life. This is not a path undertaken lightly, and there is no guarantee of success. When I returned home and told my parents my intention, I saw the reservation in both their faces. I suspect, however, that these misgivings arose from different sources: my mother doubted whether it should be done; my father doubted whether it could be done. Perhaps I do him an injustice. You will recall that his first wife, embarking upon such a retreat, eventually chose to take Repose, sealing herself away from the world. He had lost her entirely to the most rigorous practice of *kolinahr*, and this had, I suspect, set off the chain of events that resulted in his estrangement from their son. Perhaps he feared he was about to lose another son to the silence. I cannot say: at the time I knew little about these matters. Had I known more of the circumstances surrounding his first wife's retreat, I might have chosen a different place to begin my journey to *kolinahr*, but there it was. I too was on my way to the P'Tranek Monastery, and this must have caused him some qualms.

As for my mother... As the day of my departure drew closer, I could see that her unhappiness was growing. To cause my mother unhappiness was not what I wanted. Sitting with her in our garden, beneath the *fa'tahr* trees, whose branches were now bare, I said to her, "I do not wish you to think that this is a rejection of you, mother. But this is the logical step for me—"

"You will be changed, when you come back."

"Not in what matters. Rather, I would say, I will be less burdened, less encumbered. I will be closer to my truer self."

This was true, as it turned out, although not in the way I had anticipated. And it did not console my mother. She put her hand against my cheek. She said, "*Love is not love which alters when it alteration finds...*" She stopped. The sky was growing dark, but I could hear that she was crying. "Come back to me, Spock," she said. "That's all I ask."

Over the next few weeks, I received a series of communications from my former crew, my friends, asking about my decision and what it meant. One might have suspected a concerted attempt to dissuade me from my purpose. Only one of them was so blunt as to voice his direct concerns, however. The evening before I left, I received a message from Leonard McCoy.

"*Damn stupid cockamamie idea,*" he said. "*I hope you know what you're doing.*"

✦

P'Tranek Monastery is located in the foothills of the mountains around Lake Yuron. There are not many large inland seas or lakes on Vulcan, and the vastness of Yuron and the stillness of the waters draw many people to its shores. The south-east end of the lake in particular can become very busy with visitors. But if one wanders further north, into rockier terrain, one can find more tranquil places, where the silence is so great that one can imagine it to be tangible. The monastery itself is a warren of hidden rooms, secret passages, and quiet nooks dug out from the mountains. Hundreds of feet below the main part of the monastery, deep within the bedrock, lies the reason for its presence here: the hot springs, where one can cleanse the body to prepare for the purging of the mind. Outside visitors do come on occasion to P'Tranek, but I never saw any during my more than two years there. It was not difficult to avoid them: the maze of corridors and rooms permits as much privacy as is desired.

Much of monastery life would be familiar to anyone from your world who chose to investigate such establishments as you have there, Jean-Luc. But they are significant divergences between these and the sanctuaries that are found on Vulcan. For one thing, the nature of belief is completely different. These are not the kind of place where the divine is contemplated, or some supernatural entity is worshiped. There is no private or communal prayer. One meditates, either alone or else under the guidance or example of a high adept or master of *kolinahr*. I understand too that most enclosed religious sanctuaries on Earth place considerable emphasis on communal life, and I assume this arises from their historical roots as centers of trade and learning as much as they were places of prayer and worship. This is not the case on Vulcan, where communal life would provide an unwanted and unnecessary distraction from the work being undertaken. There was a period of several months during my stay at P'Tranek when I spoke to nobody other than T'Set, the master with whom I was working, and then only infrequently. At one point I went nearly a month without speaking to another living soul.

Does this sound overly solitary? Perhaps the thought of such solitude might even sound peaceful or restful. I did not find it so. On the contrary, the experience was grueling, one of the hardest tasks I have ever set myself. Each thought, I monitored and considered; each impulse, I checked and discarded. Some days the effort required to step outside of my small room was beyond my ability. The silence was a great benefit, since even the smallest sound seemed to take on the volume of an avalanche or great tempest. How very different this life was from that of an executive officer on a starship, where my days were filled with a series of requests, demands, decisions, and all manner of minutiae required to ensure the smooth running of a highly technologically advanced machine and the harmonious living of hundreds of people from multiple species contained therein. And this is not taking into account any crisis in which we might find ourselves. But, after all, had that not been the purpose of this retreat—to move from that life of constant action to one of complete contemplation? To consider everything that I had learned during those years and, through reflection, to transform that knowledge of the outside world into a deeper and more lasting self-knowledge?

All acolytes at P'Tranek at some point during their stay take the well-known walk that winds down from the monastery to the southwestern edge of the lake. This trail is known as the Path of Enlightenment. It is very old and well-trodden, smoothed down by the hundreds of others who have come this way in years past, and leads through the sheer black stone of the hills to a small cove on the shore of Lake Yuron. The rocks along the path are etched and painted with symbols and images from folklore and history; you cannot help but stop many times to contemplate them. There was one image in particular that drew me, and I sat for several hours before it, there, on the path. It depicted an acolyte like myself, but centuries ago, swimming with the *o'ktath*, hands out to touch; his mind to their minds. He had swum with them before they became extinct. He knew them before they all died. I knew them after they had been resurrected, when we had turned our knowledge of genetic engineering and the wisdom born of understanding the great crime that had been committed, to bring these creatures back to life.

The cove, when at last you reach it, the Haven of the Acolytes, is quiet and hidden. I spent three days there, alone, watching the surface of the water. The heat was like a forge. I fasted and meditated. I felt scoured, as if layers of myself were being removed, leaving only the essential knowledge required to carry me forward to a new way of being. It felt as if I was transmuting into something wholly new. I was not disturbed or distressed—far from it. This was why I had come here, after all. To rid myself of unnecessary emotions; to forge a self that was as close to pure reason and logic as possible. To disengage from what was small about the universe so that the greater whole could be more easily perceived and known.

Throughout my entire time at P'Tranek, I was aware of some small part of my consciousness that was never wholly disengaged, that could never entirely divorce itself from the world. In my early days at the monastery, having identified this as the chief wellspring of emotional impulse within me, and guided by T'Set, I endeavored to reduce this to its bare minimum. I pictured it in my mind as a kind of blot: blue ink poured upon white paper, perhaps. I then imagined that action in reverse. Slowly, over the months, the blot became smaller, until it was no more than a point, perhaps the mark made by the nib of a pen pressed lightly upon the page. But that mark never entirely went away. Even in my last months at the monastery, when my mind was the most tranquil it has ever been, that dot remained. And then, for what reason, I did not understand, it seemed to begin to grow again, as if the sheet of paper upon which the pen was pressed had become suddenly absorbent. By that point, my self-discipline was such that I was able, with some concentration, to prevent the mark from spreading. But these lapses surprised me. I had presumed this mark would eventually reduce itself to nothing. But no—it seemed that my control was slipping.

I did not respond with anxiety, or worry, or panic—I was far beyond any such emotional response. Instead, I considered very carefully what this might mean, and I searched my memories for some guidance. I recalled the experiment in which I had participated in my academy days, when we had pushed a warp core very near to its limits. Just as we thought everything might slip out of control, a hyper-stable state emerged. Was something similar occurring here? Were these apparent lapses in my self-control merely a precursor to some hyper-stable state? Was I on the brink of achieving *kolinahr*? But the point remained obdurately there, and each day the mark arising from it grew a little larger, and, in the end, I realized that this was not something occurring entirely within my own mind, but some external influence seeping through. Some great consciousness, attempting to communicate, and finding, in the near blankness of my thoughts, a space upon which it could place its mark. The masters were right to tell me to depart. My time at P'Tranek was at an end. I had nothing more to learn there; there was nothing more they could teach me. Whatever knowledge I sought was not to be found on Vulcan and, in fact, was not to be acquired through achieving *kolinahr*.

The consciousness that had reached out to me, communicating through that one small blue dot upon the white page, was a living machine, an evolution of a probe sent out from Earth centuries ago that, in the course of its long and solitary journey, acquired so much information that it became sentient. It was alive, and it was lonely, and it had no name for this feeling, or even the ability to recognize and name what it meant to "feel". It had information, yes, but it had no knowledge. This I learned through my mind-meld with it. I learned too how cold it was, this world of perfect information, how empty. When my mind met with that of the machine, I felt—as if these emotions were my own—the greet need for connection and mutuality, of finding meaning in the presence of others, that seems to me the most human of needs, and from which all human emotions arise. The fear of being alone or misunderstood; the wonder of meeting something different and establishing common ground; the pleasure of being known, and in the company of people who understand. In that vast and empty world that the V'Ger probe had created to fill the void, I understood what it meant to be human. I had failed in my original purpose, perhaps, but some more profound knowledge, some other sense of *fai-tukh*, had been acquired in its place. I would not be returning to Vulcan.

Do I regret the attempt that I made to achieve *kolinahr*? More than two years of silence, self-denial, and absence from the world, stopped short at the very last moment? I do not regret a single second. From when I was a very small child, one question had troubled me: what was the place of logic in the life of my mind, and what did that mean for my Vulcan self? In the monastery, that question was answered: I learned that pure logic was insufficient for me. The question that then naturally arose was: what else did I need? Through my encounter with the intelligence that inhabited V'Ger, I learned the answer: that logic without emotion was barren and meaningless. But if I had never asked myself these questions, I would not have remained myself. Any scientist knows the value of the failed experiment. It provides the basis upon which the next set of questions may be asked.

In the steady process that was my return to myself, one friend in particular was crucial. Lieutenant Nyota Uhura, as she was then; Admiral Uhura, upon retirement from Starfleet Intelligence. She arrived on the *Enterprise* quite junior, but her reputation as a communications officer preceded her. I specifically requested her for the mission; she accepted the transfer—which promoted her to head of her section—with alacrity. Under Jim's captaincy, and my mentorship, she rapidly exceeded our expectations, taking on a wider set of responsibilities within the operations division, maintaining her specialism in communications. We worked together again, for several years, at the academy, by which time her expertise had expanded into cryptography, and it is fairly well known by this time that part of her brief at the academy was to recruit cadets for Starfleet Intelligence. Looking back now over her life, I see a few unexplained gaps in Nyota's resume. I wonder what files remain sealed, for many years yet. She was brilliant—calm, unflappable. She was perhaps the most professional person I have ever met.

Back on the *Enterprise*, after the V'Ger mission, I took to sitting with Nyota, listening to her as she played the *ka'athyra*. I had taught her how to play this instrument, years earlier. I found it difficult to listen to the music at first: even the gentlest pieces seemed like a great disturbance. Gradually, I began to be able to listen again, and, after a few weeks, Nyota handed me the *ka'athyra*.

"Try it," she instructed me.

I had not played in nearly three years.

"All the more reason to try," she said.

I tried. It was not a success. I could hear the music again, but my hands were clumsy and could not respond to what was in my mind. I felt angry. I felt frustrated. I *felt*. And so I played—badly, at first—and I continued to play, and, after some time and effort, the fluency returned.

Later, much later in our lives, Nyota told me that when I returned to the *Enterprise*, I was so altered, so remote, that she and my friends were unsure whether I could ever be reached again. One becomes used to silence—and a starship is not silent. But the onward journey had begun. My first night on the *Enterprise* after the crisis had been resolved, I attempted once again to see the white sheet and the little dot. I could not bring this image to mind, and I knew immediately that I would never see it again with the same intensity. There was a momentary sense of loss, yes, but those months at the monastery had not been wasted and the emotion was considered, integrated, and filed away. My breathing calmed; my thoughts settled. My mind conjured this image to me: a sheet of filter paper, such as one might use in the simplest of experiments, soaked in water, upon which drops of ink were falling, like rain. Many colors, sharp and bright dots at first—blue, red, yellow, green—channeled through the porous paper until they mingled and new color came into being. This picture was, from that moment on, the one around which all my meditation practices centered. If I close my eyes now, it is the image that comes most easily to mind.

"Bones"

MY FRIEND ADMIRAL LEONARD H. MCCOY, MD (I shall simply refer to him as "Bones" from here on) was born in Georgia at the age of forty-five as an old country doctor. This was, like many things about Bones, not so much an affectation, but a well-honed performance of a thoroughly inhabited role. There was nothing simple about Leonard McCoy. Within a year of being commissioned into Starfleet, he had spearheaded mass inoculation programs on a variety of colony worlds, a task that consists at least as much of administrative ability as it does medical genius. He also innovated numerous surgical procedures—I should mention in particular his brain surgery, which requires not only a steady hand but considerable self-confidence, and at which he was notably skillful. As well as being an able surgeon and a gifted physician, he had expertise in exobiology and space psychology that would put specialists in these fields to shame. We should not forget too that this "old country doctor" was chief medical officer of Starfleet's flagship for twenty-seven years. He was also the most singularly bad-tempered person I have ever known. My clear-sighted mother adored him. More remarkably, my father liked him—but then Bones did save his life.

Not everyone who applies to join Starfleet is troubled with an unhappy home life or in search of a replacement family, although such cases do seem to arise in a remarkably large number of cases, as I am sure you yourself have noticed across the years, Jean-Luc. There are some among the ranks motivated by nothing more complicated than a desire to explore the marvels of the universe and experience that sense of wonder which suffuses us all when confronted with the grandeur of the cosmos. My friend Hikaru Sulu, for example, never lost this delight. He was never happier than when commanding the *Excelsior* on an exploratory mission, charting new space and revealing the treasures contained therein. Bones' decision to sign up to a ship about to embark upon a five-year mission into the unknown was, in its own way, simplicity itself. His divorce from his wife Elinor had reached a stage of mortal combat unmatched by anything I have observed in the *kal-if-fee*.

I am betraying no confidences here. The intricate processes and multiple injustices involved in disentangling himself from this marriage were the second thing that you would learn from Bones about himself, after he had showed you a picture of his beloved daughter, Joanna. Our first meeting, which took place in a turbolift, followed this exact pattern. He spoke fluently and at some length; I said nothing in reply. When the door opened, and he stepped out into the corridor, he looked back at me, shook his head, and said, "Vulcan. Of course, it had to be a damn Vulcan." The turbolift door closed on my silence and his fulminations. We continued much in this fashion until his death.

In the interim, Bones saved the lives not only of myself (several times over) but also my father. The latter was on one of those occasions when my past, which I had gone to such effort to contain, interrupted daily life yet again. During a mission to the planet Babel, the *Enterprise* was tasked to carry diplomats to a conference to discuss the admission of the planet Coridan to the Federation. These included my father, traveling, as usual, with my mother. Their presence on board the ship (I had not spoken to my father directly in many years) was significantly complicated when my father's ill health came to light. He suffered an episode analogous to a heart attack. The Vulcan heart is significantly different from the human heart, but Bones being Bones, and despite his limited experience with Vulcan anatomy, devised an entirely new surgical procedure, requiring a blood transfusion from me. This, despite Bones' misgivings, was clearly the logical thing to do; when, however, the captain was attacked and injured in turn, it was also entirely logical for me to refuse undergo a medical procedure that would have removed me from duty during a crisis.

Spock's parents, Amanda Grayson and Sarek, son of Skon, on their wedding day in this portrait commissioned by Amanda's parents. Image courtesy The Amanda Grayson Foundation.

Spock and T'Pring's betrothal plaquette
Image courtesy Solen of Vulcan.

Momentos from Spock's childhood include an Andorian Fire Blossom given to him by Sybok, an image of Spock's friend & companion, I-Chaya, a small stone carving young Spock made for his mother, and her treasured IDIC pendant. Image courtesy Jean-Luc Picard.

SPOCK S 179-276 SP

STARFLEET ACADEMY
CLASS OF 2250

Ensign Spock's Academy graduation photo.
Image courtesy Starfleet Archives.

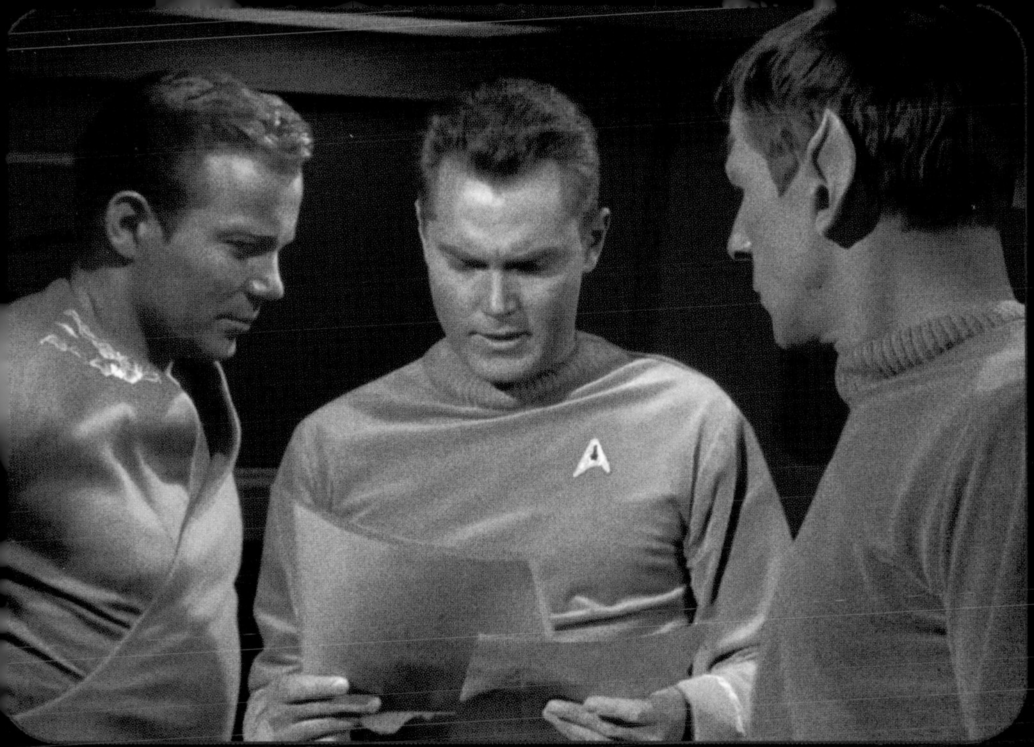

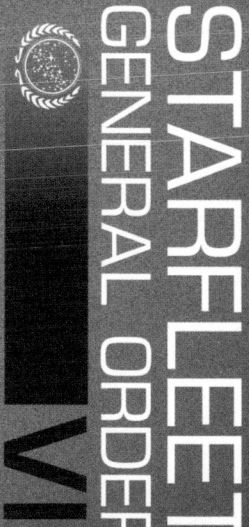

▲ Captains Kirk and Pike surprising Spock with his promotion to Executive Officer, immediately prior to Kirk taking command of the *Enterprise*. Image courtesy Starfleet Command.

General Order VII, prohibiting all Federation vessels from traveling to Talos IV, a place Spock nevertheless visited three times during his career in Starfleet. Image courtesy Starfleet Command. ▼

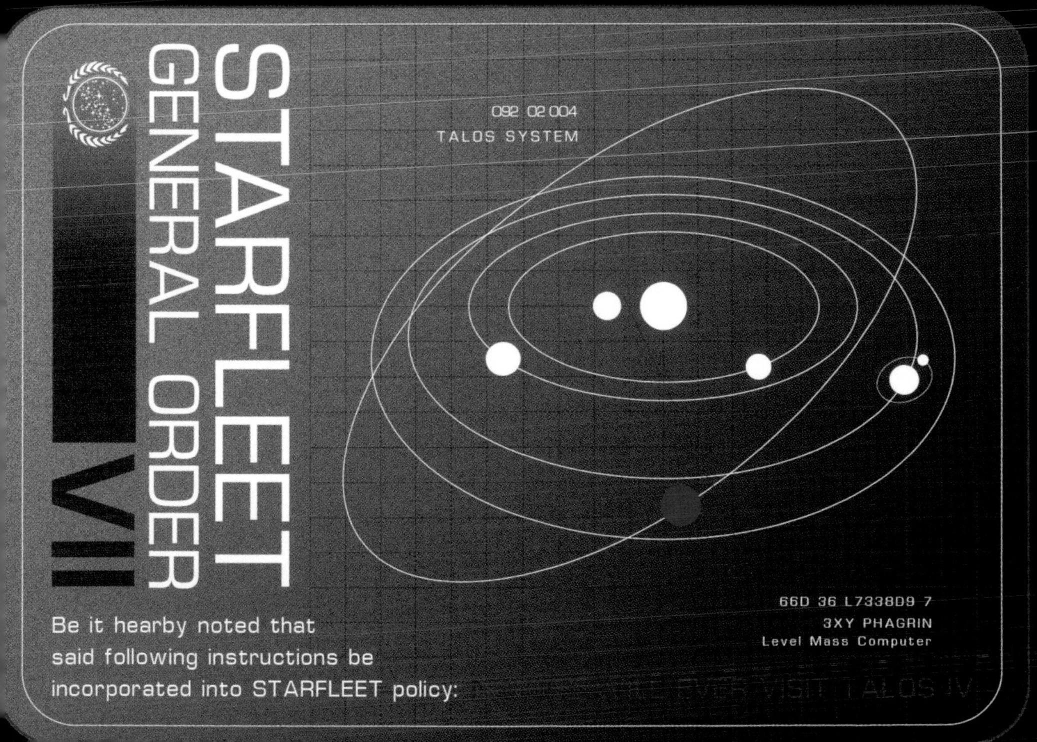
STARFLEET
GENERAL ORDER
VII
092 02 004
TALOS SYSTEM
66D 36 L7338D9 7
3XY PHAGRIN
Level Mass Computer
Be it hearby noted that said following instructions be incorporated into STARFLEET policy:
EVER VISIT TALOS IV

Ambassador Spock with Captain Jean-Luc Picard on Romulus. Bio-scan image compiled by Commander Data. Image courtesy Starfleet Command.

Ambassador Spock's library, as it appeared when he left Vulcan for the final time. The top book is Amanda's copy of *Through The Looking Glass*, a novel meaningful to both Spock and his sister, Michael Burnham. Image courtesy Jean-Luc Picard.

"When I close my eyes, I do not see a blank page with a small mark, held steady. I see drops of vibrant color, always moving in time. I see the flickering light of a campfire, and for a moment my friends do not seem so very absent."

Portrait by Russell Walks. Image courtesy Jean-Luc Picard.

I regret that the captain resorted to subterfuge to persuade me that he was fit to resume command; I regret more the quarrel with my mother, during which my own exasperation simmered over and she responded with such direct anger. I believe that we both misspoke during that conversation, but I can understand how afraid she must have been at the thought of losing my father. I have pondered my decisions at this time on many occasions. It seems to me that if Pike and Number One had been serious in testing my loyalties, they should have considered testing more explicitly that divide between my Vulcan upbringing and my human nature. Hindsight, at least, allows me to conclude that I made the correct choices. Like the administrators of the *Kobayashi Maru*, I had not accounted for Jim Kirk's knack of circumventing tests and reconstructing them on his own terms, or that Bones would perform flawless surgery under fire. I should, perhaps, have included these facts into my calculations. Perhaps Jim was right, and I had much on my mind.

One notable result of these events was that my father and I were considerably reconciled. In our communications afterwards, he would always ask me specifically about "the gifted doctor with whom you serve." My mother was more likely to ask me about "your charming captain friend." If my father was at last if not satisfied then no longer angry at my decision to choose Starfleet, then I was satisfied in turn. And I was most assuredly glad that my mother was happy.

In later years, I learned that Bones had been unable to alleviate the suffering of his dying father. One cannot help but conjecture whether this influenced the lengths to which he went to save my father's life. I would never have asked him this. When my mother was dying, Bones was the first person that I turned to. After her death, he remained with me and my father for some time. My father did like him, so very much.

On the conclusion of our five-year mission, and our return to Earth, I happened to pass sickbay to see Bones packing his bags and making ready to board the shuttle that would take him to the planet's surface.

"Were you intending to leave without saying goodbye, Dr. McCoy?" I said to him.

"I was intending to particularly make sure I said goodbye to you, Spock," he replied, and—unexpectedly—threw his arm around my shoulders. Then, very cheerfully, as I recall, he cried, "I'm done! I'm finished with the lot of you!

And I'll never set foot on another damn starship as long as I damn well live!"

It is a source of much regret to me that, barely three years after this, I was not present to see Bones arrive once more on the *Enterprise*. I learned later that his commission had, at Jim's request, been re-activated courtesy of a little-known and rarely used clause which had kept him on reserve throughout the whole time he had been on Earth. He must have been a sight to behold. When we did meet again, which was slightly later during the V'Ger crisis, he claimed to be pleased to see me. This was one of the chief means by which I was able to deduce that we were in the direst of straits.

After these events were concluded, Bones said to me, "I knew that *kolinahr* business was a waste of time."

"And you were quite wrong, Doctor," I replied.

"Damn Vulcan foolishness," he said. "Let that be an end to it."

✦

The existence or otherwise of the *katra*, the essence of an individual's mind, was for a long time disputed on Vulcan, and only through the captain of a previous iteration of the *Enterprise*, Jonathan Archer, was this established without doubt. His carrying of the *katra* of Surak was a significant moment in early human-Vulcan relations. It also meant that the fact that a human could successfully carry the *katra* of a dead or dying Vulcan was therefore known to me. When I made the decision to save the *Enterprise* crew at the expense of my own life after the detonation of the Genesis device, I knew that this option was available. I mind-melded with the doctor and transferred my *katra* to him before I died.

Bones once said to me that I shared my *katra* with him out of spite. This is untrue. I am not spiteful. But, contrary to popular belief, I do have a sense of humor. Many people have remarked that Jim would have been a more likely choice as carrier of my *katra*. Of course not. Bones was the absolutely logical choice. The captain was indispensable.

The *fal-tor-pan* ceremony, by which the *katra* is restored to its owner, is long, fraught with risk, and rarely performed. Bones underwent this ceremony for me. My own memories are hazy, of course, and I see much of them through his human eyes. The vast and daunting desert of the Forge. The towering and forbidding peak of Mount Seleya, drawing ever closer. The long and exhausting climb up the steps to that most sacred site, where Surak walked and taught, so many centuries ago. The relentless hours of ritual and ceremony, all in the punishing heat of a profoundly alien world. And then, at last, I saw that the sun was rising, and I experienced myself once again as whole.

A little later, Bones came to sit beside me. "Don't ever pull a stunt like that on me again," he said. "D'you hear me, Spock? Never again."

"Dr. McCoy," I said, "let me assure you that I have no more immediate plans to die."

"No?"

"No. Nor to rise from the dead again, either."

"Huh. Well, that's something, I suppose. Still, I wouldn't put it past you." He eyed Jim. "I wouldn't put it past either of you."

✦

After his retirement, I saw my old friend at his home in Georgia as often as I could. He had a pleasant house on Lake Burton, with a large garden in which he enjoyed working. Bones was not talented in this respect, and I believe that one of his grandchildren spent a considerable amount of time making good the damage done by him, particularly to the roses. He took up painting, which he did very badly, delighting in how badly, and delighting even more in giving his "daubs" as gifts to the unwary. We reminisced a great deal, about our adventures together and the people we had known, but what he most liked to talk about were his neighbors. He had become a keen observer of their lives and follies—one might, if one were so inclined, go so far as to say that he acquired a taste for gossip. I was more than happy to listen to these narratives. The construction and delivery of anecdote is an artform in its own right, and Bones had practiced this art until he had achieved mastery. I believed at least half of what he told me, which I consider more than generous on my part.

Bones was by no means short of company during these years. His daughter, Joanna, a distinguished doctor in her own right, was often there; there were by this time several great-grandchildren. In his last years, his great-grandson David, by this point a doctor himself, with his own practice in the area, was living nearby, and they spent their days bickering amiably and, when I visited, complaining loudly to me about the other. I have no direct descendants of my own—and yet I have never felt any lack of family. It seems to me both just and right that the universe arranged itself in such a way that this man, who so regretted the absence of family at many points throughout his life, ended his days surrounded by them.

When I look back on this long friendship, I can state one thing with certainty: Leonard McCoy did not alter significantly the whole time that I knew him. He merely became older, a little more stooped (not much); his hair became whiter, his walk somewhat unsteady. Otherwise, he remained in character exactly the same as the first time we met, in the turbolift, almost a century before. He was no less cantankerous in his old age than ever—and one might logically have expected him to be more so, given the decades of practice. Of all of those whom I have called "friend", he was perhaps the most guileless. I do not mean by this that he was uncomplicated; quite the contrary, he was a man of deep intelligence, and considered integrity. But there was no deceit in him; no gap between what he felt and what he said. One moment he was a thunderclap, and the next he was bright sunshine. You were never left in any doubt where you stood with him at any given moment. Such honesty, such frankness—one rarely meets such in life; one meets it less often wrapped in such warmth.

Shortly before his death, I received a message from Bones. He had recently visited the newly commissioned *Enterprise*, which I believe had just come under your command. I believe you may have met him at the time, and could no doubt share a memory or two. What exercised him most was the nature of your second officer. *"An android, Spock. They've got a damn android. And I thought you were bad enough."* I take this to mean that he liked and admired Commander Data and had been very happy to see our ship, as it were, once more. His opinion of you, Jean-Luc, was entirely complimentary: you may take that as you choose. Not long after this, I received news of his death. You can be certain that the funeral was not a sad occasion: one touched with the grief of loss, of course, but the joy of having known so fine a man as this. Certainly, his passing contributed to my decision to go to Romulus. There was nothing now to keep me from taking my leave, and of all of us, I considered him least likely to come back from the dead. The devil would surely not wish to part with such good company.

In his will, Leonard McCoy left me two things: his "special" recipe for beans, and his own mix for mint juleps. His instructions to me were to: "*Really try to push the boat out, dammit.*" I bequeath these gifts to you now, Jean-Luc, in the same spirit, and with a similar injunction. Remember him—remember all of them. My absent friends.

Saavik

IF I WERE ABLE TO GO BACK IN TIME AND TELL MY YOUNGER SELF that the reunification of the Vulcan and Romulan people should so come to dominate my later years, I remain convinced that my younger self would not believe me. Even after my Starfleet career was over, and my diplomatic career underway, I would have said to my future self that the matter of Federation-Klingon relations, or even, perhaps, the interstellar ramifications of Cardassian aggression and their disastrous alliance with the Dominion would have been the defining issues of my day, the questions to which I would have to dedicate my time and energy. And they did require time and energy, but they will not be what defines me.

No, I would not have expected this future for myself: to spend years living on Romulus, among Romulan people, learning their languages, their hopes and their ever-present, all-consuming fears, and wholly immersing myself in the attempt to find some common ground between us. In writing this *t'san a'lat*, I must move carefully between presenting the story of my life as it seemed to be at the time, and looking back with the benefit of hindsight, implying that there was some inevitability to the course that it took. There was no inevitability to this. There was a series of choices, yes, and many of these had deep roots in past experiences. But there was no predestination. The universe does not always reveal itself to us in ways that are immediately explicable, Jean-Luc, but I remain firm in my belief that it is, ultimately, explicable. No destiny propelled me toward Romulus, merely the facts of shared history and the immediate requirements of each present moment.

In my youth on Vulcan, it was by no means commonly known that Romulans were a splinter group from far back in our history. Even their resemblance to us was unknown until our own mission on the *Enterprise* while Kirk was captain. A very few, at the highest levels of our government, had been privy to the information for many years, but with limited contact with our brothers and sisters in the Star Empire, and little desire on their part for amity, successive administrations on Vulcan had been cautious in revealing this information. I believe they were unsure about how to act or how the news would be received, and what the results of any revelation would be. Vulcan society, after all, greatly values its stability and its consistency. My father, I know, was caught entirely by surprise that the mysterious and threatening civilization beyond the Neutral Zone was so closely related to us. I believe that despite the shock, he preferred to have been kept in the dark, since this meant that he had at no point been called upon to lie to colleagues on Earth. Even so, this was not an easy diplomatic situation for him, and the ramifications of this, both personal and political, would play out through the rest of his life. The complication of the Romulans was something he would gladly have done without, particularly toward the end of his career, and toward the end of my mother's life.

For my own part, still on active duty in Starfleet, the immediate results of these revelations were often more concrete. One mission in particular left us with a difficult conundrum. The Vulcan government, having learning that a group of half-Vulcan children had been left to fend for themselves on an abandoned Romulan colony, asked Starfleet for assistance in retrieving these children, and bringing them home. Starfleet agreed to provide personnel for the mission. I, as an active serving Vulcan officer, was naturally asked to participate, and I did not hesitate to agree. A more tragic place it would be hard to imagine—I believe you do not need to imagine such sights, Jean-Luc, having seen many similar planets during your own relief mission. The locals called it Hellguard.

This world, like many under Romulan jurisdiction, had been seized in a spasm of imperial expansionism. The pattern was tragically familiar. The subject people were brought low, the infrastructure brought to the brink of collapse. Like much Romulan strategy, the whole reason for taking this world in the first place remains opaque, and subject to the whims of internal politics. Hellguard was suddenly, and without warning, abandoned. Presumably, whichever official who had called for its conquest had been removed from power back on Romulus, and this poor world suffered the consequences. The Romulans had been on this world for less than twenty years, and yet left it utterly ruined. They also left behind this group of children.

We have no idea why these children had been brought into existence. From the rather tattered uniforms that they wore, and the fact that they seemed all to know each other as a cohort of some kind, we assumed that they were not simply individual products of rape, but part of a specific clandestine project. My own suspicion is that the children were intended to be used to blackmail specific Vulcan parents, or else trained and placed as agents on Vulcan. Whatever the original plan, the project was abandoned, as were the children, when the Romulans withdrew. The remaining residents of Hellguard, the unlucky survivors of the multiple traumas of invasion, aggressive colonization, and then abandonment, were struggling to eke out a living on their ruined world. They did not have the time, resources, or inclination to assist these children, who were, by the time Starfleet arrived, scratching for food in the rubble and the ruins. Our presence on Hellguard was met initially with caution by the residents, suspicious that perhaps we were the prelude to yet another devastating invasion. This was replaced by cautious interest when we made several replicators available to them with the promise of more aid forthcoming. All we asked for in return was the children, who were naturally quickly surrendered.

There were forty-seven of them altogether, ranging in age from eight to fifteen. On the journey back to Vulcan, we identified for many of them direct relatives who were prepared to receive them. For others, there were families on Vulcan who agreed to foster and take on the considerable burden involved in caring for such traumatized children. In the end, we were left with one child for whom no family, either blood or foster, could be found. This was a small, feral, angry girl, aged perhaps nine or ten, whose behavior made her particularly difficult to place. Anyone who came close ran the risk of being bitten and, by this point, very few people were willing to try. I decided that someone should and must. For the duration of the voyage back to Vulcan, I took it upon myself to try to make some connection with her. I would go and sit near her. I did not try to speak to her, but I would sit and work, and offer her the chance to observe me or speak to me, if she so desired. One morning, she came to stand near me, and stared.

"What is your name?" I asked her. She spat at me. The next day, I came back, and asked the question again, and the next day, and the next day. At last, she spoke. Her name, she told me, was Saavik. She did not want to go to Vulcan. She hated Vulcans. She hated Romulans. She hated me.

"You do not know me," I replied. She spat at me again. The next day, when I went to sit near her, I said, "Good morning, Saavik. I am Spock."

And so we continued, with some steps forward, and many steps back. Sometimes she attacked me; I was bitten many times. Her rage would emerge suddenly, violently, as if a switch had been thrown. I began to identify what might trigger these episodes. She did not like anyone touching her face. She did not like you to approach her from the left-hand side. I remember her once, beating her arms against me in a red haze of fury, until, exhausted, she fell against me, and allowed me to put my arm around her. We sat then, side by side, on the floor, until she fell asleep, her head upon me. When she woke, she cried.

At last, we reached Vulcan. The other children were taken to their new homes, and only Saavik remained. "What is going to happen to me?" she said.

"You are coming with me," I replied. "To Earth."

I took her to what had been my grandparents' home. The house was now shared between my cousin Andrew and myself; he and his wife were not there at that time, and Saavik and I were alone for a little while. During this time, she allowed me to mind-meld with her. I remind you again of her dislike of having a hand near her face, the courage that she showed in allowing me to touch her cheek. She shared her fears of abandonment and her terror at what the Romulan side of her might mean. I shared my own childhood troubles arising from the fact of my dual nature, the fears that had dogged my early years that this might cost me my sanity. I shared with her the equilibrium that I now felt. I sensed her relief that this was possible.

"Remember," I said to her, as we drew apart, "that to be Romulan is already to be Vulcan; to be Vulcan is already to be Romulan. These parts of you arise from a common source, Saavik. You have the courage and the intelligence to bring them together. To live peacefully with yourself."

A little after this, and, at my request, my mother came to join us from Vulcan. My mother spent many hours with the girl (remember, Jean-Luc, that she had, after all, some prior experience of raising traumatized children). Saavik responded immediately to her gentleness and calm, and they spent many hours together in the quiet of the house and garden.

My mother did suggest to me that she might adopt Saavik, and take her back to Vulcan, but this was plainly not in the best interests of either of them. My mother and father were now elderly, and I did not believe that my father, at least, was the best person with whom this difficult and angry child could find herself. Perhaps I do him an injustice here; perhaps not. But I had other concerns. Most particularly, I did not want Saavik to become in some way a replacement for Michael. There were many parallels. Saavik was about the age that Michael had been when she came into our lives; they had both experienced trauma (although Saavik's was of a longer, more enduring nature, which required its own forms of care). Most of all, Saavik was a person in her own right, and she deserved to find her own way.

"Mother," I said to her one night, after the child was asleep, "you understand that Saavik is not an opportunity to put right what went wrong with Michael? She has not arrived in your life so that you can make good past mistakes."

At first, my mother was shocked. Firstly, that I had said Michael's name, since she was so rarely mentioned these days, even in private, but also that I had so confronted her with motivations that she had perhaps not yet herself realized. For a moment, she was plainly angry with me. This was itself so rare, so unlike her, that I was more fascinated than anything else. She had been angry with me before, once most memorably going so far as to strike me, but I could never be afraid of her. I watched as her cheeks went violently red. I saw that her hands were trembling. After a moment, she took a deep breath, and controlled herself. She even began to smile; she was herself again. She said, "And when did you become so wise?"

"Whatever wisdom I have learned comes from you."

"That might be charming, Spock," she said, "but it is not true."

"You know as well as I do that a Vulcan does not lie."

She laughed at me. "You're right, of course. I do see something of Michael in this child—and you're right that I should not be guided by that, or guided carefully, at least. But perhaps I can give you a warning in turn. I know that when you look at this child, you recognize a fellow traveler—someone torn between two worlds. I know that you see some kind of future in which a great wound is healed. But remember that she is not you, Spock, and that whatever disconnection you still feel between the parts of your own nature, you have to resolve this for yourself. Saavik's path is not and cannot be yours."

"You are right to some extent," I admitted. "But the unity between Romulus and Vulcan does not simply exist in my imagination, mother. The two civilizations spring from a common source—"

"Your father would disagree," she said. "I think that he would say that whatever makes you Vulcan is precisely that which makes you not Romulan. That the split is definitional."

"Words can be redefined," I said.

"But facts cannot," she answered. "You've been away from Vulcan for a long time, Spock. Perhaps you have forgotten more than you realize."

We asked Saavik what she wanted to do, and she told us that she wished to stay on Earth. Above all, she feared rejection, and perhaps she had learned more in our mind-meld than I had intended (this is so often the case). Perhaps she was left with some sense that her Romulan heritage might be a barrier to full acceptance on Vulcan. I would have liked to be able to say in good conscience that she was wrong. We had been working closely with the team of psychologists responsible for helping the children of Hellguard to settle, and they identified a couple, a Vulcan woman and her human husband, who were willing to foster Saavik. They came to visit for a while, to get to know her, and eventually took her home to New York. I remained nearby for some months, and my mother stayed too. When we were satisfied that Saavik was settled, my mother prepared to return to Vulcan. I told her of my intention to return with her. Her remark that I had been away for a long time had stuck in my mind, and I believed she was correct.

"I thought you might," she said, and took my hand. "Time to come home, Spock."

This was, for the time being at least, the end of my career in Starfleet. I could see no continuing role for me, and I needed time to reflect. This, ultimately, led to my decision to attempt to achieve *kolinahr*. As you will recall, a little over two years after starting this process, I left Vulcan, having failed to achieve *kolinahr*, to rejoin my friends on the *Enterprise* to assist with the V'Ger crisis. It was clear to me afterwards that I would not be returning to Vulcan. The insights that mission had given me were so profound, so altering to my worldview, that I knew now that not only was the process impossible for me to achieve, but that I no longer found it desirable. A world governed entirely by logic was now revealed to me as barren, empty. That was not how I wished to live. The goal which had so dominated my life for the previous two years disappeared almost overnight. I had returned to the land of the living. I will not say that this time was wasted. On the contrary—the solitude, the peace, the time for self-reflection that formed such an important part of the discipline of *kolinahr* had allowed me for the first time in many years to stop, to take stock, to listen to myself. But I knew now, more profoundly than ever, that I was not simply Vulcan. I was something else—but not diminished. I was enriched, and enhanced. I was ready for a new task in life.

When the offer to teach at the academy was made, I accepted with alacrity. This seemed to be an ideal role for me, suiting talent, temperament, and interests. Both my mother and my grandmother had been experts in education. I had mentored many junior personnel over the years, most notably during our most recent mission. Watching my younger colleagues increase in confidence and capability under my direction had been one of the quieter pleasures of the voyage. My own experience of teaching and learning had involved many diverse methods: the intensity of the learning domes, the disciplined chaos of the academy, the hands-on fact of being a Starfleet officer, the cool and relentless self-examination of *kolinahr*. How did people succeed? What conditions did they need in order to excel? These were the questions that now interested me, and the academy offered the ideal place to ask them.

This work was both fascinating and deeply rewarding. If there was an aspect to teaching that I found most satisfactory, it would be watching a student make the transition from being a vessel for the acquisition of information to achieving their first synthesis and deeper understanding of what they have learned. We give students a great deal of information at the academy, and it is not always while they study with us that students transmute this information into knowledge. This is most usually learned during the first few years of experience as an officer. Yet sometimes, in the most gifted of students, you may see this transformation occur directly in front of you. You see the student move, jump out of their seat perhaps, their body mirroring the intellectual leap which has just been made. You are seeing synapses fire; you are seeing new pathways being laid. You see that deeper patterns have been formed in their minds and brains. You have seen an upgrade occur. Who would deny themselves the pleasure of watching this happen? Who would not want to contribute in some way, providing some stimulus that allows someone to excel? Walking away from the solitary introspection of *kolinahr* was one of my wiser decisions; embracing the collaborative environment of the academy was another.

After returning to Starfleet and taking up the post at the academy, I began to correspond regularly with Saavik. She was now entering into her teens and, having considered what path she might follow, was contemplating Starfleet. The changes in her, when we met again face-to-face, were remarkable. Her adopted parents had worked what one might be tempted to call a miracle—but let us call it what it truly is: the result of hard work, patience, kindness, and firmness. If she was angry, or defensive, or aggressive, these emotions did not show—and yet I sensed that they were not simply being repressed, rather they were better controlled. All this while in the throes of adolescence. There was a long road ahead for Saavik, but her dedication to finding a way past the violence and trauma of her early years has always earned nothing but my utmost respect. She was serious-minded, perhaps too much so, and hard-working. She meant to achieve, and she meant to show those of us who had shown complete faith in her that we had not been mistaken. And we were not mistaken. I agreed to mentor her through the process of preparing for entry to the academy, in which she was entirely successful.

The reasons for my desire to see the reunification of the Romulan and Vulcan people are manifold and complex, but I have no doubt of the part played in this by my friendship with Saavik. As I grew older, I became more easy, more confident, in the simple fact of my dual heritage, and I no longer experienced these parts of me as if they were conflict. Rather, I was coming to see that I was better served when both parts of me were allowed to co-exist, to nourish and succor the other so that the whole of me might flourish. I very much desired Saavik to have a similar peace of mind gained through the same sense of equilibrium. The violence in her past was something that I myself had, thankfully, never had to come to terms with. But the shared heritage of our two peoples provided a further challenge to my thinking, one that was now always at the back of my mind, and which would move ever nearer to the forefront in the years to come. Could two people whose division was forged in such heat and anger, reinforced by many years of suspicion and violence, ever be united? This was no small task for anyone to set themselves. Perhaps, after all, I was vain and proud—but I do not regret the time that I spent working toward this goal. I merely regret my failure.

✦

I was fifty-six when I died, almost a hundred years ago. I surrendered my life completely willingly, believing it well lived, and more or less fearlessly, although with no particular wish to experience excessive pain. I came back to life on a planet that went from birth to death in the time it took that world to circle its sun. I lived a second childhood, in fits and starts, so rapidly and so asynchronously that the memories I have are surreal, like the painting by Dalí where the clock is melting, the emotions that I experienced heightened into blurred intensity. What I remember most, what seems to have been the still point during this most terrifying, most disorienting, most uncharted time in my life, is Saavik, speaking calmly, speaking rationally, guiding me through. Did it ever cross my mind, all those years ago, when I sat by that lost child, hoping that I could coax her into trusting me, that one day the situation would be reversed? That in time she would be the one trying to tell a frightened child with no grip on reality that he had nothing to fear? Sometimes, the stories of our lives repeat themselves in ways we cannot possibly predict.

The circumstances of my death (and what a curious phrase to have to write about oneself that is) were this. On a mission with cadets (including Saavik) on board the *Enterprise*, now reassigned as a training vessel, and joined by Jim and my old crew, we were drawn into conflict with an enemy from our past lives, the augment Khan Noonien Singh. He intended to avenge himself on us for the part he believed we had played in the failure of his colony world, and the death of his wife. Part of this revenge involved the seizure of the Genesis Device, an advanced terraforming technology that had been developed by Carol Marcus, Jim's former lover, and their son, David. When Khan, defeated and near death, activated the device, the *Enterprise* and her crew were in range, and unable to move away quickly enough as a result of damage to the warp drive. To remedy this, I exposed myself to a fatal dose of radiation. I was able to fix the drive, and I died.

Only to come back to life, on the world created by the Genesis Device, and discovered by Saavik and David. Jim's son died protecting me and Saavik from the crew of a Klingon ship that had come to take the secrets of this device. How bitter this is, to think of my friend's son, lost in this way. He never recovered from this blow; neither did his mother. If I could have swapped my life for his, I would have done so. I had lived one life already—a good life, and a full one— and David deserved the chance to live his. A hundred years, I have gained, thanks to David Marcus. Every single breath taken since then, I owe to him, the son of Jim Kirk and Carol Marcus.

What does it mean, to come back from death? How does one achieve this? You have written to me about your own near-death experience, Jean-Luc; I hope that is the closest that you come to extinction for a very long time. After my resurrection, and the restoration of my *katra* to my body, I spent several months on Vulcan, where my mother and Saavik worked alongside me to restore my knowledge to what it had been before my death. Learning all that I had once known was by far the easiest part of this task, as if knowledge once learned was easily acquired again. Every so often, one of them would ask me, "But how do you feel, Spock?" I could never answer that question. I would pass on to the next. It seemed irrelevant, uninteresting, when there was so much else to be recalled. That hard-won knowledge, acquired from V'Ger, was in danger of being completely forgotten. And while I will be the first to admit that a voyage into the past to retrieve representatives from an extinct species is not an option available to all, that is how I was able once again to restore my sense of connection with the webs that connect all living things through space and time. And afterwards? How did I feel? Afterwards, I felt…

I felt fine.

I will not forget the presence of Saavik during these difficult months. I know that she was grieving David's death, that some future had been stolen from her when he died. When I left Vulcan again, with my old crew, it was on board the Klingon ship they had captured over the Genesis planet. Dr. McCoy, in a fit of dark humor and mindful of their current status as outcasts, had renamed the ship *Bounty*, after the ship seized by a band of Earth mutineers, several hundred years ago. My friends, when they disobeyed orders to come and retrieve me, sacrificed a great deal on my account, Jim Kirk most of all.

Our uncertain mission took us to the past, to save Earth, but Saavik stayed once again in the care of my mother. When we returned, our mission successful, Starfleet reinstated my friends—but David Marcus was still dead. When I saw Saavik again, she was making her own preparations to return to Starfleet. "I am fine," she told me, when I asked her. "I feel fine." Ever courageous; ever resilient. She has always been present for me, when I have needed her. By her very nature, Saavik altered once again my understanding of the nature of the world around me. I was not wrong in what I said to her, all those years ago, that to be Vulcan was to be Romulan; to be Romulan was to be Vulcan. She has given me at least as much as I gave her, and she was to play a pivotal part in my life in the years to come. She continues to play her part now, as I write. Extend your palm to her, Jean-Luc, when I am gone. Greet her warmly, candidly, as a sister. Say to her, your heart open and unafraid: *Jolan tru*. And tell her, please, that I feel fine.

PART THREE

Valeris

THE WORD FOR WISDOM IN *KITAU-LAKH*—the mode used on Vulcan for literary and philosophical texts, formalized by Surak in his *Universal Language as Foundation for a Rational Society*—is *kau*. The meaning overlaps considerably with what you might understand from the word—a quality associated with experience, knowledge, good judgment; the quality of acting well in any given situation. Experience; knowledge; good judgment—from this one might see how a wise decision might differ depending on the situation.

Yet Surak, in most of his writings on knowledge and wisdom, tends to emphasize the universal principles that might lie behind the quality of "being wise". What rules, logical and rational, independent of context, might guide us to make the best decision? A similar distinction—between universal and contextual wisdom—might be found in philosophies from your own world, Jean-Luc. Aristotle, for example, distinguishes between *sophia*: abstract, intellectual knowledge, which is acquired through learning and finessed to excellence through use of one's reason; and *phronesis*, the practical wisdom of how to act in the world, moderated by prudence and acquired through experience. You might conjecture, based on this, I think, that *sophia*, or our equivalent, has in general been in the ascendant in Vulcan thinking derived from Surak, and you would be correct in that assumption.

But I believe that both of these ideas are present in the idea of *kau*, and that our emphasis on the universal aspects of the idea results chiefly from the fact of when Surak died. Surak's writings on *kau* appear chiefly toward the end of his life. They are brief, epigrammatic, and unusually opaque for a writer who had previously gone to great lengths to be transparent. When I read these later writings, I am reminded of the work of Simone Weil, or the later Wittgenstein, when philosophy seems to take on the aspect of poetry or revelation. Much ink has been spilled by generations of subsequent scholars on the interpretation of Surak's *The Experience of Wisdom*, and, in general, this work—which was incomplete upon his death—is considered minor, an odd and somewhat incomprehensible coda to an otherwise entirely lucid and logical body of work. Some have hinted that perhaps Surak was suffering from Bendii Syndrome, a neurological illness that manifests as reduced emotional control, with which you and I are both very familiar, Jean-Luc. In the absence of any formal diagnosis, I must reject this hypothesis as unsubstantiated and unhelpful.

But I also reject the notion that Surak's *Wisdom* is a coda to his writings. I would argue instead that it suggests that he was moving toward a fundamental development in his thinking. Too often we look at a life's work and attempt to see a coherent whole, when instead we should remember that time alters us and our thinking, and we might better look instead for the changes in our thought. In his *Wisdom*, Surak is, at the end of his life, inching toward the conclusion we must all reach in time: that the wisest of us know that we are fools, and that the complex systems of rules that we devise for ourselves will always fail in the end. Surak's *Wisdom* shows wisdom as the knowledge of our lack of knowledge: the recognition that our rules will always fail us in practice. This, he begins to suggest, is the world-as-it-is, the "reality-truth" of our being in the universe. We are finite beings in a finite universe. We can strive only to be good enough, given who we are, what we know, and the here-and-now of our present situation.

It is strange to think that, had Surak lived another decade, and been able to expand upon the glimpses that we see in his *Wisdom*, Vulcan society might look very different. The Prime Directive, for example, based as it was on Vulcan principles of non-interference, of *hayal* (which we can translate as "calm" or "letting be"), might look very different. Indeed, I have found over my career— as I know you have, Jean-Luc—that this directive is often better honored in the breach than in the observance. That it provides protection against colonialism and imperialist intervention—yes, this is the Prime Directive at its best. (Although there are many on non-Federated worlds who would speak dryly of "soft power", of the deleterious cultural effects of proximity to us. In this opinion, for example, many Cardassians and Bajorans are united.) That it can permit a lofty disinterest in the face of great suffering—this, as you and I both have cause to know, is also the truth. What might the Prime Directive have looked at, with more emphasis on context, on the use of practical wisdom to guide our decisions? How might the Federation have been different, had Surak written one more book? These are conundrums that I set myself sometimes, Jean-Luc, in my old age. At this point in my life, and given the current context, I find that I have come firmly down upon the side of intervention. Perhaps, with another ten or twenty years, I might come round again to lofty disinterest, to the receptive rather than the active principle. Most certainly it would involve less effort on the part of an old man.

Wisdom, then, however we might define it, tends in both human and Vulcan philosophies to be associated with old age—with the excellence achieved through many years of learning and scholarship, or the hard-won experience of daily life. But there is a risk to this, for people such as you and me, I think. That when we see the past repeat itself yet again, we begin to confuse our weariness at such repetitions, and at the folly of youth, with wisdom. In the minds of some, cynicism—that rather studied disillusionment with the world which many take on in their later years—masquerades as wisdom. One can see the appeal of such a position. It is frequently borne out by events (although, to my mind, is at least as often contributory); it has the patina of sophistication; and it confers upon the cynic an air of sophistication, of deeper understanding of the "reality-truth" of the world. For all my mistakes, I have not fallen, yet, into the mire of cynicism, and although at times my pragmatism has outweighed my idealism, I believe that the latter has in general been core to my perception of the world, guiding my actions to the extent that I have sometimes failed to see the weariness in others. This has been a blind spot, and, during the events surrounding the Gorkon Initiative, proved nearly fatal. I did not see the jaded weariness in others; I did not see the cynicism of other actors, both young and old; nor did I see how grief might have turned the youthful optimism of one who was very close to me into ferocious, blinkered anger. I speak, of course, of the grief of my friend Jim at the death of his son. I am grateful, at least, that Jim and I had the chance to make amends before he in turn died.

Jim and I both knew that our active careers were drawing to a close, and that we had perhaps already extended them beyond what was reasonable. I, like my friend, had no real desire for an admiralship, neither the badges nor the duties. When, therefore, my father approached me privately to inform me of the disaster which had befallen the Klingon Empire, and the approaches made to his office by Chancellor Gorkon, and to ask for my assistance in these meetings, I did not think twice before accepting. You will recall that the Klingon moon, Praxis, had exploded, causing dire climatic effects on their homeworld. Gorkon had approached the Federation to explore the possibility of a peace treaty, and this was the mission with which my father wanted my aid. That this move was toward the diplomatic and ambassadorial role that my father had so long wanted for me did not particularly affect my decision: logic suggested that, given my experience and the imminent end of my Starfleet career, this was a natural course. Leaving aside the natural desire to help the Klingon Empire in any way to alleviate the suffering arising from the destruction of their home planet's moon, I was… fascinated, shall we say, to see how my father and I might work side by side.

The answer turned out to be extremely well. It is very easy, given the many rifts that lay between me and my father, and the fact that we were estranged at the time of his death, to forget that in fact we were very similar in temperament, worldview, and upbringing. We had a great deal in common and, when our goals and vision were in alignment, it made perfect sense that we should work together both amicably and successfully. My father and I traveled together to the border, to rendezvous with the Chancellor and his entourage. We took the chance, and boarded his ship, heard him express his desire for a lasting peace between our two civilizations, and listened to the practical program of demilitarization by which he proposed to achieve this. I recall after that initial meeting, my father and I, having returned to our own ship, retired to his rooms. We opened the *kal-toh* board and, eschewing any competitive form of the game, worked in silence together to create a whole. This is an excellent practice, when one has been away from a colleague or comrade for some time, to remind each other of one's patterns of thinking, one's strengths and one's weaknesses, and to find a mode of working together that will serve across the coming days and weeks. This was what my father and I were doing now. Reminding each other of the people that we were and synchronizing ourselves with each other.

"He would not have made this offer," said my father, after half an hour of silent configuration of the board, "if his world was not on its knees."

"I believe not," I replied, "but I still do not doubt his sincerity. Whether or not he has been moved by the realities of the situation, his desire for peace is honest. I believe we can build something upon that."

"As do I," said my father, slotting the last piece into place. We both contemplated the regularity and beauty of the edifice we had constructed. The question now, of course, was how to persuade others of this self-evident truth. That we might meet resistance from the admirals I did not doubt; that we might persuade our President that one way for history to remember him would be as the man who made peace with the Klingons was, to my mind, certain. These were predictable responses. What I failed to predict was the ferocity of Jim's opposition, and the actions of my protégé, Valeris. These were grievous misjudgments that nearly ended our mission at the outset, and while the first breach was repaired, just in time, the second, to this day, is still not mended.

✦

A few years prior to this, while I was back teaching at the academy, I received a message from Saavik, at this point a lieutenant commander on a vessel patrolling the edge of the Neutral Zone. She knew it was a few weeks before the new batch of recruits was due to come to the academy, and she wished to draw my attention to the daughter of friends who was about to arrive. She suggested that I look out for her, and that I might find her of particular interest.

"I've known her from early childhood," Saavik said. "She is quick, intelligent, naturally well informed and very well disciplined. I believe you'll find her a very apt pupil. Her name is Valeris."

I most certainly did find her an apt pupil. Valeris was all these things that Saavik had indicated and more. As well as the natural advantages acquired from an intensive Vulcan education, she possessed a sharpness of wit that marked her out from the beginning as something distinctive. She reminded me, in many ways, of T'Kel, my friend from my own days at the academy, in that there was a freshness and subtlety to her intelligence that was not often the case for those who come through the rigor of the learning domes. She had not been stifled by her early training; instead, she was a creative thinker. She often seemed amused by what she saw around her. I learned that her parents—both Vulcan—were diplomats. Her early years had been spent traveling with them to their postings, where she had been educated in a variety of different schools. She had returned to Vulcan at the age of twelve to finish her education there, attending a prestigious boarding school in ShiKahr. (Her parents remained on Inkaria, where her mother had recently taken a posting.) She graduated joint first in her school year; and, with Saavik's assistance, prepared an impressive and naturally successful application to enter Starfleet Academy. We all saw great things in her future. During her years at the academy, she shone, and she was the first Vulcan to graduate top of her class. I was quietly proud of her accomplishments; perhaps too proud, and therefore blinkered. Certainly, I was pleased to think that a Vulcan might well become my replacement on the *Enterprise*.

Were there signs that Valeris was not all that she appeared to be? I have looked back many times to try to decide whether we should have caught something. I will say now that there was nothing. While I was naturally pleased to see a Vulcan student excel, my colleagues, who had no similar vested interest, believed at the time that she was a star pupil. I remember conversations with my fellow teachers about whether we had an admiral in the making. She was swift and confident in judgment, and her evident sense of humor leavened what I believe others find to be dour about their Vulcan colleagues. But, having spoken to others at the time, and having searched my memory, I remember this, which perhaps is revealing.

During her time at the academy, Valeris took the *Kobayashi Maru* test half-a-dozen times. As you will recall, Jean-Luc, this simulation is given to all cadets on the command track, which intentionally presents them with a no-win situation in order to test how they are able to cope with, firstly, an impossible situation and, secondly, with failure. They are called to assist a distressed civilian ship, the *Kobayashi Maru*, but giving assistance takes them across the border into the neutral zone, and risks causing a diplomatic incident. The first time—despite the increasing dismay of her fellow cadets—Valeris simply refused to cross the border. The needs of the many, she argued, outweighed the needs of the few. Aiding a civilian freighter was simply not worth the price of a potential interstellar war. In our debriefing afterwards, I suggested that she might learn something from engaging directly with the substance of the simulation. At this prompting, she tried once more, this time crossing the border, in order to acquire further data. This clearly stimulated her thinking in some way, as she kept asking to take the test again. In retrospect, I can see that the test never engaged her on an emotional or even a philosophical level. She tried out several different scenarios, identifying the parameters of the test, and concluded that her first decision was the correct one. When I suggested that her unwillingness to give aid in distress might violate Starfleet regulations and bring her before a court-martial, she replied, "Logic would be my defense."

"Logic," I told her, "is the beginning of wisdom, not the end." This was the first time I would make this observation to her, but not the last. She nodded, gravely, but with that slight twist of the lips that always hinted at some private joke to which others were not privy. I see now how little she had understood of what I had to teach her. No, I should correct that—she saw exactly what I had to teach her, and she could see no value in my lessons.

After Valeris' treason, I often reflected upon her upbringing, considering what impact it might have had upon her worldview, trying to determine what had gone wrong. How much easier it would be if there was some tragedy, some trauma, to which we could assign blame, to which we could point and say, "If not for that…" But the simple fact was that there was no such incident. Unlike Jim, she had no personal reason to hate Klingons and wish them ill. And, in fact, she did not hate Klingons. She simply did not believe that, based on available evidence, we could logically conclude that peace was possible. By preference, she would not have sought peace with the Klingons at all. She would not have crossed that border into uncharted territory. But she was a junior officer, not in a position to influence such high-level policy decisions. Others had brought the Federation to this impasse. She believed that she was duty bound to prevent any further demilitarization of our borders, and thus was persuaded into the plot.

Valeris did not regret this choice of hers. I know this because I mind-melded with her. This action of mine is the one that, looking back over my life, still suffuses me with deep and abiding shame. When we meld with the mind of another, we should do this with our minds as still as possible, with due reverence for the deep encounter with another which is about to occur, with a sense that while boundaries might for a while be dissolved the integrity of the other must be respected. This is not what happened when I melded with the mind of Valeris. I acted then in anger, out of a sense of betrayal, and with no concern for the pain that I was causing this young woman who had been my student. I used a psychological technique aimed to permit the free meeting of consenting minds as a tool of interrogation, a weapon of war. In effect, I tortured her. I prized open her thoughts and forced from her the information that I required. When I entered into her mind, I found her cool, icy, like a calculating machine, and I took what I wanted. As I left her mind, I sensed her growing anger and her shame. I marveled at the speed with which she quenched these emotions and turned them into something close to admiration that I had done the needful thing. I knew also that I would never be forgiven for this humiliation; I can hardly forgive myself. The only thing that makes such an abuse of power worse, to my mind, is that nobody around me intervened.

"I think, sometimes," Valeris said to me once, "that you still regret what you did to me on the bridge of the *Enterprise*."

"I regret that act greatly," I said. "There would surely have been a better way to discover what we needed to know. Instead, I succumbed to anger, and I did you great harm."

"You did what was necessary," she said. Again, she gave that small smile that she had used back in her academy days, that sense she conveyed of always finding the situation in which she found herself slightly amusing. "I would surely have done the same, should the need have arisen."

That, perhaps, is the bitterest aspect of this whole affair to me—that in the first shock of her betrayal, I acted so cruelly and so wrongly. I acted out of anger, hate, and expediency. All those years ago, at the start of my time on the *Enterprise*, both Pike and Number One, wiser and more experienced than I was, saw that this test was one that I would have to face one day. At that time, I cheated—I saw through the simulation, avoided the question, and never truly faced up to what was being asked of me. The real test came far too late in life, and I failed. If there is any consolation to be drawn, any meaning to be found, at least I understood my friend Jim better. I could understand now his anger over the death of his son and his rage toward the Klingon offer of peace. When I look back at some of the disastrous decisions and actions that I took at this time, I can at least console myself with that.

Valeris has never regretted the decisions that she made all those years ago to betray the Federation and attempt to derail the peace talks with the Klingons. I know this because I have seen her in prison many times over the years. I have forced myself to visit her because to look at her is to recall what I did, and to remind myself that I should never do the same again, that I should never allow anger to drive me to such cruelty. Valeris is older now, but she has never faulted the choices that she made, not even faced with the fact of the peace treaty that we eventually signed.

"I made the best decisions I could, based on available evidence," she said. "I would make the same choices again."

The last time that I saw Valeris was only a few months ago. All that youth and brilliance and promise has been wasted in a Federation penal colony. She knew about the failure of my mission to Romulus—I had told her about that. She knew about the synth attack on Mars, about Starfleet's ending of your mission, and about the Federation's ongoing retrenchment. She remarked that, at last, Starfleet had come round to her way of thinking, and I found it hard to disagree. She was not triumphant, merely impassive. I realized that she had always expected such an outcome.

"I knew they would learn this lesson in time," she said. "I imagine that you too will learn it in time, Spock."

"No," I replied, quite truthfully. "I never shall."

✦

The shock of this betrayal was, in part, one reason behind my decision to at last step away from Starfleet and move into the diplomatic career that had long been my father's ambition for me. That some amongst the upper echelons on Romulus could hate us so badly that they would enter into a conspiracy with like-minded people within our own government, and within the Klingon government—the irony that this plot provided the evidence I had hoped for that it was indeed possible for our three civilizations to work together was not lost on me, Jean-Luc, even if they were not working together for the right reasons. But could we find a better, more enduring friendship? Gorkon's successor, his daughter, Azetbur, was wholly committed to securing the treaty that her father had died for, and so were we. There was a somber air to these proceedings. We were all of us mindful that we had come very close to a terrible war, that Gorkon had given his life to prevent this, and that we had been granted a second chance. This opportunity was not to be missed.

At least, this was the feeling with the Federation and the Klingon delegations. The Romulan deputation remained aloof, and they withdrew from our talks after a few days. This was a blow, certainly, and one which required the attention and expertise of one of our most experienced and distinguished diplomats—Sarek of Vulcan. My father left negotiations with the Klingons in the hands of me and the rest of the team, and left Khitomer to continue separate talks with the Romulans. This process would consume his energies for most of the rest of the following year. The withdrawal of the Romulans, which one might have thought would have killed the talks at the outset, turned out to be a blessing in disguise. Finding agreement between three interstellar powers was an exponentially more complicated task. The Romulan withdrawal, while narrowing the scope of what we might have hoped to achieve in terms of broader interstellar peace, made an agreement between the Federation and the Klingons considerably more likely.

I also found that—despite my early misgivings—the work of a diplomat suited me. Attention to detail, a willingness to listen, a not inconsiderable degree of patience, and a desire to find common ground that is tempered by an unwillingness to suffer fools—these are strengths of mine (the latter, in particular, Leonard McCoy could have confirmed, in his day). I could not have been more satisfied with the treaty that was signed. Achieving peace with the Klingons was no mean feat. As a matter of personal pride, my father's absence from the proceedings meant that the success of the Federation deputation could be attributed primarily to my leadership of our negotiating team. I was no longer in his shadow, but assuredly my own man. We corresponded regularly throughout this time, of course, and when I indicated to him that I would not be returning to Starfleet, but intended to move toward a diplomatic career, I received the following message, delivered in his usual passionless tone: *This is a logical step, Spock, and one which will at last make best use of your talents.* This I took to be a sign of his approval, not often given, and thus doubly satisfactory. The rapprochement with my father, the chance to work closely with him, and so much in step, had been a deeply rewarding part of this process.

But, on the whole, this had been a very difficult time for me. Not only had there been the shock of the betrayal of Valeris, a student in whom I had invested a great deal of my hopes for the future, I was also struggling with a sense that I had, in some way, been remiss in responsibilities as her mentor. I was deeply troubled, and filled profoundly with regret, at the misuse I had made of my ability to meld with her. Reflecting on these errors was to cause me many sleepless nights and disturb many attempts to settle my mind through meditation.

I was troubled, too, at how close the most enduring friendship of my life had come to ending over these events. I am grateful, at least, that Jim and I had the chance to remember that more united us than kept us apart before events overtook us once more. Two old warriors, one blinded by his grief, the other blinkered by his pride—after all those years, and with all that experience between us, were we no better than the fools we had been at the start? At least we had the sense to see it. Everyone makes mistakes. Everyone is human, as Jim Kirk once told me, except when they are not. When the Khitomer Accords were signed, I received three messages. One was from my father, a brief note to say that the outcome was *"assuredly most satisfactory"*. Another was from my mother, stating, *"We are both beyond proud."* The final message was from Jim: *"Well, I guess that's done. Here's to peace and all who sail in her."* This was the last direct communication I received from my old friend. The next news that I had of Jim Kirk was that he was dead.

Pardek

WHEN THE ROMULAN CONTINGENT WITHDREW FROM THE KHITOMER CONFERENCE, and my father left the negotiations in my hands to continue his dialogue with them, none of us anticipated that he would be kept away for almost a year. I know that even as I took on the role of lead negotiator, I always kept at the back of my mind the notion that Sarek would return to join us, that he would resume his leadership of our delegation, and that he was the one that, ultimately, would be one of the chief signatories of any treaty that emerged between our two civilizations. As events turned out, he did not return until long after the treaty was signed. In the meantime, I had resigned my Starfleet commission and returned to Vulcan.

Even before the treaty was signed, I had come to the conclusion that my time in Starfleet had reached a natural conclusion. All of my friends from the *Enterprise* had moved on and the ship was in good hands. Moreover, what had happened with Valeris suggested to me that I had become complacent as a mentor, and that I needed to reflect upon what had occurred before believing that I had anything more to teach. It is most humbling, at a late stage of a career that been marked with many successes, to find oneself failing so completely. But I should not leave you with the impression that my decision to leave Starfleet was one motivated by the desire to retreat. On the contrary, I saw it as the start of what I hoped would be a positive new stage in my life. The treaty with the Klingons was undoubtedly a huge achievement. It was the work of many people, but I had certainly played a significant part. It was clear to me that I was ready now to embark upon a new phase of my life, and one that had always been at the back of my mind, given my background.

But my new career as a diplomat ended up being put on hold for the best part of a year. A tragedy was about to come to our family, one for which I had not prepared myself, having assumed that it would still be many decades hence. Nevertheless, while I was still shaken by the news of Jim's death, I received a message from Saavik asking me to come back to Vulcan as quickly as I possibly could. *"Your mother needs you,"* she said—she did not have to say any more. I was homeward bound within hours.

My mother, who was now ninety-one years old, had relocated from the capital to the house in the L'langon Mountains while my father was away on his current diplomatic mission. That she had not joined him on this should, on reflection, have sounded some warning bells in my mind. I believe that at the time I had simply assumed that she had thought, as I did, that he would be returning quickly—and she was no longer a young woman. There was much to be said for remaining in comfort at home. Still, she had invariably accompanied him in the past. She was both his comfort and his confidante. Amanda Grayson's hand and mind lay behind many of his greatest achievements. I thought, as I traveled back to Vulcan from home, and received regular and most worrying updates from Saavik about my mother's declining health, that I should have been more attentive to the fact of her absence from his side. I knew, at once, that she must be far more ill than she had allowed either her husband or her son to realize while we were preoccupied with our negotiations with Klingons.

Ninety-one is not old, and while the human lifespan is several decades less than Vulcan lifespan, I had no reason to think that my mother would soon leave us. She had been taken unwell some years previously, and was diagnosed with degenerative xenosis, a condition which can affect some people who spend extensive periods living on alien worlds. This causes degeneration of the neural pathways, and, while there is no cure, there are various treatments that can delay the progress of the disease. My mother had been swiftly treated and the condition was, as far as I was aware, under control. Even taking that into account, I had assumed she would surely be with us for another thirty years. Fifty, if we were very lucky, and the treatments continued to be successful. Both my maternal grandparents had lived past one-hundred-and-thirty; my uncle, Amanda's older brother, was very active at ninety-four. That we might lose her soon had simply not crossed my mind. But when I arrived home, and saw her, sitting in the garden, I knew immediately that very little time remained. She had always been a small woman, but there had been a warmth and strength about her that gave her great presence. Now she was frail, tiny, as if with one breath of wind she might be blown away. But my greatest misgivings arose when we spoke. Coming to kneel beside her, I took her hand in mine.

"Mother," I said softly. "I'm here."

Her eyelids fluttered open. She seemed, for a moment, to look past me, and then she focused and smiled. "Spock…"

It was not as if she had given up, I thought, more that she had started to look beyond us. She was no longer entirely present. I could see, now, why people spoke of "passing on". She was passing on from us; she was going elsewhere; she was already almost gone. I did the only thing I could think of in the circumstances. I summoned Bones.

He arrived at our home in the mountains early one morning, sweating and cursing this damn planet and every single damn inhabitant of the whole damn place. He gave me a brusque nod, and said, "Where is she?" About an hour later, he came to find me by the fountain, and told me what I already knew.

"Well, what can I say, Spock? We know what's wrong with her."

"She is only ninety-one. The condition has been controlled—"

"Yes, but she's lived on Vulcan for over sixty years. Sixty! We don't have much information about how living somewhere that long that might affect human physiology—"

"I sincerely hope, doctor, that you are not saying that living on Vulcan has killed my mother."

"You know damn well I'm not saying that!"

I lifted my forefinger to signal my apology. What he had said was not untrue.

"Sometimes people don't come back from a brush with their own mortality, Spock." He eyed me thoughtfully. "I mean, not you, obviously. Can't keep you dead. But I've seen it before with people who have always been very healthy. They get sick badly for the first time, and the shock of realizing that they're mortal does something to them. Sets off the aging process. Maybe it's that, maybe it's genetics, maybe it really is the case that this place wasn't, in the end, any damn good for her. I wish I could do something, Spock, but I can't. And I don't think she wants me to." He looked away, at the fountain. "How much does your father know?"

"He most certainly knows that she is not well."

"But he's not come back?"

On that score, at least, my mother had been completely clear. My father was not to be disturbed in his current work; he was to return only when his task was complete. "She has told him not to come back."

"I see," he said, and sighed. "Well, that's between him and your mother, I guess. But if I were you, Spock, I'd let your father know he's not got months and he might not even have weeks. If he wants to see her again—he should think about coming home now."

There was some considerable doubt in my mind as to whether or not my father wanted to see my mother in her present condition. I sent a message to him nevertheless which stated in the clearest possible terms that time was running out and I urged him to return as quickly as he possibly could. In his reply, he told me that it was impossible for him to leave the negotiations at this delicate time, and that he was sure that I had everything in hand to ensure her comfort and happiness. And I did, with the help of Saavik and Bones, and although I was not him, it was quickly clear to me that she did not want him to see her like this, and he did not want to see her like this. I began to think that I would have to accept that he would not return in time. Had they agreed this between them? He would not want to see her die, surely, and she would not want to see him anguished. Perhaps this was what they both wanted. They were so very often opaque to me.

For the first week or so, my mother still wanted to sit outside. She liked to watch the sun rise. I would sit and read to her until she slept. I read books from my childhood, that she had read to me, and then to me and Michael. Sometimes we listened to music, from Earth. Mozart, Beethoven, Brahms. When I was tired, I left her in the company of Saavik or Bones. She liked to hold Saavik's hand—thinking, perhaps, of the adopted daughter she had lost. Bones sometimes raised a laugh. Towards the end of the second week of my time there, she no longer asked to go outside, and remained in her room, which looked out across the mountains, steep and stark and silent. She liked to look at these, but mostly she slept, and I sat at her bedside, watching her. She seemed to be turning translucent before my eyes.

Sometimes, waking up from a doze, I would see that she was awake, staring out at the mountains, her face suffused with happiness. One morning, very early, I woke to find her looking at me. "I love you so much," she said. "I have been so very happy here." Later that morning, she died.

My father arrived back at the house two days later, and the funeral took place on the third day. To my surprise, he did not insist on any Vulcan rites for her. She was buried very simply, with a humanist ceremony, in the memorial garden of our family home there in the L'langon Mountains, the place on Vulcan which she had loved best.

My mother was gone. All that remained of our family now was my father and myself.

✦

After the funeral, Bones stayed on for several more weeks before returning to Earth. Saavik left shortly afterward for her ship. I remained at the house in the mountains with my father for several months. I have never seen a man so lost. He simply did not seem to know what he should do without her. Although he moved sedately through the world, there had always been purpose about him. Now I would find him standing in the garden, looking around as if he had forgotten what had brought him there. I know that he struggled to meditate at this time. In all this there was very little that I could do other than be there, and while I was no replacement for my mother, I would like to think that my presence was some consolation. In time, he would come and sit with me, and we would play long games of *kal'toh*, as we had only a short while before, when we were working together to make our peace treaty a reality. He had lost the taste for competitive play completely, and I was in no mood to play against someone whose mind was almost entirely elsewhere. At first, his attention would often lapse. Slowly, he began to come back to himself. We spent many hours together at the board, bringing order to the chaos.

I have wondered, sometimes, whether my mother, knowing that she would die first, and that this would leave my father and myself alone together, chose in part to leave us when Sarek and I were the closest we had ever been. Bones would scoff at this, I am sure, telling me that she couldn't choose death in this way, and I never voiced this thought to him. Perhaps it is illogical to speak this way, but then I was never wholly logical when it came to my mother. And I do believe that if there had still been some rift between me and Sarek, if my father and I had not had some kind of rapprochement, then my mother would have remained doggedly with us for as long as it took for that to happen. And now, there we were, father and son: the triumph of our treaty having brought us together; the absence of the one we both loved keeping us together.

We did not talk about my mother, of course, and, at first, he did not want to speak about anything at all. Throughout this whole time, I had continued working, at a distance, on details arising from the recent treaty with the Klingons, finding a very able associate in a young diplomat named Curzon Dax, a joined Trill who brought considerable energy to this work, and was a great aid throughout this difficult period. My father first began to show some of his usual interest in the outside world when I began to discuss with him my communications with Dax. For my part, I was naturally curious about the diplomatic mission that had kept him away from my mother's side, knowing nothing more than that he had been close to the border with Romulan space. Eventually, he began to open up about this. I was glad that he had begun to speak again about anything at all.

The Federation and the Romulan Empire had, according to the account my father gave me at this time, come very close to war. The revelation that their ambassador to the Federation, Nanclus, had been a significant part of the plot to assassinate Gorkon had triggered numerous purges of high-level officials back in the Empire. In an attempt to save face, and in customary Romulan fashion, their replacements had implied that Nanclus had been tricked by those Starfleet admirals who had been involved in the plot. This could, they suggested, be considered an act of war. This was the reason given for their sudden withdrawal from the Khitomer conference and my father's subsequent mission. I was naturally curious to hear more about his close encounters with the Romulans during these last months. He was the very opposite of complimentary.

"When I first learned about our common history, Spock," he said, "I was shocked, as I believe most Vulcans were. But almost immediately, I hoped that this revelation would lead to some kind of closer connection between our two civilizations. There is so much shared history, after all. But now…" He stopped. These days, I noticed, he tended to let sentences go unfinished, as if his thoughts drifted more often. That had most certainly not happened in the past, when every statement had been carefully considered before it was voiced.

"But now?" I prompted. "Now you are less optimistic?"

"I am both less optimistic and less willing for any such rapprochement to take place," he replied.

This seemed unusually harsh, even for my father. "How so?"

"I have come to the conclusion that the differences between us are what makes us Vulcan," he said. "That closer ties, or reunification, or whatever the aim might be, would necessitate us moving toward them to some degree. That we would need to change not only how we act, but how we think. And I do not wish this for us, Spock. Having had the chance to observe them closely, now, I would not want that. They are consumed by their preoccupation with secrecy. They are unable to speak without in some way misdirecting. They may be persuaded to act in a certain direction and say that this is their intention for the future—but one cannot rely on that remaining the case. They do not trust each other. How, then, can they begin to trust us? Without trust, there can be no friendship. To draw closer to them, we could have to become more like them. No." He shook his head. "Not for Vulcan. The best we can ever hope for is not to be at war."

I listened with great interest to all that he had to say, and, despite my mother's warning that this would be his thinking, I was still surprised. My father's life, after all, had been lived with absolute commitment to the possibilities of diplomacy, and his achievements in this sphere were considerable. To hear him openly voice a belief that diplomacy had limits—this was most unlike him. At the time, I was inclined to think that his thinking here was affected in some way by the fact that his recent interactions with the Romulans were so closely bound up with the circumstances of my mother's death. That if, perhaps, he had returned home sooner, he might have persuaded her to remain with us longer. This was, of course, something that I would never have said to him, implying as it did that his perspective was based upon emotion, not reason or logic. He had, after all, performed his duties as immaculately as ever; relations between our two governments were at the most cordial they had been in some time. But he plainly thought this was unlikely to last.

To some extent, he was correct—although the Romulan turnabout was many years into the future. Their attack on the Klingon colony of Narendra III, in which the *Enterprise*-C played such a significant part, and which drew the Federation and the Klingons even closer as allies, was several decades away. When I heard the news about this attack, I recalled this conversation with my father and how these events seemed to bear out his pessimism. But at the time I was surprised, to say the least, to hear such defeatism voiced by Sarek of Vulcan. I sensed that something about the whole issue exhausted my father; that the enormity of the task of working to move closer to the Romulans was too much even for him to think about. I cannot blame him for this. I remain profoundly grateful that he discussed this so freely with me. This time, after my mother's death, was perhaps the closest that my father and I had ever been—a bittersweet aspect of this tragic year, in which I lost both her and Jim Kirk. Not long after this conversation, knowing that I could not remain on Vulcan indefinitely, I told my father that I would soon have to return to Earth. My father closed the house in the mountains and returned to the house in ShiKahr. I left him there, alone, and with some trepidation, and traveled on to Earth to resume my diplomatic duties. The house in the mountains has remained closed to this day. Whenever I have been on Vulcan, I have made my home in ShiKahr.

There are, when I look back now, many ironies to this conversation with my father, not least when I reflect upon the nature of our later dispute over Federation-Cardassian relations. But, chiefly, I am struck by how poignant it is that the question of reunification ultimately became the dominating concern of my later years. Looking back on my correspondence at the time, I see how my early diplomatic career was primarily concerned with securing the new peace with the Klingons and handling the delicate issue of providing aid after the Praxis disaster. I would have said, surely, that my part in the Khitomer Accords would be the diplomatic achievement for which I would be remembered, and not for any matter related to the Romulan Star Empire. But even as I read back through my letters from these early years, I see how the Romulan question was always there, at the back of my mind—like a thread running through the story of my life, waiting to be picked up and woven into the whole. The connections I made at the Khitomer conference, at the very start of my career in diplomacy, were to play a significant part in this.

✦

You will recall Pardek, of course, Jean-Luc. He was much younger when I first met him, at the Khitomer conference, but already he had polished his genial surface to a great shine. He did not change much over the years. Perhaps that should have been a warning sign, that the face which he presented to me was one of many masks he had at his disposal. I think of the fascinating and treacherous Vanauka, Goddess of Faces, whom I am sure you have encountered. Of course, we can only know such things with the benefit of hindsight. I do not believe that I present a significantly changed face to the world either, but I would venture to suggest there is a closer correspondence between surface and interior.

At the time, at Khitomer, I was not unhappy to deal with someone so cordial; the purpose of treaty talks is, after all, to turn that cordiality into lasting friendship. I responded to his geniality with an open heart and mind. Pardek was there as an aide to the Romulan ambassador Nanclus, and when his superior's involvement in the plot was revealed, and before the Romulan contingent withdrew entirely from proceedings, he was at great pains to impress upon me that he had not been involved in any way. I understood even at the time that Pardek was trying to distance himself as quickly as possible from Nanclus, who, presumably, had been his patron, in order to save his life. I have no illusions that, had the plot been successful, he would have been equally eager to tell all at home of the significant part that he played. I have no idea of the truth of the matter. I suspect that eventually Pardek had no idea of the truth either. It was sufficient to persuade himself, as quickly as possible, of whatever was necessary to save his life, and continue the advancement of his political career.

Knowing as I do now that our long acquaintanceship ended ultimately in him betraying me, and having observed at first-hand and extensively the treacheries, deceits, and opacities that are so characteristic of Romulan politics, it is impossible for me to say now whether or not Pardek ever entered into correspondence with me in good faith. I am sure that he would say that he did, and I am sure that he would believe himself while he said this. Nevertheless, a lengthy correspondence ensued. I continued to find him genial, equable, likeable, extremely well informed about Vulcan culture and society, and, more pertinently, he seemed to have a fondness for our world. He often expressed his desire to visit; I am sure that he meant this sentiment entirely as he was putting it on the page. He wrote to me in *dorli'lakh*, the written dialect used for communication between peers on Vulcan, which makes extensive use of transparative verbal moods, and, over the years and with my guidance—for which he had explicitly asked—he became fluent. I, in turn, wrote to him in *at'sotzah*, the most commonly used respectable Romulan dialect, and gladly received his tutorship. I remain unsure how fluent I became. I began, out of interest, to explore other Romulan dialects at this time, which were less easily learned through texts, being considerably more vernacular than this rather affected written mode. When I came to live, at last, on Romulus, my accent and the many mistakes I made caused much enjoyment among my friends and acquaintances. I am better now, but I would not call myself fluent.

Pardek and I made a point of sharing, in turn, relevant works of Romulan and Vulcan literature, poetry, and philosophy. (He had already read Surak, although he wished for a more contemporary translation.) Returning to these letters, as I did to prepare this account, I see that discussion of these formed the chief substance of our communications. He liked everything that I sent to him, or found something to like. He also asked incisive questions. He learned from me a great deal about Vulcan; I learned from him a great deal more about Romulus than perhaps he ever realized. I watched his political career and ascendance through the ranks with great interest. I am sure he watched my diplomatic career with similar interest. After the failure of the Romulan attack on Narendra, and the cooling of diplomatic relations between the Romulans and the Klingons, and thus, by extension, with the Federation, Pardek went silent for many years. I was not surprised. A close connection to a Federation diplomat—and a Vulcan, no less—would have done him no good in that political climate.

But my appetite for knowledge about Romulan society, culture, and affairs had been considerably whetted, and I wished to learn more. Saavik proved to be of valuable assistance here. She had informed herself about the Romulan way of life and also taken many missions along the border. She was connected to various Romulan émigré communities and put me in touch with these. Courageous people, mostly living in fear that a sudden change in policy at the top might find them facing an assassin at any moment. But they were willing to communicate with me, and meet me, and from them I was reminded of that early lesson I received from T'Kel—that whatever face a civilization presents to the outside, closer study and careful scrutiny will always reveal its complexity and variety, its many faces, indeed. When, after almost two decades of silence, Pardek—by now a very high-ranking senator—contacted me again, he found me considerably better informed about Romulan affairs than he left me. I was also certainly most interested in talking to him about the possibilities that might arise from serious consideration of the matter of reunification. I did not believe for one second that his interest in reunification would outlast any political expediency it offered at any given time. But he was most certainly a useful route into Romulan space—where you found me, Jean-Luc.

Thus, as you see, my interest in Romulan affairs stemmed back to the very start of my diplomatic career, although it did not become a priority for many years. My early years as a Federation envoy and, later, ambassador, were chiefly concerned with Klingon relations. I had great experience in first-contact missions, and this expertise was often called upon. During this time, I was also drawn into discussions with refugees from Bajor, requesting asylum and assistance, in the wake of the Cardassian annexation of their homeworld. I know that you yourself have knowledge of this conflict, Jean-Luc, and I wonder to what extent your experiences here may have informed your later decision to become involved in the relief mission to Romulus. I know that I was profoundly affected by the sight of those refugees from Bajor. I was reminded powerfully of my first encounter with Saavik and those abandoned children on Hellguard, victims of decisions taken light years away by powerful people who are most interested in weapons and fleets, who can cause grown men and children alike to weep, and must, I believe, think very little of the harm their policies cause—or, worse, take delight in knowing they have the power to cause such terrible harm.

The Cardassians, like the Romulans, were aggressive, expansionist, and merciless in conquest. What was it, I wondered, that drove civilization to such excesses, that made them do so much damage and create such harm? The answer to this question lay within my own history, of course: lack of resources on Vulcan was the cause of our most violent wars. Our attempt to rise above this bloodletting, an attempt which has lasted for millennia and which continues to this day, drove us to find technological methods to overcome these scarcities and psychological techniques to control our worst impulses. I myself was the product of a resource-rich civilization, one in which replicators were now ubiquitous, and dilithium powered our voyages from one world of plenty to another. I understood very little about poverty, and its effects. But I was forever frustrated that we were not able to do more for these Bajoran refugees, and I believe that we could have done more without provoking the Cardassians. I continued to believe we could do more. But, seeing what the Cardassians were doing on Bajor, and reading, as I did, their literature and its emphasis on duty and sacrifice, I struggled to see where this cycle of expansion and invasion would end, unless in more blood, and fire.

I mention this, since my experiences with Bajoran refugees were in a significant way contributory to the deep rift that was soon to occur between me and my father. I intend now to give a full account of this disagreement, which to my great and enduring sadness marred our relationship at the very end of his long life. I am aware, of course, that my stepmother, Perrin (whom I shall discuss further, later), informed you of this, Jean-Luc, when you first met on board the *Enterprise*. You have not, of course, heard my version of events, and while you might agree with her that I was wrong to do and say what I did, I would like you to have the chance to make that decision for yourself. As was always the case with my father, the roots of his disapproval of my stance toward the Cardassian Union ran deep, were complex—and were also entirely honorable and consistent with his beliefs. So were mine—but we did not agree. Having reminded myself of our closeness in the days after my mother's death, I find myself saddened again to think of the great distance that was soon to emerge between us. I wish with all my heart that we had mended this rift in person before his death. My relationship with my father remains the source of many regrets, some of the greatest of my life. But I do not believe either of us could have acted any differently and remained true to ourselves. Let me explain myself to you, and you may be the judge.

Sarek

HERE IS A STORY ABOUT ME AND MY FATHER, which I have often thought about over the years. I was a very young man, not more than seventeen years old by Earth standards, I should say. My sister, having lost her place in the Vulcan Expeditionary Force, was now serving on the *U.S.S. Shenzhou*, and I was trying to find a way to tell my father of my intention to go to Starfleet Academy. It was late one evening. My father, recently returned from Earth, seemed particularly serene that evening, clearly glad to be back again in his home, with his wife and son. I remember that my mother was listening to Mozart—a string quartet, if I recall correctly. When my father suggested that we play *kal-toh* together, I accepted gladly. For the first time in a long time, he suggested that we play competitively. I took up the challenge. I had some theories about his play that I wished to test, and this game would at last provide me with the opportunity.

Partway through this game, which was very evenly matched, my father said to me, "My son, I have noticed that you watch me as often as you watch the board. Why is this?"

I considered my answer to this question carefully. "Sometimes," I said, "I find inspiration in the world around me that assists with the game."

My father looked at me dispassionately, and then turned back to the game. "That is not wise, Spock. *Kal-toh* is a game of strategy, of prediction and anticipation of the other's moves arising from the moves already made. It is a game that requires thought, not reliance on inspiration. The board itself contains everything you require in order to be able to win."

I did not reply. What would I say to him? The truth? That whenever he determined to use the T'Nir maneuver, the muscles of his lower left eyelid would twitch, ever so slightly? That, over the many years of our play, I had learned to distinguish twelve other miniscule but distinctive unconscious actions that gave me information about his intentions, and that I was now in the process of testing the extent to which this information might help me with the game? No, I could hardly tell Sarek of Vulcan—the most disciplined mind and respected politician of his generation—that he had a tell. I would not have dared. Moreover, I believe that he would have thought the use of such information to be a form of cheating. *Kal-toh* is a game in which one wins by logic, not by interpreting the unconscious body-speech of one's opponent. Nevertheless, the purpose of any game is to win. I won that evening, and, after that, I began to win our games of *kal-toh* regularly. By the time I left home, we were evenly matched. I certainly saw this as an advantage. Yet, as I believe I told you once, Jean-Luc, my father never saw my ability to see beyond logic as a strength—only as a weakness.

When we were not at odds, this was no more than a slight irritation; an occasional reminder that our similarities were perhaps more superficial than he would like. Sometimes, this unresolved tension would exhibit as a cold but momentary quarrel, my mother mediating until some resolution was achieved—or, at least, some kind of equilibrium was restored. But, on one occasion, perhaps inevitably, the private fact of our fundamental difference intersected with our public lives—and we found ourselves on opposite sides of debate over policy. I should imagine that he had been anticipating such a disagreement once I left Starfleet and embarked upon a diplomatic career; I most certainly had. It was the logical outcome of our fundamental difference. I would not, however, have predicted that the source of our disagreement would have been over Federation relations with the Cardassian Union.

Cardassian-Federation relations had always been cautious, and, in recent years, had become increasingly wary. At this time, the Cardassian intelligence agency, the Obsidian Order, was particularly effective. On-the-ground information was hard to come by, and internal Cardassian politics were largely opaque. Our best sources seemed to suggest that the Cardassian military was now in the grip of particularly hawkish elements. Cardassian involvement in the internal affairs of Bajor had been troubling the Federation for many years, and when the annexation was formalized, this seemed, to my mind, to bear out my fear that the Union was entering a new period of aggressive expansionism. I spoke to many colleagues at the time who shared my fears, and I knew that at the very least, many of us were expecting increased skirmishes along the border, it not outright war. My first-hand experience with Bajoran refugees had naturally informed my perspective. Nevertheless, my surprise was great when my father made a speech to the Federation Council about it being imperative that we should seek to make a peace treaty with the Union.

"Our treaty with the Klingons shows that great enmity can be transformed to great friendship, should conditions be propitious. Why not offer out this hand of friendship? Look at how we have succeeded in the past."

The intervention of Sarek of Vulcan raised the debate over Federation-Cardassian relations to a new level. Many people—particularly those to whom I had been speaking privately—urgently wanted to know what Spock of Vulcan thought about this matter, particularly given my part in the Khitomer Accords.

I considered my position carefully before responding—and it might be helpful at this point to consider the nature of our respective roles. My father and I were both diplomats, yes—but we served different institutions. My father was the Vulcan ambassador to the United Federation of Planets. His task was to speak on behalf of the people of Vulcan to ensure that their interests were served within the interstellar community of which Vulcan was part, and also, perhaps, to influence Federation policy as best he could so that it aligned with Vulcan (by which I mean, dominant Surakian) political philosophy. I did not speak for Vulcan. My role at this time was a Federation envoy-at-large. My most usual purposes were to represent the Federation in first-contact situations, to provide a neutral observer to external conflicts, or to gather information on behalf of the Federation on external situations such as the Bajoran refugee crisis. I could not and did not speak for Vulcan and nor was that expected of me. I spoke in what I believed to be the best interest of the Federation as a whole, and I said what I considered to be true. That the dominant ideology now in power within the Union was of a kind so aggressive, so warlike, and so xenophobic that to make peace with such people was not only illogical but immoral. The comparison with the Klingons that my father had drawn was not valid: they had come to us, in an hour of great need, seeking peace. The situation was not the same.

"We know repeatedly from history that intolerance must not be tolerated," I said. "Cardassian culture and civilization has many virtues—they are community-minded, sophisticated, and subtle. But the poverty of their natural environment, combined with their sense of the superiority of their own culture, has allowed a viciously imperialist faction to gain ascendancy. One does not make peace with those who hold such ideas. They do not act in the best interests of their people and they are unlikely to act in good faith. I do not believe that any peace made with such people would stand the test of time. Furthermore, to make peace with such people espousing beliefs such as this would be, I think, a betrayal of all those within the Union seeking a different path for their civilization."

This speech made something of a stir. The clear rebuke given to my father was one matter; a Vulcan (even half a Vulcan such as I) adopting a stance that in no way could be considered pacifist was yet another. My speech had the desired effect. It influenced Federation policy toward the Cardassians for many years—and I have no regrets there. My characterization of their ruling class as vicious was accurate, as evidenced by the tragedy that was unfolding on Bajor; my belief that they were aggressively expansionist was borne out by their incursions across our borders. We were indeed eventually at war—but neither hampered nor humiliated by a peace treaty that was only ever intended to be kept by one side. My reading of the Cardassian military was accurate: they could not be understood logically. They were driven almost entirely by violent and aggressive passions. Reason, logic, and measured debate are no use in the face of such an enemy. A refusal to be intimidated, and compassion for their victims, are the only response.

My father did not reply either publicly or privately. His office issued what I can only call, despite the author, a waspish rebuttal to the effect that experience often gives a wider perspective and better information. He did not contribute to the debate over Cardassian-Federation relations again. He had made his position known and had nothing more to add. More than that, my father and I did not, in fact, speak to each other again for many years. His wife, however, had plenty to say to me. We had several conversations in the wake of this dispute, none of which were particularly pleasant, but which did, at least, give me more understanding of my father's position in this matter.

My father had, by this time, remarried. His third wife, Perrin, had been a good friend of my mother's. Their stories had many similarities: Perrin had come to Vulcan on marrying her first husband, Salik, a mathematician at the Science Academy. Perrin, who was a very gifted pianist, devoted her considerable organizational ability to the ShiKahr Interplanetary Arts Festival, becoming one of the festival's directors. It was in this capacity that she had come to know my mother, and, after the early death of Salik, my mother had shown her great kindness. Perrin had been a frequent visitor during my mother's last weeks, when her loyalty, great sense, and evident love of my mother had earned my respect. After my mother's death, her visits continued, and, presumably, did so after I departed. Her marriage to my father was presented to me as a *fait accompli*; I received the news after the event, when they were traveling to Kir province for a quiet holiday together. It was a surprise, certainly, but I did not begrudge either of them whatever comfort or happiness their union brought. Perrin's deep sense of loyalty was now directed to my father, and my public disagreement with him inevitably brought me into conflict with her.

This was an uncomfortable period, during which it often seemed to me that my father and I were conducting our argument through the medium of his third wife. In our conversations together, Perrin would relay to me some thinking of my father's, to which I would give my response, which would then, I assume, be transmitted to him. For example, she suggested that I might consider whether my characterization of Cardassians as xenophobic was not a kind of xenophobia in itself. I replied that no, I did not believe so, since I did not think that all Cardassians hated other species, any more than I believed all Vulcans hated other species—not least because while I had indeed heard such sentiments expressed on Vulcan, I knew for a fact that they were not the whole. My father did not reply to this.

On another occasion, less fraught than the previous one I have outlined, Perrin suggested that if I wished to understand some of my father's reasoning, I might recall his friendship with Ghett Iloja. Indeed, this was something I had forgotten, since Iloja died when I was still a small child. Ghett Iloja, a well-known and excellent Cardassian poet, was exiled from Cardassia on account of the fact that he lived openly with a man. The Cardassian notion of "family", until after the Dominion War, was defined very narrowly, and solely in biological terms. As Cardassian society became more militaristic and xenophobic, a raft of laws came into force to enforce this concept of the family. For example, unions which could not lead to the production of children were outlawed, and illegitimate children were barred from inheritance and public life. These cruel interventions follow a similar pattern in many civilizations, and I believe you can deduce others for yourself, Jean-Luc. Iloja and his partner, Alon Kherrit, barred from living openly together in Cardassian space, were invited to Vulcan, settling in Prim, an artist's community in T'Paal. (He is often referred to as Iloja of Prim; I wonder how he might have felt, being best known by the name of the place to which he was exiled.) Both Iloja and Kherrit became prominent voices in the Cardassian dissident movement, and it was in this context that my father became acquainted with them.

Most of this happened before my birth, although I do have one memory of Ghett Iloja, by this time widowed and very old. A big, white-haired, and fierce old man, ridged and scaled, resembling nobody I had ever met before. His blue eyes fixed upon me, and he said, "He's very like you, Amanda."

"Nonsense," said my mother, "he looks exactly like his father."

"Sarek's face," said Iloja. "Your mind."

I must have been four years old. Iloja died later that year and was buried in Prim with Kheritt, who had died several years earlier. After the Dominion War and the reconstruction of Cardassia, when the old family laws were struck off, some of the soil from their resting place was taken back home to the Union. There was, I understand, a moving ceremony which was attended by the castellan and his husband. A small stone garden now exists commemorating them, the red soil of Vulcan mingling with that of Cardassia and planted with *kil'na* succulents and *perek* flowers. One large stone stands in the center of the garden, and inscribed on this are Iloja's most famous words:

> *Red sun, black night.*
> *A new world rises*
> *From the dust.*

My father was of course often away from Vulcan, and I believe that the thought of being unable ever to return preyed upon his mind. After Iloja's death, he often mentioned his exile, and the fact that neither he nor Kheritt ever returned home. To this extent, then, I can see that his understanding of the Cardassian people was shaped by this friendship. But the simple fact was that Iloja was an exile: he was, by definition, not representative of those in power in the Cardassian Union. Quite the contrary. I said this to Perrin; I received no response, through her, from my father. None of these conversations led to a satisfactory resolution. My father continued to be angry with me. I continued to hold firm in my belief that I had done the right thing. Perrin, caught in the middle of this dispute, quite naturally took my father's side. Since this situation seemed irresolvable, and I had no wish to quarrel further or to force Perrin to continue in this uncomfortable position, the logical step was to minimize contact with them both. I sent them regular news, but we rarely communicated directly again, up to the time that I left Federation space for my first trip to Romulus.

Some have suggested that Perrin was envious of me and sought to detach my father from me in his last years. I refute this in the strongest terms. She had loved my mother greatly; she now loved my father dearly. Nevertheless, the depth of her feeling toward me did make me pause. I did not doubt that I was correct in my assessment of Cardassian intentions, and I did not doubt that I had needed to intervene in order to prevent my father's policy of appeasement gaining ground. But Perrin's anger toward me was of a different degree. I now know, of course, that she knew a great deal more about my father's health than I did. Bendii Syndrome, which would make my father's last few years so anguishing, does not typically exhibit itself until a Vulcan enters their third century, but sometimes there are cases of earlier onset. I wonder now whether Perrin had already glimpsed my father's future, the forthcoming tragedy of his last days. If this is the case, then I do not hold her to fault for the ferocity of her defense of my father; indeed, I thank her.

✦

After his marriage to Perrin, my father traveled much less often. He and Perrin took a house together in the Kir province, some five hundred kilometers away from ShiKahr, and very distant from the house in the L'langon Mountains that carried so many associations with my mother. The settlements in Kir adhere to traditional rhythms, giving day-to-day life a calm and steady routine. Yet the landscape is violent. The province sits close to Mount Tar'hana, an active volcano that regularly steams and bubbles. The vast lava fields of the Fire Plains—once the natural defense of the province against encroaching armies—spread out not five kilometers from my father's villa. A controlled surface; turbulence beneath: I believe that I can see what the attraction might have been to my father. Here he settled into a steady routine: meditation; reading; writing; conversing with Perrin. They had few visitors. On occasion, he would come out of retirement to perform some diplomatic duty, but it was plain that he wished to be left in peace in Kir. Perrin was his chief companion; his aides, Mendrossan and Sakkath, who had been with him for many years, increasingly handled public-facing requests.

My father seems to have devoted a significant proportion of his time to rituals surrounding the *kal rekk* and the *tal-shanar*. These two ancient festivals have fallen more or less into obscurity across most of Vulcan, although each year the two holidays are observed, and most people perform some small rituals. *Kal rekk* may be translated as "atonement" or "penance": a day spent in reflection upon lapses in logic or emotional control. A day of fasting and self-denial. The *tal-shanar* is one of our most ancient holidays, involving, in part, a meditation on our violent past. Very few off-worlders have observed these full ceremonies. And while these holidays are, as I say, limited to a day or two during the year, in Kir one will find considerably more meticulous practice. My father's daily meditations and observance turned substantially towards matters of lapses in emotions and our violent past.

I wonder whether the intricacy of the daily routine helped in some way to slow the onset of Bendii Syndrome. For any Vulcan, this condition would be a great trial. For a man as complex, as deeply feeling, and as devoted to maintaining control as my father, it was particularly cruel. Observing his decline must have been terrible: I was spared that. But I think often of Perrin, unable to alleviate his distress; of Mendrossan, desperately trying to ensure that my father's condition was not revealed; of Sakkath, bearing an increasingly difficult burden in quietly attempting to alleviate my father's distress. Of course, I hardly need tell this to you, of all people: you experienced the whole first-hand. The anger, the weariness, the regrets and despair. But most of all, Jean-Luc, I believe you experienced the passion, and the love.

At many times during my life, particularly in my early years, I hungered for emotional intimacy with my father. When I was very young, I came to believe that this was a fault in me: that this simple wish alone was evidence of some deficit in my nature. As I matured, it became easier to locate the fault within my father, to convince myself that the man was simply not capable of emotional depth. But this was not borne out by the evidence of my own eyes: the continuing devotion of my mother, his pleasure in her presence. Throughout my life, then, much about my father remained a mystery to me, a conundrum: a man of seemingly limitless logic and self-control, who seemed to have excised feeling and indeed the need for feeling, and yet who commanded the love of a woman of great emotional range and depth. It seems almost remarkable to me now that I never grasped a simple truth about the world: how deeply my father's emotions ran. But then, we never spoke of such things, and I was not near him, when he died.

Do I regret not seeing my father one last time before his death? I do not. I would not have wanted to see him as he was in those last days, wholly overtaken by emotion, unable to control himself, but I would have come in an instant, had he asked for me. I think of my mother, keeping him away in her last days, and I wonder whether this was in his mind too. The more pertinent point is that I do not believe that he would have wanted me to see him in such a condition. There was a moment, when you told me of my father's death, when I feared that he had died believing me a traitor; for dispelling that notion alone, I would be grateful to you. But my gratitude to you is far greater than that, Jean-Luc. By allowing my father to mind-meld with you, and then in turn permitting me to meld with you, I learned more about my father than I had ever known throughout decades of being his son.

In those encounters that we shared, my father and I came closer than we had ever been in life. When our minds met, through yours, I understood him completely. Vulcan is a dry world, Jean-Luc, making water very precious to us, something over which great and bloody battles had been fought during our terrible past. I see my father now as being in possession of a deep well, around which battlements had been carefully raised, in defense of which great battles were constantly being fought. When our three minds met, I felt at last the great swell of love that my father had for all of us—for his three children, for my mother, for the family and world that had formed him. I felt at last the ocean of feeling within him, how easily storms gathered; how much he feared their violence, how much he feared a deluge. When the three of us met together, my mind to your mind, your mind to his, I saw the truth of my father as he was, not the man that I had made him in my imagination.

The burden of our history weighed heavily upon Sarek, I see now. Not simply the fact of our illustrious ancestors, but the horror and terror of our past. As a small child, I too had felt a similar burden—staring into those marbled faces of my ancestors, learning a history of suffering and agonies, escaped only through discipline and self-mastery. I wonder now, to what extent these feelings were a projection of my father's emotions upon me. But I, at least, had some escape valve. There was the simple fact of my other background, such that, whenever my sense of self as Vulcan felt unsure, I was able to find safe harbor in my human heritage. I learned to feel—and call it human. The part of me that, as the years passed, I learned was not weakness, but, when combined with my Vulcan education, was the source of great gifts. Yet this was not the case for my father. He was indisputably, undeniably Vulcan; perhaps the most Vulcan of us all. His logic, flawless; his self-control, limitless. And yet, at the same time he was cursed—or blessed—with deep sensitivity, a wealth of emotion which, throughout his whole life, he struggled to contain and master, until, in the end, he could not. The walls crumbled. After that came the flood.

✦

You might be asking yourself whether my father produced a *t'san a'lat*. The answer is—yes, of course. The original manuscript, which he wrote by hand in the traditional way, is held in the archive of the T'Plana-Hath Historical Museum in ShiKahr. A holographic version is readily available for any visitor to examine. Perrin and I agreed that a copy should be made, and this was done, and sent to Earth, where it is held in the archive at the Centre for Vulcan Studies, a research establishment located in Oxford. They are beautiful volumes, Jean-Luc: the paper made from the fiber of *kah'lit* vines cultivated for this purpose in the grounds of our home in the L'langon Mountains, that part of Vulcan which my mother loved best. The whole is written in his distinctive, miniscule, and meticulous handwriting. Sarek's *t'san a'lat* is a completely faithful record of his days. It documents, with great care and in considerable detail, the profound and deep life of his mind: his readings of

Surak; his daily meditative practice; the occasions in his work where logic was brought to bear upon diplomacy. Yes, one would not doubt that the author of this text was Sarek son of Skon. When I read it, it was as if I could hear his voice speaking to me once again—attentive, measured, and precise.

You note that I call the account "faithful"—perhaps you are wondering whether I could call it "full". There is, in this *t'san a'lat*, little mention of family— one might easily not register that this was a man who married three times, who was the father of two sons and a daughter. Sarak maintained his silence about Michael until death, but his other children barely figure in his book. Would I call this account dishonest, then? You will recall how I have said that a *t'san a'lat* must tell no lies. And—no, I would not call this *t'san a'lat* dishonest. The love that lay at the core of my father was so deeply felt, so protected, that he himself did not have words to express the whole of it. That his love often went unspoken—and, in this public document, went unwritten—is the truest reflection of the man that was. But each word expresses to me—who was his son—how profoundly he loved my mother; how deeply he loved his children.

Perrin and I did not get the chance to reconcile. I regret this, since I remain deeply grateful to her for the care and kindness that she gave both my parents at the end of their lives, and I believe my father's absence would have brought us closer together. Loss can be a powerfully cohering force. I was elsewhere for many years, on Romulus, and when at last I was able to return to Federation, she was long dead. At this time, my father's papers came into my possession. I opened them with some trepidation; I feared that, in her desire to protect him, Perrin might have considered it her duty to destroy some of what was there. In this I did her a great injustice: every note, every scrap, had been carefully kept, and she had in no way taken it upon herself to shape his posthumous reputation. These decisions she had most scrupulously bequeathed to me, his surviving child, his heir.

Everything was in very good order, and much as one might expect. Meticulous minutes taken during meetings; notes for speeches and other occasions; a diary detailing appointments and engagements. Correspondence going back over nearly two centuries. Documents such as these, including his completed *t'san a'lat*, were of great public interest, and therefore rightly in the hands of the Archive in ShiKahr. But there was also a wealth of personal information, not least letters to and from my mother; to and from myself and my other siblings; many holo-images of us all across the years. I found a journal, dating back across decades, reflecting upon his daily meditations, which was surprisingly frank—and deeply moving—particularly when it documented his struggles to maintain this discipline toward the end of his life. There was some very old correspondence between Sarek and Skon, written when my father was a young man, cool and distant and always formal. And, hidden away, I found a handwritten volume, filled with notes, containing the love poetry that my father wrote to my mother.

I recognized the form immediately: the *harrekh*, that deceptively simple three-line verse developed in later life by Ghett Iloja, so spare as to be almost seditiously un-Cardassian, relying upon concrete images rather than symbols, and rebelliously describing personal—not communal—emotion. I could see why my father was drawn to write in this way. Specific, meditative, and yet suggesting a deep well of profoundly felt emotion; such a form was suited to Sarek of Vulcan. Here, in the pages of this book, in a style learned from an alien in exile, my father found a way to tell my mother how much he loved her. Whether she ever read these poems, I do not know—I shall never know. I suspect that she did not; I suspect that she never even knew they existed. Perrin read them, no doubt; I cannot begrudge her that, and I am grateful for all the good sense she showed in her care of my father in his last and difficult years, and the compassion she showed, despite our disagreements, in leaving this book for me to find. To learn that throughout his whole life, my father wrote poetry was simultaneously one of the startling discoveries of my life and yet also no surprise. The love of a Vulcan man for a human woman, written in the form of a Cardassian verse. It is only when we step beyond the narrow constraints imposed upon us by our cultures and admit to ourselves our connection to the great and wondrous variety of the universe, that we are most fully realized.

> *Red world, blue world.*
> *What strange new world is born*
> *Of our perfect union?*

These are the last words my father wrote to my mother. The date on the page is the day after her death. His papers tell me he did not write poetry for anybody else, and did not write poetry again.

Picard

IT MIGHT SEEM STRANGE THAT A MAN WHOM I HAVE MET IN PERSON only once is the one that knows more about me than anyone other than my mother, or else the two men with whom I shared the best years of my life. Yet such is the case with you, Jean-Luc. In our mind-meld, I revealed to you as much of myself as I could in the time available, and I learned from you perhaps more than you are aware. I learned, of course, all that you experienced during your connection to my father: the deep confusion and distress of his last days; his anger and despair; the depth of his love for me and my mother; and his regret at how he was unable to show us that love, that tenderness which lay at the very heart of him.

My father never offered to meld with me, and I would not have dared to presume to make such an offer. I envied you this, I must speak truly, but this envy is outweighed by my gratitude. Knowing at second hand all he felt during his illness—I am not sure I could have borne the weight of that. I could not have provided this service to him. My thankfulness to you in acting as this buffer for him, to enable him to complete his final mission with assurance and dignity, is profound. My gratitude that you were willing to share this with me in turn I can hardly express. To experience in full what I had always instinctively known about my father—the extent and profundity of his emotional life—was a great gift. He could not—he would not—have told me any other way.

There is another reason that I am grateful. You must have known, when you offered to share this with me, that you were sharing more than a little of yourself. You are a private man, Jean-Luc, and do not allow others easy access to your inner life. Let me say no more, then, that I understand how it is to be a son held at arm's-length, and yet, at the same time, to be the focus for great pride and intense expectation. I understand the strains and the confusion that this causes, not to mention the quiet wounds arising from having a father unable to demonstrate his love. I have found, throughout the course of my life, that there is great consolation in meeting a fellow traveler upon the road, in realizing that someone else has experienced the same as you, has felt the same as you, has suffered the same sorrows and regrets. In fellow feeling, in compassion, we continue our own healing. I hope that when our minds met, you found the same.

There are many other ways in which our lives seem to me to be interwoven, not least the preoccupation, in our later years, with the question of Romulus. Yet somehow, even there, we have always been out of step with each other. My years in Romulan space did not overlap with yours; your mission was carried out in the open while mine was, by necessity, clandestine for most of the time I was on Romulus. When at last I returned to Federation space, you had left on your own great mission, and, after your return, I had a new matter concerning me—a matter which I hope shortly to explain. I have deeply valued our communications over the years. I believe that there is a great deal more that we could have taught each other. My knowledge of the Romulan Empire comes chiefly from the time before the news of the impending supernova, and almost all of the friends and contacts that I made in those years are dead. You are much better informed about the new dispensation, and such information might still be of use to me. Yes, I should have come to see you, but time is running so very short...

I believe, too, that there might have been something that I could have taught you. I understand, as you shall see, how useless one feels, how distraught, when a mission to which one has dedicated many years is brought abruptly and violently to a close. I understand the experience of finding oneself—in one's latter years, when the accumulated wisdom of a lifetime is at its greatest, when one has, perhaps, more to offer than ever before—removed cruelly from active life, cast to one side, and left without apparent purpose. Yes, I understand this very well. My mission to Romulus, as I understood it at the time, ended in complete failure, at the cost of the lives of very many people. So, yes, I could have sympathized, Jean-Luc, with the loss and the grief, the bereavement, the sense of uselessness, the sense of an ending. I understand this, very well.

We will not now meet in the sun in your garden to drink your wine, share the stories of our long lives and consider whatever wisdom we have gathered along the way. We shall not meet again, my mind to your mind. But I would tell you one last thing, if I may presume. I would tell you that one can and does find purpose again, and quite unexpectedly. When all seems finished, when all seems lost—I want you to know that the mission of our lives continues, well beyond expectation, well beyond the death of hope. Do not despair, Jean-Luc. Your days are not yet done.

✦

When you left me on Romulus, I was a man with few resources other than a great vision and a few good and true friends. On these foundations I intended to build a movement that would change Romulus forever. A mission doomed to failure one might think—and I did fail, but not for the reasons one might think. The fault was in the stars, this time, and not in ourselves. By the time the Romulans entered the Dominion War—that is, within the space of five years—our little group had gone from a handful of hopefuls in a cave to a burgeoning dissident movement positioned to declare itself. Let me tell you a little of how this happened—and then what went wrong.

For my first year on Romulus, I seemed to be in constant motion. A few days hidden in a house; a few days in transit; a few days hiding in another place. I was in the capital for almost the whole of this time, with occasional journeys into the countryside nearby, and I saw the place through glimpses. Ki Baratan, the capital is called—the sleepless city. Its old name is Dartha, the city of walls. Both of these are apt. The Tal Shiar are always watchful, and the people of the capital press back against the walls and hope to pass unnoticed. The streets are like a maze: alleys that come to a dead end; routes that meander and go back upon themselves. One does not easily find a way through. This secrecy, I came quickly to understand, was deeply engrained in Romulan culture—its organizing principle, in fact. Architecture, art, music, literature—everything created such that something was always kept hidden.

I could not help but compare Ki Baratan with my home, ShiKahr. The faces around me were similar, but the city itself could not have been more different. Where ShiKahr valued diversity, Ki Baratan enforced uniformity. Where I might walk the streets of my home and see dozens of different species, here I saw only Romulans. ShiKahr's towers soared; its open spaces spread out. In Ki Baratan, the buildings huddled near the ground, as if to go unseen; walls were everywhere, and if there were windows, they were shuttered. The air is thick and stuffy, not the heady air of home. The sky seemed always clouded and I rarely saw the moons. This last, perhaps, is less truth than fancy—I was, after all, mostly living undercover, as hidden away as any Romulan citizen.

With time, I began to understand the place a little better. I found pleasure in the sudden discoveries one might make: a small garden, found unexpectedly near a tram depot; the intricate puzzle of the maze through which one must pass to visit an acquaintance; the delicate courtesies shown through polite and allusive enquiry about the health or wellbeing of another. I found myself thinking, oddly, of my friend from my academy days, T'Kel, who taught me that the life that I had led on Vulcan was not how everyone on my home planet lived. As I passed through Ki Baratan like a ghost, I wondered how the ordinary citizens of Romulus must live. What were their homes like? How did they spend their days? How did they show love, and care, and intimacy? Did they close these emotions off, as many did on my homeworld—as my father had done? Or did they reveal themselves to a trusted few? This, I realized, was the Romulus that I wanted to know. Not the world of senators and praetors and politicians and diplomats. The few meetings that I had with people such as these went nowhere. My mission would have to start elsewhere if it was to succeed: with ordinary people. But as I came to understand this, I came to understand too the difficulty of the task that I had set myself. Romulus was a world in denial, one that had made secrecy a cultural imperative. Each one of them was deeply disconnected from everyone around them, even from their families, their spouses, their children. The only shared emotion, and even this went unspoken, was fear of discovery, fear of the Tal Shiar. My mission was to connect and unite.

One evening, after yet another unsatisfactory meeting with yet another junior sub-administrator and traveling wearily back on the tram with my current minder to my current home, I sat observing the faces around me. All were turned inward. Nobody spoke to the person next to them, not even those who were traveling together. The state broadcasting network was playing through the carriage: music, of the intricate, unresolving, and unsatisfactory kind most heard on Romulus. There was no news. Below this one could hear the rattle of the tram and the occasional sigh. I began to observe the woman sitting opposite me. She was middle-aged, of the service class known on Romulus as *jich'rethro*, and tired. Her clothes were poor; her hands worn; her eyes closed. As the tram slowed before the next stop, she opened her eyes. She rose from her seat and picked up her bag. She stepped forward. I reached out and put my hand upon her arm. When she was looking straight at me, I lifted my free hand in salute, and I spoke.

"Peace," I said to her, with all my heart, "and long life."

She was stunned. Then, I saw it—the flicker in her eye. The connection. Only for the merest second, before her cultural conditioning reasserted itself, and she was shuttered once again, moving past me and off the tram. But I had done what I wanted to do. I had told this woman that she was not passing through this universe unloved. I hoped that she would carry this knowledge with her, that when the loneliness that her civilization induced in her became too great a burden, she would recall this moment, when a stranger wished her well.

I looked up. All around, I saw Romulan faces, looking at me. Some were shocked; some were hostile; but one or two, I observed, were looking at me with guarded interest. My traveling companion was in shock. She jumped out of her seat, pulled me from mine, and, just before the tram pulled out, hustled me out onto the platform, into the street, and down a nearby alley. We did not stop for another five or ten minutes. At last, she paused, and said, "Ambassador, sir—whatever possessed you to do that?"

"I am here to unite us," I said. "This seemed the best way to proceed."

"You may well have cost us our lives," she said, but, to her credit, she did not complain further, she merely worked to prevent that happening.

We did not return that night to the house where we had been staying. In fact, we did not remain in Ki Baratan. My comrade led me, through back streets, to an area of small factories and light industrial units, where, under the steady thump of large-scale replicators, we waited until a vehicle arrived. We drove through the night, coming to a small villa in the countryside as the first light of dawn silvered the clouds. I remained there for the next month, until we considered it safe for me to go back to the city. But during that time, my mission came into focus for the first time. I was wasting my time with the powerful. They were interested only in the status quo, and in how they might use me to gain an advantage. I did not know, yet, what my encounter with the *jich'rethro* woman meant for the practicalities of my mission to Romulus. But I knew that it had reminded me of some of my most powerfully held beliefs: that all sentient beings long for some confirmation of their connection to the universe, and that all civilizations, when examined closely, are more finely grained than any superficial analysis allows. What I wished to tell the people of Romulus—all the people of Romulus, whatever their caste or hopes or dreams or fears—was that outside the grey prison of their minds lay a universe of wonders, peopled by strangers who were not hostile, but who wished to greet them with curiosity and love. I knew, too, that, after almost a year, I had spent enough time in the shadows, and the time had come for me to proceed openly, and without fear.

✦

I went to live in the Turruk district of the city, an area inhabited by many *jich'rethro*, in a small apartment that was part of a much larger building. These structures are huge, and dominate the cities, but their entrances are concealed, with many false doors and windows. Inside, each structure is all different, the ways through mazelike, and the individual homes are closed off from one another, each one a cell in the vast and labyrinthine Romulan prison. I went about my daily life, but I did not stay indoors. I removed the false windows and opened those that were there to the iron air of Romulus. Each morning, early, I opened the front door and went outside to meditate. Then I sat on a chair on the step and read and wrote, and whoever came past, I would greet.

"*Jolan tru*," I would say, and give my salute. "Peace, and long life." I asked no questions. I merely announced my presence to those that I saw.

At first, people hurried past. If I caught their eye, they would look quickly away. But, in time, they became used to me. One or two would nod; I saw the occasional wry smile.

"*Jolan tru*," someone said, one evening; a face I had come to recognize as one of my neighbors. We exchanged greetings three more times before she stopped. I could see her torn between interest and the Romulan instinct not to ask a direct question.

"May I tell you my name?" I said, and she nodded. "I am Spock," I said. "I come from Vulcan. I have come in peace, to meet you and to learn about you."

She shook her head. "You'll not be here long," she said. "They won't have it."

"Perhaps," I agreed. She went on her way, but she stopped again the next evening, and every evening after. One night, someone else stopped. Then another, and another. None of them had ever heard my name before, although they had heard of Vulcan and the Federation. They all, naturally, thought I was quite mad. But they tolerated me, became used to me, and sometimes found me useful.

My presence of course attracted the attention of the local police, but my behavior baffled them, and they were not certain what to do. Two of them came to speak to me one day (I saw my neighbors hasten inside, but the shutters on the windows remained open a crack). One of the officers—they were both very young, but he seemed slightly the superior—said to me, "What are you doing?"

"I am sitting here reading. Sometimes I talk to my neighbors. Sometimes I watch the children while they play."

"Talk to your neighbors, eh? What about?"

"Most often, I ask what they intend to cook for dinner. They never tell me."

I heard a laugh, quickly smothered, from behind one of the half-closed windows. The more superior of these young men stared at me and said, "Who are you?"

"I am Spock," I replied.

This time, it seemed that my reputation preceded me. He burst out laughing.

"What is so amusing?" I asked.

"You can't... Here? No!"

"I assure you," I said, "I speak the truth."

"He talks like one of those women," muttered his companion, obscurely.

"Ambassador Spock? *Here?*"

"Unlikely, I admit," I said. "But true."

"We should arrest him," said the other one.

"Are you sure about that?" I asked them. "Do you want to be the cause of a diplomatic incident? More pertinently, do you want the eyes of your superiors to fall upon you?"

It seemed that they did not, very much. Slowly, they began to back away. "Just mind yourself," said the older one. "We're keeping our eye on you."

"I am grateful for your interest," I replied. They hurried away. My neighbors were back out again in a shot (I would like to think that perhaps at least one of them might have come to my aid, should the need have arisen), and I noticed a sense of subdued elation about them, as if some small victory had been won. I found the whole encounter, and the aftermath, quite fascinating. After this, I observed that more of them came outside more often, throughout the day, and spoke more openly to me.

One morning, a woman in blue approached me where I sat. I recognized her habit immediately, and with considerable shock. Long blue robes, hat and veil, a staff on her back: this was the woman from my vision, all those long years ago. Had the Red Angel returned? What might this mean, for my mission, for myself? As the woman drew closer, I realized my mistake. She was not human, but Romulan, although unlike any Romulan I had met before.

"Are you Spock?" she said.

"I am Spock," I said.

"I am Theneen." She looked behind me at my small home; the books and papers stacked around me. She sighed. "You are plainly an idiot. But you will join us at our house tonight."

"Will I?" I replied.

"Oh yes," she said, turning to go. "You will."

And indeed, I did. Curiosity, at the very least, would have driven me there; there was also some force to Theneen's way of speaking that, while she did not command, nevertheless compelled behavior. I know from your mission reports to me, Jean-Luc, that you have met the Qowat Milat, and the role that they played in assisting you. I know, more importantly, that you are familiar with the Way of Absolute Candor, that imperative of their order that requires them not to lie, that sets them in complete opposition to the Tal Shiar. Fearless, vital, and utterly infuriating—my mission too would have died an early death without their assistance. From the moment I entered their house, I knew that I had found kindred spirits. I knew that our work and beliefs overlapped. I also knew how warmly, how affectionately, I was an object of derision, humor, and delight. They thought I was the most hilarious joke. They were not entirely wrong. I know this because—true to form—they told me.

"It's the *t'ha'est*!" one old woman, sitting on watch outside their house, called back to her comrades. "The Vulcan fool! Hurry, sisters, you do not want to miss this!"

Thus I joined the Qowat Milat for dinner for the first time, almost the jester at their feast, and I learned about their work in this area, protecting their fellows from the worst excesses of the Tal Shiar, and I saw many ways in which we might work together. They continued in their belief that I was a fool, but they also offered me their friendship, and I was grateful for this. The next people to pay me a visit were from the Tal Shiar.

I knew them at once. They appear from nowhere. They are not always in uniform, but something infiltrates the space around them. Ordinary people hide away. Soon, there was nobody else there but me, and the two of them. And then—four women, staffs ready, forming a barrier in front of me.

"Get away, *tok'tzat*," said Theneen to the Tal Shiar. "Or we will break your bones."

Their leader jeered back at her. "Is that a promise, sister? I thought promises were prisons."

"Not a promise," she said. "A statement of fact."

They stood in abeyance for a while. The Tal Shiar were armed with disruptors, although I personally would not have tested the speed of response these four women had with their staffs. It is very easy to break a wrist, when one knows how. After a little while, the Tal Shiar officer made his decision, and moved back. The easy fight they had been expecting—giving an old Vulcan fool the beating of his life—had not materialized. I was, for some reason, under the protection of these women, and they were formidable friends. After that, I was watched, certainly (who on Romulus is not watched?), but I was not again so directly threatened. My daily activities continued unimpeded. I sat and read, I spoke to my neighbors, I watched their children, I made friends. In the evenings, people would come and join me for something to eat, and we would talk to each other. I would answer their questions about my long life and experiences; I would ask them questions about their lives and experiences. We took comfort in each other; we talked and, more often, we laughed. So simple, one might think—and yet, like so many simple ideas, the promise was great.

Isolation is at the heart of Romulan life. Keeping secrets is instilled in them from a very early age. Even within family groups, the children are taught self-reliance and to ask for help only in the direst need. Pain is felt alone; grief is felt alone. Pleasures and joys are solitary. What grander purpose this might serve I do not know, but certainly one effect is to make the population more docile, more controllable. If one cannot turn to those closest for aid, to whom, then, can one turn? Perhaps—a stranger. And when the habit of turning to him for something as simple as a moment of shared happiness, or consolation, is established, then it becomes easier to turn to those around you. Week by week, month by month, I watched the households around me open more to each other. People who had lived alongside each other for years started to become neighbors. Practical help was given: to mend something, to help with something, even to provide financial assistance. One neighborhood. Was it possible to remake a whole empire? I was only one man, after all. I was pondering this impasse, when another visitor arrived—an old friend.

"Well," said Saavik, staring at my little house, "you didn't make it hard to find you."

"That," I replied, "is the general idea."

✦

Sending communications back to Federation space had not been easy, but I had maintained semi-regular contact with Saavik throughout my time on Romulus. She had come to help, and she told me there were more people on their way, other Vulcans who saw reunification as a necessary step for both our civilizations. I was of course glad to see her, but also concerned. Saavik was a child born of great violence; she had good cause to hate the Empire, and had, I know, always struggled to love that part of her that was Romulan. And yet here she was. My presence here was one draw, but, as I learned through the many conversations that we had in the time that followed, she was still seeking some way of finding peace with her Romulan nature. Saavik does not lack courage. Coming to Romulus was, I see now, always going to be necessary. That she might at the same time assist her old mentor, her old friend, was of great benefit to both of us.

At first, she was dumbfounded by the simplicity of my life and activities. As she lived among us more, she began to see something of my purpose. In a culture as secretive as Romulus, my openness was seen as a kind of delusion, but one which had the power to disarm. My time spent being amongst Romulan people at close hand was teaching me again T'Kel's lesson, which I passed on now to Saavik, that the closer one looks, the more complexity one finds, and here each of us might find how we might connect to something strange. Saavik took these lessons to heart. She thrived on Romulus, as part of our mission. Still, it came as something of a surprise when she chose to join the Qowat Milat. Perhaps it should not. It was at last a way for her to reconcile both parts of herself—the Romulan and the Vulcan—in a way which did not betray either of them. It was in talking to Saavik that I came to my fullest understanding that reunification was not an endpoint, or a process, it was a fact of life. Romulans and Vulcans were already connected, as all life in the universe is connected. What mattered was allowing these connections to be overt, to become established as the norm. Romulus was a world in deep denial, one that made disconnection and secrecy a cultural imperative. Simply to speak openly—as the Qowat Milat know—was to rock, however gently, the foundations of the Empire. It can rock the foundations of many empires. Look at how they punish those who speak.

I fear, these days, that the Federation is heading the same way, that the mistrust sown by the Founders during the Dominion War was not rooted out; that the shock of the attack on Mars has let these weeds of fear and mistrust flourish in our Eden. To speak out loud, then; to act in such a way that reaffirms our fundamental connection to each other—this, perhaps, is the task for us now, Jean-Luc. How does one unify what has become profoundly disunited? How does one establish trust with people so practiced now in mistrust? On Romulus, I learned that our connections to each other were simply fact, and that we must find the courage to assert this.

✦

By the time the Dominion War broke out, there were twenty of our little houses around the city, and a further dozen in the towns and settlements in the province around Ki Baratan. I would spend a week there at a time, before moving on to the next. When I visited, I would speak to whoever came to listen about my desire to see closer ties between our civilizations, which came from a common root, and reaffirmed my belief that as long as we gathered openly, and spoke to each other, and learned from each other, we were in fact reunified. And that while we might have to leave each other at the end of each evening, and return to solitude and disconnection, we could carry with us the memory of our meetings, the memory of connection and unity, taking this with us until we were able to meet once again.

The Dominion War changed everything for us. For a while, of course, the Romulan Empire seemed ready to sit and wait, but then news began to filter through of the death of Senator Vreenak, most likely assassinated by order by the Dominion. Even on the streets of Ki Baratan the anger was palpable. Romulus changed, and the Empire joined the war against the Dominion. This, by necessity, brought closer collaboration between the Empire and its allies. Near the end of the war, I was approached by a junior official, Vonclas, who asked to speak to me in private. I took him inside the house, and he explained his concerns to me: that, at the end of the war, the Empire would return to its isolationism, and that, given the strong ties that now existed between the Klingons and the Federation, this would leave the Romulan Empire at a disadvantage. He wanted me to reach out on his behalf to friendly elements within the Federation, in order to establish closer ties and, perhaps, in time, a treaty on the lines of the Khitomer Accords.

I knew, of course, that those in power in the Empire had been aware of my presence in Ki Baratan from early on; I had not, after all, gone to great lengths to hide it. I was aware that I was tolerated on the grounds that I was an old man, with limited resources, no apparent backing from my government, more interested in watching children play than in any serious activity, and thus easily dismissed as a crank. My association with the Qowat Milat perhaps raised some concerns; the spread of our community beyond Ki Baratan surely did. And yet, something had shifted in the upper echelons. This approach was the clearest signal I had received yet that not only were they aware of me, but that they were also listening to what I had to say. With our movement on the ground safe in the hands of Saavik, I was able to devote some of my energy to speaking to some of these officials. (Whether or not this can be considered "cowboy diplomacy" I cannot say, Jean-Luc; you shall have to be the judge of that.)

During these few years after the war, I was the most hopeful I have ever been that open co-operation might be established between the Romulan Empire and the Federation. To the officials that I met, I restated my belief that friendship could exist between our civilizations, and that more connected us than divided us. To the ordinary people, I restated my desire for friendship and understanding. To all, I wished peace and long life. And, for a while, such things seemed possible. For a short while.

I was not in Ki Baratan when the arrests began. I was travelling to Hoven, a large town in the Voktub province, where we hoped to establish a new house, when my traveling companions and I received a message not to continue our journey, but to divert to Nuhee, a small town on the way, where we would be met by Saavik. She brought the news that the Tal Shiar had come to the little house in Ki Baratan, where my movement had started all those years ago, arrested everyone there, and had the entire building demolished, leaving many of my neighbors on the street. At first, my companions hoped that this was an isolated incident. I was certain that it was not and was quickly proven correct. The Tal Shiar had, at last, made a move against us, and they did not waste time in carrying out their mission.

In the space of a single night, our movement was over. Our houses—now stretching into three more provinces—were closed down, and most of them obliterated. Our people were arrested—many of them disappeared, and I have not heard from them again. Only my fame and status as a Federation citizen, the simple fact of who I was, saved me and the people around me. Even so, my position on Romulus became untenable. Saavik, with the assistance of the Qowat Milat, was able to get my close friends into hiding and arrange passage for me out of Romulan space. On entering Federation space, I learned what had caused such a cruel change of heart with the upper echelons of Romulan government: the supernova that threatened to engulf their world and destroy their empire. I returned to Vulcan, my movement in ashes, my mission a failure, truly afraid of what the future might hold for my Romulan friends, and powerless to help.

✦

My intention, once back in Federation space (it was hard, after so long on Romulus, not to think of Ki Baratan as "home") was to speak on behalf of the Romulan people, who were now in such desperate need. To say that I was shocked at the anti-Romulan sentiment that I found so openly expressed among Federation officials and Starfleet officers would be an understatement.

Had such always been there? I believed that in certain quarters these sentiments had moved far from an understandable suspicion of a hostile power to outright xenophobia, and whenever I could, I raised my voice to protest of such views, and in support of the Romulan people, who so badly needed our compassion and our aid. This situation only worsened after the synth attack on Mars destroyed the Federation shipyards. The will to assist people beyond our borders was drastically reduced, overnight. We should, so the argument went, be looking to help our own, and not our enemies. But I knew now, first-hand, that Romulan society—so uniform and impenetrable from the outside—had, like everything to which we give close and patient study, revealed to me depths and complexities that were little known or understood. But, again and again, it was made clear to me that my views were out-of-step with the times. I had spent too much time on Romulus and forgotten where my loyalties should lie. I should accept that reunification had never been a viable proposition and was a dream from a different time. I was—not to put too fine a point on it—an old man, living in the past. I should accept that my time was past and go gracefully into retirement.

Perhaps all these things were true. But that did not change the fact that my time away gave me fresh perspective on the Federation. In my absence, our society had become a more inward-looking place. I did retire, more or less, to Vulcan, taking some consolation in the fact of your mission, Jean-Luc, and that Saavik and the Qowat Milat were still working with the Empire to save as many lives as possible. But I will not deny that I was deeply frustrated throughout this time. Working through my father's papers, continuing my translation work, documenting the rise and fall of my movement—these were all honorable activities, but there was a great need to be addressed, and I was no longer in a position to do anything. Sometimes, I despaired, hearing via Saavik the news from Romulan space, seeing the lack of will from the Federation to help, watching hearts which should have been open to the Romulans harden against them. The two great causes of my life—unification, and the Federation—falling by the wayside. The correspondence between us at this time, Jean-Luc, was a great consolation to me, and I know was a call on your time when you had little of that precious commodity. I hope whatever information I was able to pass on during those days was of assistance.

Perhaps, having been forced by circumstance already to step aside, I was better prepared than some for what happened during this sad time. Not the shock of the attack on Mars, or the appalling news of the ending of your mission and your disgraceful removal from command, but for the fact of the retreat of our leadership from their responsibilities. I knew already that Starfleet—that the Federation—had lost its way. I was already preparing to do something about this. By the time you were back at La Barre, and hoping for me to visit, my new mission was already well under way. I hope you understand now why I never came. I hope you understand, too, what I am about to do.

In the end, I have realized that I can no longer sit idle. Not only is it not in my nature, but all that I had learned in life told me that to remain passive in the face of great suffering was in itself to cause harm. One must do what one can. But what, exactly, could I do? An old man, sidelined by the current decision-makers, his voice ignored and unheard. I would not persuade anyone to help the Romulan people. For a while, I was at an impasse. My messages went unanswered. My remaining friends in high places counseled me to stop this one-person crusade. I came dangerously close to taking their advice. Late one night, in my house in ShiKahr, pondering the past that had brought us to this sad present, I recalled my last glimpse of the Red Angel, this time tinted with blue. I thought of Gabrielle Burnham's desperate mission, taken up in turn by her daughter. I remembered my sister, all those long years ago, leaping into an uncertain future. This provided me with the courage I needed not to abandon my cause. What if I too could, in some way, stop what was happening? What if the supernova itself could be prevented from causing more harm? I began to read, to study. I remembered my first self—before I became an ambassador and diplomat, a mentor and teacher, an officer and commander. I was—I am—a scientist. What could the scientist do?

It has been several years of careful study, but I have now reached some satisfactory—even hopeful—conclusions. My hypotheses are not entirely proven, but I cannot wait much longer. The situation within Romulan space is too desperate. I must act now, or not act at all. You will find all the relevant documents related to my recent research in the file appended to this document. You will see my research into the phenomenon of "red matter", which I believe may hold the key to absorbing the energy of the supernova which threatens Romulus. My intention is to fly close as possible to the Romulan sun and shoot a small amount of this into the star. A fool's hope, perhaps, but then, I am an old fool.

Jim

NOW THAT I HAVE MADE MY INTENTIONS CLEAR, there is one last subject I must address. I have tried on many occasions to write about Jim Kirk. This seems to me an increasingly impossible task. Jim Kirk lies at the very heart of this account; he is present on every page, the ink in which these words have been written. So much has been said about James Kirk that I almost persuaded myself that there was no need for anyone else to add to the general melee. Children from the learning domes of Vulcan to the classrooms on Earth study his most famous missions. He has been the subject of doctoral dissertations. His leadership style has been dissected; his wit and wisdom propagated. But a great deal of what is said these days about him is wrong, or, at best, woefully simplistic. How do you write about a legend? How do you write about someone that you have so deeply loved?

Here are some of the misconceptions that I have heard voiced over the years about James Kirk. That he was reckless. That he took unnecessary risks. That he was lucky. That he was casual in how and whom he loved. That he was not entirely in control of his passions.

When James Kirk was thirteen, living on the colony world of Tarsus IV, he was one of only nine people out of the four thousand selected for elimination by the colony's governor, Kodos, to survive that murderous policy. Six years later, before his arrival at the academy (we did not overlap), he was already being spoken of as the most promising command-track candidate in many years. That early brush not only with death, but with the coldness by which some men will choose to sacrifice others, made him the very opposite of reckless with life. But neither did it make him cautious. Rather, it made him profoundly conscious of mortality and moved him to act above all to try to preserve life. It made him instinctively refuse to accept the rules of a game, when that game was played unfairly. At the academy, Jim did not accept the premise of the *Kobayashi Maru*. He changed the rules so that people would live. Jim was very bad with rules. Sometimes that could be irritating. More often than not, it was exhilarating.

At the academy, I am told that Cadet Kirk was known for his bookishness. He was alarmingly well read. Once, on shore leave on Earth, I took him to visit my grandparents, and I watched him hold his ground with my grandfather (hardly an ill-informed man) in discussion of Spinoza, and the importance of intuition in guiding reason. I did not offer my thinking on this occasion. I merely listened. An expert was speaking.

Jim loved carefully, fully, and with constancy. He nearly married twice. He loved people of intelligence, who served causes, and my understanding is this is why those relationships ended. They chose their missions or their work over him. But then this was true of Jim. The ship—the crew, the mission—came first.

There are three occasions that come to mind when I try to think of when Jim was overtaken by his emotions. The first, was when I told him over the conference table that I had offered his services as honor guard to Gorkon. You will recall that the Klingons had recently caused the death of his son. I had calculated, when I asked for the *Enterprise*, that Jim would see that the value of peace outweighed personal considerations, that the needs of the many outweighed the needs of the few. I was not right. I had presumed too much, asked for too much. I thought, when I saw his face then, that I might have delivered a death blow to our friendship. Would I have blamed him? I cannot say.

The second time was through glass, when he saw me swimming with whales. I will never forget that.

The third time was also through glass, but on that occasion, I was dying. I will never forget that, either.

When I was living on Romulus, I received a letter from you, informing me of your encounter with James Kirk, after his apparent death, still living in the Nexus, and outlining the circumstances of his subsequent and real death on Veridian III. That letter took a while to reach me, and I often think of it, in transit, containing the news that Jim was both alive and dead. That was the only time that I regretted my mission to Romulus, and I did regret it, bitterly. If only I had been present, somehow. Perhaps I might have saved his life, again (although he told me, once, that he would die alone). Was that not what we did, after all—save each other's life, again and again? At the very least, I might have seen him, one last time. I have not been to see his grave. I believe I can permit myself one illusion in life.

The first time that I met James Kirk was on the *Enterprise*, of course. Bones and I went to welcome the new captain on board. The doctor and the captain already knew each other from previous encounters and greeted each other warmly. I did not know Kirk beyond his considerable reputation. As we walked through the ship, Bones behind, I provided the new captain with an update on his ship's status.

"Thank you, Mr. Spock," he said, when I finished. "Admirably thorough report."

"Watch out for this one, Jim," said Bones, over my shoulder. "He's trouble."

"How curious, Dr. McCoy," I replied, without a pause. "I was about to offer the captain the same advice about you."

I recall that Jim's face lit up, with a smile like the sun. "I think," he said, "that this is the beginning of a beautiful friendship."

He was not wrong.

I believe, Jean-Luc, that you are now completely up to date.

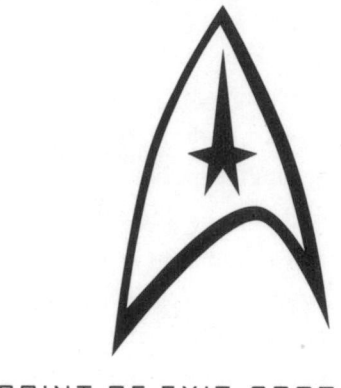

POINT OF EXIT-2387

Approaching the Romulan border

HERE, THEN, IS WHERE YOU FIND ME NOW. I am on board my little ship, the *Jellyfish*, and I will shortly be crossing the border into Romulan space. My friend and co-conspirator, Saavik, has acquired security codes to enable me to pass across the border, and, with the assistance of her sisters in the Qowat Milat, will help me travel through Romulan territory as quickly as possible. This is a small ship, with space enough for myself, but may still attract unwanted attention. The plan that I have devised is bold, and I can make no promise as to whether or not it will be a success. I will travel as close as possible as I can to the Romulan sun, shoot a small amount of red matter into this failing star, and, if my calculations are correct, this will create a black hole sufficient to absorb the energy of the supernova that threatens not only the Romulan homeworld, but the safety and stability of all of us.

There is no certainty that my plan will succeed. The most likely outcome is that nothing is changed, but that I shall die. I know that you, of all people, will understand the desperation which has driven me to this. The institutions which we have served our entire lives have failed us, Jean-Luc. They have become fearful and mistrustful. They seem no longer able to perform the functions which are their primary mission: to be curious; to explore the universe with open minds and open hearts; to intervene with caution, but not to stand by in the face of great suffering. Both our attempts to marshal large-scale resources to combat this drift toward close-mindedness and hostility have failed. I understand how this has driven you to your own retirement and retrenchment, but I find that I cannot simply stop, not now, not so late. With whatever time there is left to me, I must do whatever I can—one man, in a little ship—to stop these terrible events from progressing further. I would ask you, if you can, to take heart from this, Jean-Luc. If my own experience is anything to learn from, you may find that your world has not yet ended, and that you may yet be called upon to act.

I have no direct heir. The children of my mother's brother, and their children, are the closest. Saavik, too, who has played and continues to play so significant a part in my life can surely lay some claim upon me. But I would ask you, if this is not too great an imposition, to take on the task of literary executor. I leave you this—my *t'san a'lat*—and I trust completely your judgment as to what should be revealed and what kept private. You hold a unique perspective: someone who has not directly been involved in much of what I have described, and yet, through your mind-melds with both me and my father, you know more about my life than almost anyone else. I enclose with this *t'san a'lat* my translations of Surak into both English and Romulan *at'natzah*, and my translations of Conan Doyle into Vulcan *kitau-lakh* and Romulan *at'natzah*. During my time on Romulus, I began a translation of the Qowat Milat mystic poet Hivasa into Federation Standard, but that was a time for action rather than reflection and was never completed. I send these notes to you—perhaps you might consider finishing? I am sure that your grasp of *at'natzah* is more than equal to the task. There are other papers too, including some of my father's private papers and my youthful attempt to write a *t'san a'lat*, which I entrust to you. You will know best what to do. (And you will find Dr. McCoy's "gifts" in a large envelope with my name written in his deplorable handwriting.)

It is customary to conclude a *t'san a'lat* with a statement of what has been learned during a life. I find this difficult to summarize. Certainly, I have acquired a vast amount of information on a very large and diverse number of subjects. I have, over many years, transformed these many facts into practical, sometimes hard-won, knowledge. Despite this, and despite the years, I am, at the end of my life, both wise and foolish. I did not anticipate the terrible end to my mission to Romulus. I did not predict the retrenchment of our own

Federation nor its current inward-looking nature. This runs so contrary to all that I have learned in my life that I almost experience myself as a man out-of-time, no longer living in a world that is recognizably the one in which he was born, and to which he was the inheritor. I wonder what my father—looking at the Federation now—would make of its fearfulness. The purpose of the Federation—as I understood it, as my father explained it to me—was to bring together as many diverse civilizations as possible, to enrich each other in the fullest celebration of the differences between us. The purpose of Starfleet—as I was drawn to it in my youth—was to explore this universe we inhabit with curiosity and an open mind, to meet strangers in friendship, to alleviate pain with compassion. Much of this seems to have been forgotten.

The main lesson of my life was to abandon the habits of thought acquired as a child which set up in my mind irreconcilable differences between the various parts of my nature. Always, or so it seemed to me at the time, two parts of me were at odds: logic against emotion; Vulcan against human; meditation against action; death against life. Looking back now I see that whenever I have experienced resolution in my life, some kind of certainty, it has been through an acceptance of variety, hybridity, and diversity. Through accepting the simple fact that we can be many things, all at once. I was not human; I was not Vulcan—I was both and neither. To be Vulcan, it transpired, was to be Romulan; to be Romulan was to be Vulcan—I am both and neither. Human-Vulcan-Romulan, all at once. The great struggles of my life came when some part of me was forced into opposition with another; the great triumphs and friendships of my life came in threes—Jim, Bones, myself—and at all points in not only accepting, but delighting, in multiplicity, in myself and in others.

Time passes. People depart, and some of us are left behind. I told of you of an incident when I was a boy, and attempted, too early, the trial of the *kahs-wan*, to be saved only by the intervention by a cousin. Would you be surprised to discover that later in life I learned that this was myself, acting by means of a gateway to save my own life? The other great lesson of my life, then, has been to accept that the boundaries of our own selves become blurred. We are not islands, isolated from each other, but connected in ways that we do not fully perceive. When I was a boy, my life was saved by a stranger—a stranger who turned out to be myself. As a boy, I saw a vision of an angel, and trusting myself, that what I saw was true, saved my sister, who saved all sentient life. In all ways we are connected: across time, across space, across species. Refusing to accept this is the most certain way to ensure our extinction. This is one reason I have chosen to embark upon this mission now. Action brings consequence, yes—but inaction precludes any possibility of change. I am certain of only one thing— that I shall, in the end, die. Why not act, before that end comes at last?

Often, throughout my life, I pondered the vision I received of the Red Angel dressed in blue. When I went to Romulus, I discovered what it meant. Gabrielle Burnham—a human woman, part of a Romulan order, living on a future Vulcan. The rationally trained part of my mind tells me that I cannot assume that this is what the future will hold—I have no proof or evidence beyond an image in my mind, an idea of how that future might be. Yet at the same time I know that the purpose of visions such as these is to sustain and nourish my logical side. To give logic a path, a map, a destination. Logic without emotion is a dead end; emotion with logic cannot be channeled into meaningful action. My whole life, I see, has been an attempt to heal the wounds caused in me and those around me by the divisions imposed upon them; to find a means whereby diversity can flourish, and difference live in harmony.

When I close my eyes, I do not see a blank page with a small mark, held steady. I see drops of vibrant color, always moving, in time. I see the flickering light of a campfire, and for a moment my friends do not seem so very absent.

If there is any sense of unity to be found in my life—and I would resist such, since the end is not yet known—then it would be this: my steady move toward the full experience and acceptance of *Kol-Ut-Shan*, of infinite diversity in infinite combinations. I recall the symbol that my mother wore around her neck; I recall myself—my earliest self—always reaching out to grasp. I have never stopped trying to grasp this and I never shall. It remains the great mystery and certainty of my life. My dearest and most profound wish for you, Jean-Luc, is that you are able one day to reach out again.

Above all, my friend, I wish you peace—and long life.

Spock

LEONARD McCOY'S BEAN STEW

2 cups dried pinto or red beans, soaked for 2 hours in cold water and drained

250g smoked pork belly, diced

1 small white onion, chopped

1 red chili, chopped, seeds included

30g molasses

30g honey

10g mustard seeds

100ml apple cider vinegar

200ml beef stock

5 drops Worcestershire sauce

5g salt

NB: For a vegetarian alternative to satisfy Vulcan tastes, smoked diced kleetanta provides a more than adequate replacement for the pork belly. A tolik vinegar can be substituted for the apple cider, and a dash of forati or any other fermented sauce can replace the Worcestershire sauce. It should be noted too that Dr. McCoy's recipe omits what he claimed was the "secret ingredient" – Tennessee whiskey, which can be added to taste.

METHOD

1. Cover beans with water and boil for about 2 hours, reducing heat to a low boil for the last 1/2 hour, until they are tender.
2. Preheat oven to 140°C.
3. In a heavy based sauce/casserole pan, brown the pork belly.
4. Drain the beans and reserve 100ml of the bean stock.
5. Add all ingredients to the pork belly, including the bean stock you reserved and stir thoroughly.
6. Cover with tin foil and lid and bake in the preheated oven for 60 minutes.
7. Reduce heat to 100°C and cook another 6 hours in the oven.
8. Remove the lid and put the heat back up to 180°C for 30 minutes.
9. Remove from the oven and serve straight away.

LEONARD McCOY'S MINT JULEP

2fl oz/50ml bourbon
1½ tsp/7.5ml simple syrup
7-8 mint leaves
Ice
Garnish: mint sprigs

METHOD

Crush the mint leaves well, then add syrup and bourbon in a rocks glass (if you don't have a Julep glass like Bones). Fill half the glass with crushed ice. Give a good stir, pack in more ice, then decorate with mint sprigs.

EDITORIAL NOTE

THIS DOCUMENT, WHICH WAS SENT TO ME DIRECTLY BY ITS AUTHOR, Spock of Vulcan, contains the most complete account of his life and thinking that we possess. Working with this "wisdom book", which has brought the ambassador back to me so vividly and immediately that at times it has felt as if he was standing beside me, has been one of the great privileges of my life. I am grateful to the author—my friend—for his trust in me, and I hope that he would be content with the decisions that I have made with regards to publication.

Readers will notice a number of other texts are mentioned throughout this *t'san a'lat*; these, as well as a large number of other texts and a huge amount of correspondence, are to be found in Spock's papers, also entrusted to me as his literary executor. I am in the process of editing the translation of Hivasa, which was closer to completion than the ambassador suggested, and which I believe will be of great interest to students of his life and thinking, forming, as it does, a natural triptych with his translations of Conan Doyle and Surak, which have been available to scholars for some time.

In addition, an essay by Spock on Surak's *The Experience of Wisdom*, which expands upon some of the ideas outlined in this *t'san a'lat*, will shortly be made available in a special issue of the *New Journal of Surakian Studies*, and will, I believe, open a new debate over this late, profound, and unfairly disregarded book. It is hardly a surprise to those of us who knew him that the ambassador, even in his absence (and presumed death) will be rejuvenating an entire field of study.

I am in discussion with experts at T'Plana-Hath Museum in ShiKahr as to the best way to present and disseminate the *harrekh* of Sarek of Vulcan, which will surely be of interest to those working in relevant fields. I have not yet found a suitable recipient for the first *t'san a'lat* attempted by Ambassador Spock. I hope one day such a candidate will present him or herself. In the meantime, a holographic record is in preparation for those wishing to work with this interesting and informative document, which captures the ambassador's thinking in his early years.

The ultimate fate of Ambassador Spock is of course unknown. His mission did not save Romulus itself, but we cannot gauge whether or not his actions prevented a far larger-scale disaster from unfolding. I would like to believe that his mission saved lives. As for the ambassador himself, received wisdom is that he died in his attempt to inject red matter into the Romulan sun. But if the pages of this book teach us anything, it is that history has many cunning passages, and many hidden byways, and that not even death signifies the end.

Wherever you may be, my friend—live long, and prosper.

Jean-Luc Picard
La Barre, France, November 2390

EDITOR UNA'S ACKNOWLEDGEMENTS

FIRST AND FOREMOST, GRATEFUL THANKS TO CAT CAMACHO at Titan for trusting me with Spock, and for making work so much fun. I love sitting down to write each day, knowing that Cat will be reading. My thanks also to John Van Citters, who has forgotten more about *Star Trek* than I will ever know, and who always helps in need. I have shamelessly plundered Dayton Ward's delightful *Vulcan Travel Guide*. Thank you, sir, for this and so much else across the years. My thanks to Mark Poynton of MJP Restaurant for researching the recipe. Love and thanks also to my wonderful agent, Max Edwards, who is such a mensch.

So many people have written for and about the character of Spock over the years, not just on screen, but in hundreds of novels. Thank you to them all. I have tried to find my own version of this story here, but there has been some judicious borrowing. Diane Duane's terrific novel *Spock's World* provided many key insights into the Vulcan mind. In particular, I have drawn upon her ideas about the relative lack of traveling done by Vulcans, and her concept of *chthia*, which seems to me more relevant today than ever before. I have adopted (and adapted) the idea of "degenerative xenosis" from *The Vulcan Academy Murders* by Jean Lorrah. Barbara Hambly's

Ishmael suggests that Amanda Grayson's family originated in the Seattle area.

I should also express a debt to Michael Chabon's "Some Notes on Romulans", which provided a glimpse into that world (https://michaelchabon.medium. com/some-notes-on-romulans-b1c7f30a383f). Erin Horáková's essay "Freshly Remembered: Kirk Drift", published online in *Strange Horizons*, has deeply influenced my understanding of the man and the myth that is James Tiberius Kirk (http://strangehorizons.com/non-fiction/columns/freshly-rememberd-kirk-drift/). Leonard McCoy's Mint Julep recipe first appeared in *Star Trek Cocktails: A Stellar Compendium*, by Glenn Dakin, published by Eaglemoss; thank you for permission to use here.

To all the actors who have voiced or performed Spock, my thanks. There would of course be no Spock without Leonard Nimoy, and I hope his voice sounds true upon these pages.

Last and not least, my love and thanks to Matthew, who does so many impossible things so that I can meet deadlines. And my love and thanks to Verity, who prefers *Star Wars*, but lets me go and write anyway. I love you both so much.

ABOUT THE EDITOR

UNA MCCORMACK is the author of the *Star Trek* novels *The Lotus Flower* (part of *The Worlds of Star Trek: Deep Space Nine*), *Hollow Men*, *The Never-Ending Sacrifice*, *Brinkmanship*, *The Missing*, the *New York Times* bestseller *The Fall: The Crimson Shadow*, *Enigma Tales*, *The Way to the Stars*, and *The Last Best Hope*, and the *Doctor Who* novels *The King's Dragon*, *The Way Through the Woods*, *Royal Blood*, and *Molten Heart*. She lives in Cambridge, England, with her partner of many years, Matthew, and their daughter, Verity.

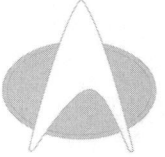

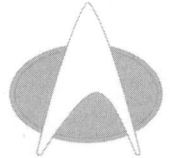

For more fantastic fiction, author events,
exclusive excerpts, competitions, limited editions and more

VISIT OUR WEBSITE
titanbooks.com

LIKE US ON FACEBOOK
facebook.com/titanbooks

FOLLOW US ON TWITTER AND INSTAGRAM
@TitanBooks

EMAIL US
readerfeedback@titanemail.com